Short Stories of the Far East

SHORT STORIES OF THE FAR EAST

David Daniels
57 The Boulevard
Sea Cliff, N.Y. 11579
U.S.A.
1-516-759-0063

Graham Brash (Pte) Ltd
Singapore

36-C Prinsep St
Singapore 0718

ISBN 9971 947 62 5

Acknowledgements

We are grateful for permission to include in this book stories by the following authors:

Hubert S. Banner, *Out of the Jungle*: to the author

W. Somerset Maugham, *Footprints in the Jungle* (from *Ah King*): to the author and Wm Heinemann Ltd

Pearl S. Buck, *The Frill* (from *First Wife and Other Stories*): to the author, Methuen & Co. and Creativity Inc.

Henry Peterson, *The Sword of Ridicule*: to the author

Dale Collins, *The Victor*: to the author

Joseph Conrad, *The Lagoon*: to the Trustees of the Conrad Estate and Ernest Benn Ltd

Ernest Bramah, *Kin Yen, the Picture Maker* (from *The Wallet of Kai Lung*): to the author

Kathleen Wallace, *The Head*: to the author

Reginald Campbell, *The Justice of Suan Hli* and *The Hut in the Paddy Fields*: to the author

Achmed Abdullah, *One — Not Two*: to the author

John Grant, *Cress*: to the author

Dorothy Black, *No Ladies' Man*: to the author

Sidney Denham, *The Prison of Sunset*: to the author

"Afghan", *Huqm Chand, an Eastern Triangle*: to the author

Coutts Brisbane, *Pain Bestowing Consequences*: to the author

Contents

OUT OF THE JUNGLE

By

HUBERT S. BANNER

THIS tale—the story of Heather Campion's foolish scepticism, and of the shocking event which abruptly transformed her into a more credulous, and therefore infinitely wiser, woman—was given to me by Max Herrick, of the Federated Malay States Forestry Department, and he told it in the jungle at sunset, the place and season proper to such eerie narrations.

To explain my presence in that remote glade, I must begin with the statement that I was visiting Malaya to investigate, on behalf of a certain "learned society," the truth or falsity of a report that some recent geological discoveries in the interior of the Peninsula shed an entirely new light upon the distribution of the aurignacian culture. A dry-sounding mission, you may think, and I will not deny that it was dull. Dull enough, at all events, to make me welcome the sight of a stalwart, essentially English-looking figure silhouetted against the gold and crimson of the sundowning.

"Oh, hallo," the man said, turning at the sound of my footsteps and peering through the gloom at me. A moment later I recognized him as Herrick, whom I had met a few days previously at the "Spotted Dog" Club in Kuala Lumpur, and simultaneously he knew me, too. His glance rested on the handful of Malays in my train, provided by the generosity of the Geological Survey Department.

"Didn't know fossils were nocturnal in their habits," he said, grinning.

"They're not," I told him. "We're on our way back to camp—near that limestone rock." I pointed out a precipitous crag that towered above the jungle a mile or so away. "And what are you doing in this God-forsaken spot, if it comes to that?" I queried, glancing curiously at a little camp pitched on one side of the glade.

"Just mapping a new bit of reserved forest . . . Come, I think a drink's indicated."

We chatted for a while, then sat smoking in silence and listening to the multitudinous voices on the jungle's awakening night-life. Suddenly, Herrick startled me by snatching up a rifle and aiming it towards the far edge of the clearing. But before he could pull the trigger one of his Malays broke into excited speech. Herrick pulled a rueful face and lowered his weapon, swearing beneath his breath.

"There, it's gone," he muttered disgustedly.

"What's gone?" I demanded. "I saw nothing."

"Your eyes aren't trained. . . . There was a deer."

"Why didn't you shoot, then?"

"Because Abdul here said he recognized it as a ghost-deer, and begged me not to. He said it would be asking for trouble."

"A ghost-deer!" I echoed. "But surely you don't believe in such nonsense?"

"Of course not," Herrick answered impatiently. "I'm not an absolute fool."

"Then why pay any attention?" I persisted.

"Because I can't afford to have Abdul think I am an absolute fool. He'd lose all respect for me at once."

Then Herrick began to initiate me, out of his long experience, into the dæmonology of that bogey-ridden land. And as I listened, I began gradually to suspect that Herrick himself had not wholly escaped the taint of its all-pervading superstitions. Not, of course, that he gave active credence to the idle tales of the Malays, but rather that he appeared to regard it as tempting fate to controvert them. His attitude seemed to be that only fools presume openly to challenge the ancient wisdom. In his secret heart a man may scoff, but let him at least lend no tongue to unbelief. At his peril does he, who is here to-day and gone to-morrow, deride lore which, for only one brief moment of eternity, he encounters in its passage from the dawn of thought towards centuries yet infinitely distant.

I might have rejoined, perhaps, that an outlook which was well enough for the ancient Greeks did not necessarily become an officer of the F.M.S. Forestry Department. But before I could open my mouth Herrick began to tell me the story of Mrs. Campion . . . "a yarn with a certain amount of the Greek irony in it," was how he described it . . . and by the time he had finished I felt less sure of my ground. . .

I will not tell the story as I received it, for Herrick, like so many men who spend long stretches of their lives in solitude, was an uneasy raconteur, one whose words fell slowly from him and were not always adequate. Here, however, is his narrative as I have tried to reconstruct it.

Heather Campion, the wife of the district officer at Bunga

Kenanga, had been "out" for about a year. When first Peter introduced his bride to the British community, she had been hailed on all sides as "just the very wife for him," what with her good looks and her pretty manners. Now that she had been in Malaya long enough to find her feet, however, the community was not so sure after all, and even the Resident had been observed to purse his august lips at mention of her name, an omen far from encouraging to a district officer. For Heather showed signs of developing into that most terrible of social scourges, a woman with a mission; and the devil of it was that her reformative zeal was directed at the one object to which above all, as an official's wife, she should have given a wide berth—Malay tradition.

It did not take Peter Campion long to realize that trouble lay not far ahead if Heather persisted in making an open parade of her contempt for those age-old beliefs which are as the very core of the Malay soul. And in due course he took occasion to point out to her the unwisdom of her ways.

"You're riding for a fall, Heather-blossom," was how he put it.

For perhaps a minute Heather did not answer, but continued to turn over the pages of a magazine which had that evening arrived in the mail. But presently she let it fall in her lap and sat staring out over the veranda-rail into the velvety night. It had been raining heavily, but the downfall had come to an abrupt end. The drenched earth and vegetation were exhaling a heady fragrance. Cicadas were shrilling in the glistening trees, as though determined to drown the hoarse outcry of the legion frogs. From the Malay village, whose lights glimmered deep down in the valley, beyond the muttering river, drifted a sweet-sad tinkle and throb of native music.

"I simply can't see it," Heather said at last. "Here you are, Peterkin, a district officer, plunked down in the wilds among these primitive people. And here I am with you, ready and anxious to do all I can to help. . . What are we here for? Don't say it's just to keep the country in order for the benefit of the merchants and planters, because I know you wouldn't be here if you thought that was all."

"Certainly not," Peter agreed.

"Very well, then," pursued his wife, "isn't it our absolute duty to try to educate the people out of these stupid superstitions that hem them round on all sides? How can they ever really progress under such a handicap? Take Fatimah, for example."

Fatimah was the Campion's sewing-maid and the wife of their head "boy." She had, a few evenings since, presented her lord and master with a lusty son. Encountering an old Malay man of dubious aspect at the compound gate, Heather had demanded his business, and, on learning that he was the local sorcerer—summoned to weave spells for the undoing of any evilly disposed birth-spirits that might arrive in the guise of night-owls, polecats, truncated human heads, and the like—had sternly forbidden him to enter the premises. The most obvious result of her interference was that the head boy had sulked and glowered and skimped his work ever since. Hence the origin of the present discussion.

"Exactly," said Peter; "as you say, take Fatimah. She and Achmed are making themselves thoroughly miserable with the notion that the kiddie may have to go through life under a birth-curse. And all because you wouldn't stand for a little harmless hocus-pocus."

Heather stood up abruptly and walked to the head of the steps leading down to the garden.

"Sorry, Peterkin," she said, "but I just can't see it like that. The 'hocus-pocus,' as you call it, is keeping these wretched people back in the Middle Ages."

If only she wouldn't take herself so infernally seriously, Peter reflected with some measure of irritation. True, during their courtship in England, he had often enough voiced a fervent conviction that she would prove "a real help" to him in his work. But he had never visualized her assistance as extending farther than the gracing of garden parties and dinner tables, the maintenance of amiable relations with the local chiefs' wives, and, possibly, the occasional beguilement of some senior official. No sooner, however, had she acquired a working knowledge of the Malay tongue—and her flair for languages had made that a speedy matter—than here she was, obsessed with this ridiculous notion of attacking native superstition. Already she had bitterly offended several influential Malays by attempting to "cure" their women-folk of beliefs that were an integral part of the structure of their complex etiquette. And now she had even alienated their own servants. In short, she was definitely becoming, not a help, but a handicap. The Malays were certain to complain. Before long the Resident would be sending for him . . .

"It can't be done with a rush, Heather," he expostulated. "It's a matter of centuries and centuries of education, and we've only been in the F.M.S. half a century yet."

"Nonsense!" snapped his wife. "One's got to be a little ruthless, that's all . . . I'd weed out these superstitions like—like dandelions."

"Their roots go far, far too deep for that, my dear."

"I'll believe it when it's proved to me. Until then I shall go on doing my level best to enlighten these poor people whenever I get the chance."

"Let us hope the proof won't come in too terrible a form when you do get it—as you certainly will," Peter answered moodily, striking a match with unnecessary violence to light his pipe. To ease his feelings he shouted for Achmed and ordered him to bring a *stengah*.

He was in the act of raising a whisky-and-soda to his lips when a scrunch of sandals upon the gravel arrested him, and into the oblong of light cast by the veranda lamps emerged a picturesque and venerable figure. The stranger was a Malay, yet something in the shape of his black velvet cap and the hang of his *sarong* betokened that he was not of the Peninsula. The face was wrinkled like a walnut and terminated in a straggling fringe of white beard, but the eyes were lively and bright with intelligence. Murmuring a respectful greeting, he squatted on the steps and proceeded to open the cloth bundle he carried over his shoulder, displaying a varied assortment of brassware and silverwork.

"We are in need of nothing, thank you," Peter said at once. Heather, however—possibly just because he had made the assertion with such complacent certitude—crossed the veranda and began to examine the old fellow's wares piece by piece. Presently, she picked up a little silver bracelet.

"I think I'll buy this as a peace-offering to Achmed," she suggested. "He'd love it for the baby."

Peter had no objections to offer to that; on the contrary, he considered it an excellent plan. So Achmed was summoned and presented with the trinket, and the sulks vanished from his countenance like mist at the touch of the sun. As his cyes took in the details of the pedlar's appearance, however, something like consternation sprang into their depths. The hand he extended to take the bracelet began to tremble so violently that he all but dropped it from his grasp; his voice, as he spoke his thanks, was unsteady and pitched a half-octave above its normal tones. On his way back towards the kitchen regions he halted to cast a final glance over his shoulder at the stranger, and this time there was no mistaking his expression: it was eloquent of positive terror.

The old man snorted contemptuously as he packed up his stock-in-trade. "Yonder goes a fool, tuan," he observed, looking up at Peter with a sour smile.

"Quite possibly," the district officer answered curtly. But Heather was curious: her proselytising soul cried aloud for explanations.

"Why was he frightened?" she demanded in her direct fashion, so different from the circumlocution which, according to the Malay code, is essential to good manners.

"Because he is a fool, mem—like the children who pelted me with mud and stones only this afternoon. We grow accustomed to such folly, we of Korinchi."

He appeared disinclined to say more, but he was not proof against Heather's methods. By dangling before his cupidity a half-promise to buy a brass salver she gradually elicited the explanation of Achmed's strange behaviour. It was simply that he firmly believed, like every other Peninsula Malay, that all the inhabitants of Korinchi, in Sumatra, possessed the power of transforming themselves at will into tigers!

"An idle tale, mem, and void of truth," the pedlar concluded apologetically.

"I should hope so, indeed!" Heather exclaimed. "As though any man could change himself into an animal!"

To her great astonishment, though, the old fellow implored her to be silent. His eyes had grown wide with alarm; he cast panicky glances into the shadows of the garden.

"Speak not thus, mem!" he begged. "It is perilous to tempt the powers of darkness."

"But you yourself said, not a moment ago, that the tale was void of truth!" Heather's voice held pained accusation.

"Nay, nay, I did but say it was an idle tale that we of Korinchi be the tiger-men. . . For assuredly it is well known of all men that such demons there are. Indeed, I have spoken with men who had encountered them. Myself, I have beheld the secret place in the forest whither they repair at nightfall to assume their tiger shape."

Heather became ominously calm, but a faint sneer played round her lips.

"How interesting!" she commented. "May I ask how they accomplish it?"

The pedlar threw another hasty look over his shoulder before answering. When he spoke it was almost in a whisper.

"They crouch with their brows pressed to the ground, mem. Then, very, very slowly they turn a somersault, thus"—he illustrated the motion with his hand—"and behold! even as they turn, a tail sprouts forth, stripes come rippling up through the texture of their skin, their teeth become long and sharp, and their nails are changed to cruel talons. . . Thus transformed, they steal forth in search of prey, make their kill and gorge themselves withal. Then, in the black hour before daybreak, they return, heavy with meat, to that same place of evil enchantment, where they regain human form by turning another somersault—backwards this time. And having effected that, they stealthily creep back to their homes, and there sleep through the daylight hours till once more the setting of the sun drives them forth upon their hellish business."

Heather threw back her head and laughed loudly.

"Did you ever in your life hear such utter bunkum, Peterkin!" she demanded.

But Peter did not answer. His eyes were fixed upon the scattered lights of the village down there in the valley, and upon the inky blackness beyond, where he knew that the sombre, inscrutable ocean of jungle rose, wave upon wave, to the feet of the distant mountains. In his ears rang, not his wife's challenging words, but the plaintive cadences of the Malay music, the solemn rumble of the river, and the forest's innumerable murmuring voices. Against the background of their timeless message Heather's laughter was like the crackling of thorns . . .

To the old vendor of brassware that laughter was insupportable.

"*Aia!*" he exclaimed, his voice quivering with mingled terror and indignation, "the mem may laugh if it pleases her, but within the week I will bring her proof that the things whereof I spake are even so. By the beard of Mohammed I swear it—I, Sudrono."

His eyes were ablaze with resentment; as he shouldered his pack and shuffled away in the direction of the village, his lips worked convulsively and he made gestures of senile anger with his hands.

"Wait, I haven't bought the brass tray yet," Heather called after him.

"I will not sell it to you!" he answered, and that refusal to trade may be considered as the measure of his perturbation. Sumatra folk do not lightly throw away the chance of profit.

Heather, with a contemptuous snort, sat down and picked up her magazine again, but presently, finding herself beginning to yawn, she went off to bed. Peter, however, remained in his chair on the veranda, struggling with the vague unease that would not leave him. Of course, Heather was right in principle, he reflected, but she was very wrong in practice; the East would not suffer itself to be hustled on to enlightenment, however nonsensical its conceptions. Were they invariably so nonsensical, though, after all? Peter had been in Malaya enough years to feel not quite certain any longer of what was credible and what preposterous.

A hundred things had happened in his experience which could not be fitted into an outlook governed by the rigid rules of British commonsense. . . But no, it did not do to think on those lines. You had to keep a firm hold on commonsense out here; once let go of that sheet-anchor, and you would speedily find everything else was slipping from your grasp—efficiency, judgment, even decency . . .

He stood up and stretched himself, and as he did so there floated through the still air from some remote spot the querulous snarl of a hunting wild beast. Twice—three times—the savage voice sounded its plaint, rose to a full-throated roar, then throbbed away into silence. An almost forgotten line of the Psalms entered Peter's mind: *"The lions roaring after their prey do seek their meat of God."* Only, of course, in Malaya they were not lions, but tigers and leopards. And was it always of God they sought their meat? More likely of the devil, if that old pedlar were to be believed. Well, Heather had shown plainly enough what she thought of his nonsense—too plainly, perhaps . . .

As Peter got into bed, memory gave back to him another isolated tag, but this time it came from a hymn. *"Nor powers of darkness me molest,"* it ran. He fell asleep with it repeating itself over and over in his mind, and it was confusingly mingled with the roars of the distant creature imploring sustenance of Heaven—or hell . . .

As Sudrono shuffled away into the darkness, his normally placid old heart seethed with contemptuous disgust. True, the world would be a pleasanter place for himself if the ancient tradition of the were-tiger should somehow be exploded; each trip to the Peninsula—and he made several in the course of a year—involved braving innumerable insults and even, sometimes, active persecution. On the other hand, how could one imagine the Malays ever ceasing to believe in that which was no mere idle legend, but proven fact? Everyone knew, for example, the true story of the man who knocked on the door of a peasant's hut one night, begging the favour of a torch to light him through the jungle; and how the children of the householder, peeping from a dark corner in the garden, were terrified to see a striped tail hanging down from beneath the stranger's coat. . . Still, Sudrono often wished that local notions placed the home of the were-tigers in some district other than Korinchi. That part of the tradition, at least, was purest nonsense.

Infinitely deeper, however, than Sudrono's annoyance arising out of this unjustified accusation, was his anger at the presumption of the district officer's wife. Who was this pale upstart, in the name of Allah's mercy, that she should dare to laugh aloud at the lore which had come down in the keeping of the Malayan folk, passed on from father to son in unbroken chain since the world's beginning? Besides, what transparent hypocrites these English were! They scoured the deep sea in fire-ships and the face of the earth in devil-carriages; they rode the heavens like angels of Paradise; from the empty air they plucked speech and music. And yet, notwithstanding all these cogent evidences to their own command of magic, they scoffed at the older-established sorceries of Asia. Let them scoff, though: he would show them—yes, he, Sudrono!

He passed the night in the corner of a buffalo-byre, odiferous and a-crawl with vermin, where even the herdsman's smouldering fire of coconut husks could not dispel the clouds of mosquitoes. For to the man of Korinchi none would give lodging in their homes. Fresh in their minds was the experience of a smallholder in a neighbouring village who, taking pity on just such another, had offered him a night's shelter. In the morning there had been found a gaping hole in the *attap* wall of the fowl-house, and all the chickens had been missing. Simultaneously, the Korinchian guest had fallen sick, and then, O all-revealing dispensation of Allah! he had vomited forth clouds of feathers.

Sudrono took the road early, ill-rested and cantankerous, and that day it was a path of tribulation. Here and there he made some trifling sale, but for the most part the inhabitants of the hamlets which he visited whisked their children indoors at his approach and sullenly declined to trade. And as he met their forbidding faces, some scowling with hatred, others blank with terror, Sudrono cursed afresh the foolishness that insisted upon locating in his home-district the domicile of the fiendish beasts in human shape.

Noontide found him weary, dispirited, and a little feverish after his bad night. He was now traversing a plateau set between two ranges of hills. It consisted chiefly of ricefields, and there were few trees, therefore, to give him shade from the cruel sun, which glowed like a steel boss set in a canopy of brass. Sudrono felt as though his very veins were being scorched dry; his feet dragged ever more painfully through the clogging dust, and the fever-devils were pounding the core of his brain with red-hot hammers. Presently he came to a wayside spring; the splash and gurgle of its thin trickle made the sweetest music he had ever heard. But there was a woman there, and she had but that moment begun to fill the first of her two bamboo vessels; it would be minutes before she was finished.

Suddenly, the woman chanced to look up and see him patiently waiting there, his tormented eyes fixed on the crystal thread of water. Without a word she picked up a coconut-shell cup, held it beneath the spout until it was full, and handed it up to him.

"The blessing of Allah be upon you and all your house," the old man muttered indistinctly as he took it from her.

"You have come far?" the woman questioned. Then, as her eyes took in the details of his appearance, a momentary expression of fear flickered in their depths. "But I see that you have," she added timidly; "you are of Sumatra—a Korinchian."

"Yes, I come from Korinchi," Sudrono confessed in a listless voice. He desired to be polite, but could think of nothing beyond the deliciousness of the cool water; life was flowing back into him with every gulp.

"Ah!" The woman's long-drawn monosyllable spoke volumes. For a few moments she was silent, and Sudrono wondered whether perhaps she was regretting now that she had given him that blessed draught.

"You look harmless enough," she ventured presently; "yet I have heard—they say——"

"Needless to tell me what they say," the pedlar broke in; "much wicked nonsense is told of us Korinchians. . . Yet only yesternight I listened to a speech more wicked and more foolish than all the things they say of us. It was the speech of a white woman."

Again the other ejaculated: "Ah!"—implying this time that in that instance the foolishness of the utterance could be taken for granted.

Encouraged by her interest, Sudrono narrated the story of the district officer's wife and her insolent denial. Also he told of his own rash oath to bring, within a week, proof that the things whereat she scoffed had a real existence. "How I may accomplish it I know not," he concluded, "though God will doubtless point a way. But I have sworn it, and by some means I will fulfil my vow, lest I be shamed."

He spoke vehemently, for by this time, what with fatigue and fever, the blasphemy of Mrs. Campion had assumed portentous proportions in his mind, and her prospective humiliation had become an obsession.

"That should be easy," the woman answered surprisingly. "Listen: does your way take you to Hatimanis?"

"It is there I plan to pass the coming night."

"Good. Go, then, to the headman of Hatimanis and beg

from him a bone of the heifer that was slain outside the village two dusks ago. These three months and more has the Striped One taken constant toll of the Hatimanis cattle, but till now none was ever quick enough to set eyes on him. This time, though, a herdsman chanced to come upon the dead heifer while the killer yet crouched over it, and—you have doubtless heard that sometimes the 'somersault-tigers,' if they be taken by surprise, change back to human shape all in a moment and by no will of their own?"

"And with truth; for behold, so it came to pass at Hatimanis, no less. Even as the herdsman approached, a form sprang from the heifer's carcase and melted into the shadows. For an instant of time the herdsman saw it clearly in the moonlight, and *it was the form of a man.*"

"But will the white woman accept the bone for proof?"

"Ask the headman for a writing with it."

For some while longer they conversed, while Sudrono ate his mid-day rice and inwardly praised Allah for having sent this woman across his path—a sensible woman, who, far from becoming tongue-tied with terror at the very sight of him, as most were, had actually offered the solution of his problem. All would now be well; on his return to Bunga Kenanga he would be in a position to save his face. For it never occurred to Sudrono that Mrs. Campion might conceivably reject the heifer's bone as trustworthy evidence, even when accompanied by a "writing." The Malay peoples, for all their subtlety, are in some respects astoundingly simple.

Having finished his meal, the pedlar bade a courteous farewell to the woman and resumed his way. Now that a practical idea had been presented to him, he felt immeasurably lightened in spirit. The fever had left him, the sparkle had returned to his eye, and his feet dragged less than before his encounter. And as though fortune were anxious now to compensate with lavish hand for her former defection, trade began to improve. In one village Sudrono sold three bracelets, in another a set of betel-nut utensils and two pairs of ear-rings.

So preoccupied did he become with his bargainings that he failed to keep a tally upon the passage of time. He left the flat, rice-growing area and ascended into the jungle-covered foothills by the road which would bring him to Hatimanis; but he had no conception of the lateness of the hour when he took the upward path, and it was with a sense of shock, therefore, that he suddenly noticed the swift tropical dusk commencing to gather when he still had some miles to travel.

The spot in which he found himself was wild with a savage desolation sufficient to strike terror into the most valiant heart. To right and left stretched a sea of *alang-alang* grass, shoulder-high, from which rose occasionally scrubby trees that were distorted by the twilight into the semblance of terrible goblins. Ahead, the trees massed themselves of a sudden into a dense grey-green wall, and the pathway, plunging down a steep declivity, vanished into the black shadows beneath their intermeshed branches as abruptly and completely as though it had entered a tunnel driven through a hillside.

Grimly forbidding though this vista was, however, Sudrono had no choice but to go forward. With a muttered prayer on his lips he descended the slope, and a few moments later the forest had engulfed him. The blackness now resolved itself into a greenish-gloom, as though he were walking in some cavern at the bottom of the sea. Save for an occasional scuffling of birds or monkeys preparing for the night high overhead in the leafy roof, the forest was filled with a deathly and oppressive hush: a quietude so profound that the snapping of a dry twig beneath Sudrono's feet sounded like a pistol-shot.

He had progressed for perhaps a mile when a sudden commotion brought him to a halt with wildly thumping heart. To the uninitiated ear it might have seemed a noise harmless enough—merely a frenzied chattering among the monkeys and birds. But Sudrono had been brought up in the understanding of jungle-lore. He detected at once that the sound was not stationary, but that it travelled through the forest ceiling in a meandering line, subsiding into a querulous murmur in one quarter even as it mounted to a climax of panic in another. There was but one interpretation possible: some dangerous animal, some hereditary enemy of the humbler jungle dwellers, was threading a stealthy path along the dim, green corridors below. But where? Even Sudrono's trained ears could not tell him, in that vast cathedral-gloom of tree-boles and undergrowth and looping tendrils, from what direction the ominous alarms were sounding; sometimes they seemed to come from the right, sometimes from the left; one moment they were in front, the next behind. He stood hesitant, throwing terrified glances into the shadowy aisles on either hand, and again his tremulous lips framed a whispered prayer for protection. But even in his prayers he was scrupulously careful to refer to the prowling brute as "He of the Hairy Face"; for all Malay folk know the disastrous consequences of mentioning the tiger by name.

The prayer was scarcely finished when a devilish uproar burst out, abruptly and quite close at hand. It began with a staccato, coughing snarl; then, after an instant's pause, came roar upon roar, mounting in frightful crescendo until the very roof of the forest seemed to shiver to their crashing reverberation. Hearing that dreadful noise, Sudrono felt his soul shrivel within him. The tiger, he knew, had pounced at some creature—and missed. Those roars, sinking now to a hoarse, rasping murmur, had been the wild protest of his disappointment and impotent fury. Before, he had been a shadowy presence, full of caution, procrastinating in the hope of certainties; but now he would be a raging fiend incarnate.

Sudrono began to run, but his running was a sorry performance. His knees quivered under him, scarcely adequate to bear his weight. Sweat poured down his face, half blinding him. His breath came in wheezing gasps. More than once tree-roots brought him down sprawling in the soggy mess of decayed vegetation that formed the forest's floor. In the extremity of his anguish he no longer made any attempt to move quietly. The brassware in his sack clanked at every lurching step, and he even began to babble aloud the ancient Malay ode of tiger-propitiation:

The buffalo is big, the buffalo is mighty;
The foe dreadeth his horns, his horns hard and sharp,
And his pointed hooves that trample his fallen enemy.
Yet stronger than the buffalo art Thou!
Haîlah! Haîlah!
Strong is man; he turneth the wood, the iron he forgeth;
He bendeth the buffalo to the yoke and compelleth his toil.
But stronger yet than man, and more wily, is the Great Lord.
The Great Lord is man's friend, wishing him no ill.
Haîlah! Haîlah!

The final "Haîlah" tailed off into a sob, however, for now, almost level with him, Sudrono could hear the unmistakable crackle and swish of a heavy body thrusting its way with reckless precipitancy through the undergrowth. Every instant he expected to see the foliage parted by the striped devil's snarling and ferocious mask.

He was half dead with fright—almost arrived at a stage, that is to say, at which he would have simply collapsed to earth and awaited his end—when a sudden bend in the path most unexpectedly revealed the answer to his prayers. This answer took the form of a tiger-trap—an oblong cage of stout bamboos lashed together with rattans. At the end facing Sudrono was the entrance, topped by a door heavily weighted with logs and poised in such fashion that it would crash down in its guiding grooves the instant the bait inside the trap was touched.

This contrivance stood back a little from the track, and in all likelihood it would have escaped Sudrono's notice but for the circumstance that the moon was now rising. A ghostly radiance filtered down through the foliage; the trap stood out in sharp relief against a background of silver. With a sob of thankfulness the pedlar stumbled across the intervening space and flung himself through the doorway. A moment later he had grasped the piece of dog's flesh which served as bait. The door descended with a thud, and there he crouched in the semi-darkness, shivering and whimpering in the nervous reaction from his agony of fear.

Presently, when he felt able to move again, he peered forth through a narrow slit between two of the bamboos, and that which he beheld froze the marrow in his bones. A gigantic tiger was standing in the middle of the pathway, and its eyes were fixed on the trap with unwavering concentration. The moonlight struck into their yellow-green depths, to shine forth from them again bearing a message of chill, pitiless savagery; it displayed in clear detail the round, uncompassionate skull, the wrinkled nose and stiff, bristling whiskers; crowning horror, it revealed a thin trickle of hunger-saliva that dripped from the grinning mouth, sparkling like a dribble of diamonds.

For some little while the beast stood thus, gazing; then, abruptly, it walked over to make closer inspection. As it passed slowly along the row of bamboo bars, sniffing at each interstice in turn, its breath filled the cage with a hot, nauseating stench. Failing to find a weak spot in the nearer side, it went round to the other wall and the back, and finally sprang on to the roof, where it discovered a narrow opening near the middle. Through this it thrust its leg as far as it would go, and for five minutes that seemed like as many hours Sudrono squeezed himself into a corner while the huge paw, with claws distended, scooped to and fro within a few inches of his face.

Finding its efforts in this direction unavailing, the tiger presently descended and gave itself to attempting to wrench the side-bars apart, heaving and grunting in a temper that mounted from moment to moment. When this also proved fruitless, it flung itself down on its side and tried to gnaw its way in, but the bamboos were set too close to afford its jaws a purchase. Then it retreated a few feet and emitted a succession of roars, as though hoping that that voice of terror would cause the bars to collapse like the walls of Jericho. And at last, with backward-lingering glance and waving tail, it began to stalk slowly away towards the thickets. It had not gone more than half a dozen yards, however, when round it whirled and came rushing back, snarling with

For five minutes that seemed like as many hours Sudrano squeezed himself into a corner while the huge paw scooped to and fro within a few inches of his face.

baffled rage, to apply itself anew to the bamboos and their rattan bindings.

Throughout the night this went on, the tiger alternately making frenzied attacks on the trap and seeming to give up in disgust, while Sudrono sat huddled in his corner, shivering with mingled cold and terror and muttering broken prayers. But as time wore on the intervals between the onslaughts became longer and longer. Several times the brute vanished for half an hour at a stretch, and after one such disappearance, which was just when the eastern sky was beginning to pale in preparation for the dawn, it did not return at all.

With daybreak the birds sent up their pæans of joy, and accompanying them went the thanksgivings of Sudrono for what seemed no less than a miraculous deliverance. He crawled to the door and attempted to raise it, but it proved too heavy for his old muscles, so he sat to wait in patience for assistance. And before another hour had gone by it came, for from the direction of Hatimanis appeared some ten or twelve Malays, led by the village headman himself. As their eyes fell on the dropped door their chatter abruptly ceased, and they rushed forward with excited shouts to investigate the "catch." The headman bent down and screwed up his eyes to look through an interstice. Then with a sharp intake of his breath he started back.

"A man!" he exclaimed.

"In sooth, a man," Sudrono confirmed; "but a man who is chilled and weary and sorely affrighted. . . Therefore release me quickly, I implore you."

One of the villagers moved to the door of the trap as though to comply, but the headman checked him with a gesture. He stooped again to peer more closely between the bars.

"It would seem from your attire, O stranger," he said slowly, "that you are of Korinchi. . . How come you to be in this trap?"

"I entered it to preserve myself from Him who Walks the Forest by Night."

Dead silence greeted the explanation, and Sudrono suddenly experienced a cold, sinking sensation in the pit of his stomach.

"Free me, I beg of you," he repeated urgently. His voice held a sharp note of apprehension.

"The Striped One," the headman pronounced in a judicial manner, and addressing his companions rather than Sudrono, "has ravaged our herds these last three months. Worse than this, he has slain the children of our loins."

"But surely it cannot be in your minds that I—I, Sudrono—bear the guilt of these foul deeds?" the pedlar protested. He was in the throes of real terror now, for he knew beyond all possibility of doubt, from the embarrassed demeanour of the villagers round about, that this was just exactly what they did believe.

"If that were so," he continued, his panic rising when he saw no sign of relaxation in the grim faces gathered around, "should I not still wear the Striped One's guise? How should I have regained human semblance—*here?"*

The chief, however, gravely shook his head.

"It is well known," he retorted, "that They of the Somersault do oft-times change their form all in an instant—through some shock of fear, for example."

His words reminded Sudrono suddenly of his conversation with the woman at the spring.

"But I was journeying to Hatimanis only to seek out yourself," he declared desperately. "I was minded to ask you for a bone of the heifer that was killed two days ago."

He could not have thought of anything more unfortunate to say. At once the headman demanded how he knew of that killing, and the story about the woman who had given him water was received with derisive laughter.

"But I swear to you, with the sole of your foot upon the crown of my head," the pedlar insisted, "that I am wholly innocent of this charge! I have wrought ill to no man. I am a peaceful trader. I swear it—I——"

"Such a one would forswear himself and think no shame, the headman interrupted.

"But you must believe me, you *must!"* screamed Sudrono, seizing the bars and shaking them frenziedly. "Search the ground: you will find my foot-marks."

The headman cast his glance perfunctorily over the trampled terrain.

"Far as the eye can see," he pronounced, "are the Hairy-faced One's prints and none other. . . . But come, we waste words." He turned to one of the villagers. "Abdul, one of those children slain was yours; therefore let your hand serve our common need. Take my lance and mount upon the trap. What is to do, let it be done quickly and with mercy."

The man addressed as Abdul accepted the weapon, tested its point with his thumb, and clambered up as directed. For one age-long moment Sudrono's agonized eyes watched in petrified fascination the bright spear-head as it descended through the narrow opening in the roof and shaped its direction. Then, swift as lightning, came the great darkness. . . .

Herrick ceased speaking and fumbled in his pocket for matches. The velvet curtain of night had dropped over the land, and the rim of a huge orange moon was poking over the still tree-tops. Somewhere in the ghostly forest a questing beast shattered the silence with a savage roar.

"Indeed a pretty bed-time story," I commented dryly. "Is that the end?"

"Yes and no," was Herrick's answer. "I happened to be dining with the Campions when the police brought poor old Sudrono's body there on the way to the mortuary. The assistant commissioner called Campion outside to look at it, and explained the business so far as he'd been able to unravel it. Campion came back a bit white about the gills.

"Heather," he said, "do you remember what that old pedlar promised you?"

"He promised to bring proof of the existence of were-tigers," Heather answered, wondering why he looked so queer.

"Well," Peter went on, "he hasn't managed that, exactly, but he's done the next best thing. He's brought you absolutely conclusive proof that you'd better mind your own business in future. . . . I told you these things were not just—dandelions. I hope you'll be satisfied. Come and see for yourself."

"And was she satisfied?" I asked.

"Mrs. Campion," said Herrick, blowing down his pipe to remove an obstruction, "is universally held up as the perfect model of a district officer's wife."

FOOTPRINTS IN THE JUNGLE

By

W. SOMERSET MAUGHAM

THERE is no place in Malaya that has more charm than Tanah Merah. It lies on the sea, and the sandy shore is fringed with casuarinas. The government offices are still in the old red *Raad Huis* that the Dutch built when they owned the land, and on the hill stand the grey ruins of the fort by means of which the Portuguese maintained their hold over the unruly natives. Tanah Merah has a history and in the vast labyrinthine houses of the Chinese merchants, backing on the sea so that in the cool of the evening they may sit in their open loggias and enjoy the salt breeze, families dwell that have been settled in the country for three centuries. Many have forgotten their native language and hold intercourse with one another in Malay and pidgin-English. The imagination lingers here gratefully, for in the Federated Malay States the only past is within the memory for the most part of the fathers of living men.

Tanah Merah was for long the busiest mart of the Middle East, and its harbour was crowded with shipping when the clipper and the junk still sailed the China seas. But now it is dead. It has the sad and romantic charm of all places that have once been of importance and live now on the recollection of a vanished grandeur. It is a sleepy little town, and strangers that come to it, losing the energy brought with them, insensibly drop into its easy and lethargic ways. Successive rubber booms bring it no prosperity, and the ensuing slumps hasten its decay.

The European quarter is strangely silent. It is trim and neat and clean. The houses of the white men—government servants and agents of companies—stand round an immense *padang,* agreeable little bungalows shaded by great cassias, and the *padang* is vast and green and well cared for, like the lawns of a cathedral close; and indeed there is in the aspect of this corner of Tanah Merah something quiet and delicately secluded that reminds you of the precincts of Canterbury.

The club faces the sea; it is a spacious but shabby building; it has an air of neglect, and when you enter you feel that you intrude. It gives you the impression that it is closed, really, for alterations and repairs, and that you have taken an indiscreet advantage of an open door to go where you are not wanted. In the morning you may find there a couple of planters who have come in from their estates on business and are drinking a gin-sling before starting back again; and latish in the afternoon a lady or two may perhaps be seen looking with a furtive air through old numbers of the *Illustrated London News*. At nightfall a few men saunter along and sit about the billiard-room watching the play and drinking *sukus,* and perhaps four may be found to make up a rubber of bridge. It is only on Wednesdays that a shadow of gaiety may be seen, for then the gramophone is set going in the large room upstairs and people come in from the surrounding country to dance. There are sometimes no less than a dozen couples then, and it is even possible to make up two tables of bridge.

It was on one of these occasions that I met the Cartwrights. I was staying with a man called Gaze, who was head of the police, and he came into the billiard-room, where I was sitting, and asked me if I would make up a four. The Cartwrights were planters and they came in to Tanah Merah on Wednesdays because it gave their girl a chance of getting a few dances. They were very nice people, said Gaze, quiet and unobtrusive, and played a very pleasant game of bridge. I followed Gaze into the card-room and was introduced to the Cartwrights. They were already seated at a table and Mrs. Cartwright was shuffling the cards. It inspired me with confidence to see the competent way in which she did it. She took half the pack in each hand—and her hands were large and strong—deftly inserted the corners of one half under the corners of the other, and with a click and a neat, bold gesture cascaded them together.

It had all the effect of a conjuring trick. The card-player knows that it can be done perfectly only after incessant practice. He can be fairly sure that anyone who can so shuffle a pack of cards loves cards for their own sake.

"Do you mind if my husband and I play together?" asked Mrs. Cartwright. "It's no fun for us to win one another's money."

"Of course not."

We cut for deal and Gaze and I sat down.

Mrs. Cartwright drew an ace, and while she dealt, quickly and neatly, she chatted with Gaze of local affairs, but I was aware that she appraised me. She had shrewd eyes and they observed you with keenness, but also with good humour.

She was a woman somewhere in the fifties (though in the East, where people age quickly, it is difficult to tell their ages), with white hair very untidily arranged, and a constant gesture with her was an impatient movement of the hand to push back a long wisp of hair that kept falling over her forehead. You wondered why she did not, by the use of a hairpin or two, save herself so much trouble. Her blue eyes were large, but pale and a little tired; her face was lined and sallow; I think it was her mouth that gave it the expression which I felt was characteristic of caustic but tolerant irony. You saw that here was a woman who knew her mind and was never afraid to speak it. She was a chatty player (which some people object to strongly, but which does not disconcert me, for I do not see why you should behave at the card-table as though you were at a memorial service) and it was soon apparent that she had an agreeable knack of badinage. It was pleasantly acid, but it was amusing enough to be offensive only to a fool. If now and then she uttered a remark so sarcastic that you wanted all your sense of humour to see the fun in it, you could not but quickly see that she was willing to take as much as she gave. Her large, thin mouth broke into a dry smile and her eyes shone brightly when by a lucky chance you brought off a repartee that turned the laugh against her.

I thought her a very pleasant person. I liked her frankness. I liked her quick wit. I liked her plain face. I never met a woman who obviously cared so little how she looked. It was not only her head that was untidy, everything about her was slovenly: she wore a high-necked silk blouse, but for coolness she had unbuttoned the top buttons and showed a gaunt and withered neck; the blouse was crumpled and none too clean, for she smoked innumerable cigarettes and covered herself with ash. When she got up for a moment to speak to somebody, I saw that her blue skirt was rather ragged at the hem and badly needed a brush, and she wore heavy, low-heeled boots. But none of this mattered.

And it was a pleasure to play bridge with her. She played very quickly, without hesitation, and she had not only knowledge but flair. Of course, she knew Gaze's game, but I was a stranger and she soon took my measure. The teamwork between her husband and herself was admirable; he was sound and cautious, but, knowing his game exactly, she was able to be bold with assurance and brilliant with safety. Gaze was a player who founded a foolish optimism on the hope that his opponents would not have the sense to take advantage of his errors, and the pair of us were no match for the Cartwrights. We lost one rubber after another, and there was nothing to do but smile and look as if we liked it.

"I don't know what's the matter with the cards," said Gaze at last, plaintively. "Even when we have every card in the pack we go down."

"It can't be anything to do with your play," answered Mrs. Cartwright, looking him full in the face with those pale blue eyes of hers; "it must be bad luck, pure and simple. Now if you hadn't had your hearts mixed up with your diamonds in that last hand you'd have saved the game."

Gaze began to explain at length how the misfortune, which had cost us dear, occurred, but Mrs. Cartwright, with a deft flick of the hand, spread out the cards in a great circle so that we should cut for deal. Cartwright looked at his watch.

"This will have to be the last, my dear," he said.

"Oh, will it?" She glanced at her watch and then called to a young man who was passing through the room. "Oh, Mr. Bullen, if you're going upstairs, tell Olive that we shall be going in a few minutes." She turned to me. "It takes us the best part of an hour to get back to the estate, and poor Theo has to be up at an unearthly hour in the morning."

"Oh, well, we only come in once a week," said Cartwright, "and it's the one chance Olive gets of being gay and abandoned."

I thought Cartwright looked tired and old. He was a man of middle height, with a bald, shiny head, a stubbly grey moustache, and gold-rimmed spectacles. He wore white ducks and a black and white tie. He was rather neat and you could see he took much more pains with his clothes than his untidy wife. He talked little, but it was plain that he enjoyed his wife's caustic humour and sometimes he made quite a neat retort. They were evidently very good friends. On his side there was admiration of her oddness and eccentric personality, and on hers gratitude for his appreciation and confidence. It was pleasing to see so solid and tolerant an affection between two people who were almost elderly and must have lived together for so many years.

It took but two hands to finish the rubber and we had just ordered a final gin and bitters when Olive came down.

"Do you really want to go already, mumsey?" she asked.

Mrs. Cartwright looked at her daughter with fond eyes.

"Yes, darling. It's nearly half-past eight. It'll be ten before we get our dinner."

"Damn our dinner," said Olive gaily.

"Let her have one more dance," suggested Cartwright.

"Not one. You must have a good night's rest."

Cartwright looked at Olive with a smile.

"If your mother has made up her mind, my dear, we may just as well give in without any fuss."

"She's a determined woman," said Olive, lovingly stroking her mother's wrinkled cheek.

Mrs. Cartwright patted her daughter's hand, and kissed it.

Olive was not very pretty, but she looked extremely nice. She was nineteen or twenty, I suppose, and she had still the plumpness of her age; she would be more attractive when she had fined down a little. She had none of the determination that gave her mother's face so much character, but resembled her father; she had his dark eyes and slightly aquiline nose, and his look of rather weak good-nature. It was plain that she was strong and healthy, her cheeks were red and her eyes were bright, she had a vitality that he had long lost. She seemed to be the perfectly normal English girl with high spirits, a great desire to enjoy herself, and an excellent temper.

When we separated, Gaze and I set out to walk to his house.

"What did you think of the Cartwrights?" he asked me.

"I liked them. They seemed to me very nice people. They must be a great asset in a place like this."

"I wish they came oftener. They live a very quiet life."

"It must be dull for the girl. The father and mother seem very well satisfied with one another's company."

"Yes, it's been a great success."

"Olive is the image of her father, isn't she?"

Gaze gave me a sidelong glance.

"Cartwright isn't her father. Mrs. Cartwright was a widow when he married her, and Olive was born five months after her husband's death."

"Oh!"

I drew out the sound in order to put in it all I could of surprise, interest, curiosity, and eagerness to know more. But Gaze said nothing and we walked the rest of the way in silence. The boy was waiting at the door as we entered the house, and after a last gin *pahit* we sat down to dinner.

At first Gaze was inclined to be talkative. Owing to the restriction of the output of rubber there had sprung up a considerable activity among the smugglers, and it was part of his duty to circumvent their knavishness. Two junks had been captured that day and he was rubbing hands over his success. The go-downs were full of confiscated rubber, and in a little while it was going to be solemnly burnt. But presently he fell into silence and we finished without a word. The boys brought in coffee and brandy and lit our cheroots. Gaze leaned back in his chair. He looked at me reflectively and then looked at his brandy. The boys had left the room and we were alone.

"I've known Mrs. Cartwright for over twenty years," he said slowly. "She wasn't a bad-looking woman in those days.

Always untidy, but when she was young it didn't seem to matter so much. It was rather attractive. She was married to a man called Bronson—Reggie Bronson. He was a planter. He was manager of an estate up in Selantan and I was stationed at Alor Lipis. It was a much smaller place than it is now; I don't suppose there were more than twenty people in the whole community, but they had a jolly little club and we used to have a very good time. I remember when I first met Mrs. Bronson quite clearly.

"There were no cars in those days and she and Bronson had ridden in on their bicycles. Of course, then she didn't look so determined as she looks now. She was much thinner, she had a nice colour and her eyes seemed larger. They were very pretty blue eyes, you know, and she had a lot of dark hair. If she'd only taken more trouble with herself she'd have been rather stunning. As it was she was the best-looking woman there."

I tried to construct in my mind a picture of what Mrs. Cartwright—Mrs. Bronson as she was then—looked like from what she was now, and from Gaze's not very descriptive remarks. In the solid woman, with her well-covered bones, who sat rather heavily at the bridge table, I tried to see a slight young thing with buoyant movements and graceful, easy gestures. Her chin now was very square and her nose decided, but the roundness of youth must have hidden this: her unlined skin was pink and white, and I could well imagine that the careless way in which she dressed her abundant hair gave her a peculiar charm. At that period she must have worn a long skirt, a tight waist and a picture hat. Or did women in Malaya still wear the topees that you see in old numbers of the illustrated papers?

"I hadn't seen her for—oh, nearly twenty years," Gaze went on. "I knew she was living somewhere in the F.M.S., but it was a surprise, when I took this job and came here, to run across her in the club just as I had up in Selantan so many years before. Of course, she's an elderly woman now and she's changed out of all recognition. It was rather a shock to see her with a grown-up daughter; it made me realize how the time had passed; I was a young fellow when I met her last, and now, by jingo! I'm due to retire on the age-limit in two or three years. Bit thick, isn't it?"

Gaze, a rueful grin on his ugly face, looked at me with faint indignation, as though I could help the hurrying march of the years as they trod upon one another's heels.

"I'm no chicken myself," I replied.

"You haven't lived out in the East all your life. It ages one before one's time. One's an elderly man at fifty, and at fifty-five one's good for nothing but the scrap-heap."

But I did not want Gaze to wander off into a disquisition on old age.

"Did you recognize Mrs. Cartwright when you saw her again?" I asked.

"Well, I did and I didn't. At the first glance I thought she reminded me of someone I knew. It didn't occur to me that I hadn't seen her for twenty years, and she'd changed. I thought it was someone I'd met on board ship when I was going on leave and had known only by sight. But the moment she spoke to me I remembered at once. I remembered the dry twinkle in her eyes and the crisp sound of her voice. There was something in her voice that seemed to mean: You're a bit of a damned fool, my lad, but you're not a bad sort, and upon my soul I rather like you."

"That's a good deal to read into the sound of a voice," I smiled.

She came up to me in the club and shook hands with me. "How do you do, Major Gaze? Do you remember me?" she said.

"Of course I do."

"A lot of water has passed under the bridge since we met last. We're none of us as young as we were. Have you seen Theo?"

For a moment I couldn't think who she meant. I suppose I looked rather stupid, because she gave a little smile, that ironical, quizzing smile that now I recalled so well, and explained.

"I married Theo, you know. It seemed the best thing to do. I was lonely and he wanted it."

"I heard you married him," I said. "I hope you've been very happy."

"Oh, very. Theo's a perfect duck. He'll be here in a minute. He'll be so glad to see you."

I wondered. I should have thought I was the last person Theo would wish to see. I shouldn't have thought she would wish it very much, either. But women are funny.

"Why shouldn't she wish to see you?" I asked.

"I'm coming to that later," said Gaze. "Then Theo turned up. I don't know why I called him Theo; I never called him anything but Cartwright; I never thought of him as anything but Cartwright. Theo was a shock. You know what he looks like now; I remembered him as a curly-headed youngster, very fresh and clean-looking; he was always neat and dapper. He had a good figure, and he held himself easily, like a man who's used to taking a lot of exercise. Now I come to think of it, he wasn't bad looking—not in a big, massive way, but graceful, you know, and lithe. When I saw this bowed, cadaverous, bald-headed old fellow with spectacles, I could hardly believe my eyes. I shouldn't have known him from Adam. He seemed pleased to see me; at least, interested; he wasn't effusive, but he'd always been on the quiet side, and I didn't expect him to be."

"Are you surprised to find us here?" he asked me.

"Well, I hadn't the faintest notion where you were."

"We've kept track of your movements more or less. We've seen your name in the paper every now and then. You must come out one day and have a look at our place. We've been settled there a good many years, and I suppose we shall stay there till we go home for good. Have you ever been back to Alor Lipis?"

"No, I haven't," I said.

"It was a nice little place. I am told it's grown. I've never been back."

"It hasn't got the pleasantest recollections for us," said Mrs. Cartwright.

"I asked them if they would have a drink, and we called the boy. I daresay you noticed that Mrs. Cartwright likes her liquor; I don't mean that she gets tight or anything like that, but she drinks her stingah like a man. I couldn't help looking at them with a certain amount of curiosity. They seemed perfectly happy. I gathered that they hadn't done at all badly, and I found out later that they were quite well off. They had a very nice car, and when they went on leave they denied themselves nothing. They were on the best of terms with one another. You know how jolly it is to see two people who've been married a great many years obviously better pleased with their own company than anyone else's. Their marriage had evidently been a great success. And they were both of them devoted to Olive and very proud of her, Theo especially."

"Although she was only his step-daughter?" I said.

"Although she was only his step-daughter," answered Gaze. "You'd think that she would have taken his name, but she hadn't. She called him daddy, of course—he was the only father she had ever known—but she signed her letters Olive Bronson."

"What was Bronson like, by the way?"

"Bronson? He was a great big fellow, very hearty, with a loud voice and a bellowing laugh; beefy, you know, and a fine athlete. There was not very much to him, but he was as straight as a die. He had a red face and red hair. Now I come to think of it, I remember that I never saw a man sweat as much as he did. Water just poured off him, and when he played tennis he always used to take a towel on the court with him."

"It doesn't sound very attractive."

"He was a handsome chap. He was always fit. He was keen on that. He hadn't much to talk about but rubber and games, tennis, you know, and golf and shooting; and I don't suppose he read a book from year's end to year's end. He was the typical public-school boy. He was about thirty-five when I first knew him, but he had the mind of a boy of eighteen. You know how many fellows, when they come out East, seem to stop growing."

I did indeed. One of the most disconcerting things to the traveller is to see stout, middle-aged gentlemen, with bald heads, speaking and acting as though they were schoolboys. It is as though from the time they first pass through the Suez Canal no idea had ever entered their heads, and they continue, though married and the fathers of children, and though they may be at the head of large businesses, to look upon life from the standpoint of the sixth form.

"But he was no fool," Gaze went on. "He knew his work from A to Z. His estate was one of the best managed in the country, and he knew how to handle his labour. He was a damned good sort, and if he did get on your nerves a little, you couldn't help liking him. He was generous with his money, and always ready to do anybody a good turn. That's how Cartwright happened to turn up in the first instance."

"Did the Bronsons get on well together?"

"Oh yes, I think so. I'm sure they did. He was very good-natured, and she was very jolly and gay in those days. She was very outspoken, you know. She can be very funny when she likes, even now, but there's generally a sting lurking in the joke; when she was a young woman and married to Bronson it was just pure fun. She had high spirits and liked having a good time. She never cared a damn what she said, but it went with her type, if you understand what I mean; there was something so open and frank and careless about her that you didn't care what she said to you. They seemed very happy.

"Their estate was about five miles from Alor Lipis, and they used to ride in most evenings about five. Of course, it was a very small community, and men were in the majority. There were only about six women. The Bronsons were a godsend. They bucked things up the moment they arrived. We used to have very jolly times in that little club. I've often thought of them since, and I don't know that on the whole I've ever enjoyed myself more than I did when I was stationed there. Between six and eight-thirty the club at Alor Lipis twenty years ago was about as lively a place as you could find between Aden and Yokohama.

"One day Mrs. Bronson told us that they were expecting a friend to stay with them, and a few days later they brought Cartwright along. It appeared that he was an old friend of Bronson's. They'd been at school together—Marlborough, or some place like that—and they'd first come out East on the same ship. Rubber was not very good at that time, and a lot of fellows had lost their jobs. Cartwright was one of them. He'd been out of work for the greater part of a year, and he hadn't anything to fall back on. In those days planters were even worse paid than they are now, and a man has to be very lucky to put by something for a rainy day. Cartwright had gone to Singapore. They all go there when there's a slump, you know. It's awful then. I've seen it. I've known of planters sleeping in the street because they hadn't the price of a night's lodging. I've known them stop strangers outside the 'Europe' and ask for a dollar to get a meal; and I think Cartwright had a pretty rotten time.

"At last he wrote to Bronson and asked him if he couldn't do something for him. Bronson asked him to come and stay till things got better. At least it would be free board and lodgings, and Cartwright jumped at the chance, but Bronson had to send him the money to pay his railway fare. When Cartwright arrived at Alor Lipis he hadn't ten cents in his pocket. Bronson had a little money of his own—two or three hundred a year, I think—and though his salary had been cut, he had kept his job so that he was better off than most planters. When Cartwright came, Mrs. Bronson told him that he was to look upon the place as his home, and stay as long as he liked."

"It was very nice of her, wasn't it?" I remarked.

"Very."

Gaze lit himself another cheroot and filled his glass. It was very still, and but for the occasional croak of the *chik-chak* the silence was intense. We seemed to be alone in the tropical night, and heaven only knows how far from the habitations of men. Gaze did not speak for so long that at last I was forced to say something.

"What sort of a man was Cartwright at that time?" I asked. "Younger, of course, and you told me rather nice-looking; but in himself?"

"Well, to tell you the truth, I never paid much attention to him. He was pleasant and unassuming. He's very quiet now, as I daresay you noticed. Well, he wasn't exactly lively then, but he was perfectly inoffensive. He was fond of reading, and he played the piano rather nicely.

"You never minded having him about. He was never in the way, but you never bothered very much about him. He danced well, and the women rather liked that, but he also played billiards quite decently, and he wasn't bad at tennis.

"He fell into our little groove very naturally. I wouldn't say that he ever became wildly popular, but everybody liked him. Of course, we were sorry for him, as one is for a man who's down and out, but there was nothing we could do, and—well, we just accepted him, and then forgot that he hadn't always been there. He used to come in with the Bronsons every evening and pay for his drinks like everyone else. I suppose Bronson had lent him a bit of money for current expenses, and he was always very civil. I'm rather vague about him, because really he didn't make any particular impression on me. In the East one meets such a lot of people, and he seemed very much like anybody else.

"He did everything he could to get something to do, but he had no luck. The fact is, there were no jobs going, and sometimes he seemed rather depressed about it. He was with the Bronsons for over a year. I remember his saying to me once:

"After all, I can't live with them for ever. They've been most awfully good to me, but there are limits."

"I should think the Bronsons would be very glad to have you," I said. "It's not very gay on a rubber estate, and as far as your food and drink go, it must make very little difference if you're there or not."

Gaze stopped once more and looked at me with a sort of hesitation.

"What's the matter?" I asked.

"I'm afraid I'm telling you this story very badly," he said. "I seem to be just rambling on. I'm not a damned novelist, I'm a policeman, and I'm just telling you the facts as I saw them at the time; and from my point of view all the circumstances are important. It's important, I mean, to realize what sort of people they were."

"Of course. Fire away."

I remember someone—a woman, I think it was the doctor's wife—asking Mrs. Bronson if she didn't get tired sometimes of having a stranger in the house. You know, in places like Alor Lipis there isn't very much to talk about, and if you didn't talk about your neighbours there'd be nothing to talk about at all.

"Oh no," she said. "Theo's no trouble." She turned to her husband, who was sitting there mopping his face. "We like having him, don't we?"

"He's all right," said Bronson.

"What does he do with himself all day?"

"Oh, I don't know," said Mrs. Bronson. "He walks round the

estate with Reggie sometimes, and he shoots a little. He talks to me."

"He's always glad to make himself useful," said Bronson. "The other day when I had a go of fever, he took over my work, and I just lay in bed and had a good time."

"Hadn't the Bronsons any children?" I asked.

"No," Gaze answered. "I don't know why; they could well have afforded it."

Gaze leant back in his chair. He took off his glasses and wiped them. They were very strong, and hideously distorted his eyes. Without them he wasn't so homely. The *chik-chak* on the ceiling gave its strangely human cry. It was like the cackle of an idiot child.

"Bronson was killed," said Gaze suddenly.

"Killed?"

Yes, murdered. I shall never forget that night. We'd been playing tennis—Mrs. Bronson and the doctor's wife, Theo Cartwright, and I; and then we played bridge. Cartwright had been off his game, and when we sat down at the bridge table Mrs. Bronson said to him: "Well, Theo, if you play bridge as rottenly as you played tennis, we shall lose our shirts."

We'd just had a drink, but she called the boy and ordered another round.

"Put that down your throat," she said to him, "and don't call without top honours and an outside trick."

Bronson hadn't turned up. He'd gone in to Kabulong to get the money to pay his coolies their wages, and was to come along to the club when he got back. The Bronsons' estate was nearer Alor Lipis than it was Kabulong, but Kabulong was a more important place commercially, and Bronson banked there.

"Reggie can cut in when he turns up," said Mrs. Bronson.

"He's late, isn't he?" said the doctor's wife.

"Very. He said he wouldn't get back in time for tennis, but would be here for a rubber. I have a suspicion that he went to the club at Kabulong instead of coming straight home, and is having drinks, the ruffian."

"Oh, well, he can put away a good many without their having much effect on him," I laughed.

"He's getting fat, you know. He'll have to be careful."

We sat by ourselves in the card-room, and we could hear the crowd in the billiard-room talking and laughing. They were all on the merry side. It was getting on to Christmas Day, and we were all letting ourselves go a little. There was going to be a dance on Christmas Eve.

I remembered afterwards that when we sat down the doctor's wife asked Mrs. Bronson if she wasn't tired.

"Not a bit," she said. "Why should I be?"

I didn't know why she flushed.

"I was afraid the tennis might have been too much for you," said the doctor's wife.

"Oh no," answered Mrs. Bronson, a trifle abruptly, I thought, as though she didn't want to discuss the matter.

I did not know what they meant, and indeed it was not till later that I remembered the incident.

We played three or four rubbers, and still Bronson did not turn up.

"I wonder what's happened to him," said his wife. "I can't think why he should be so late."

Cartwright was always silent, but this evening he had hardly opened his mouth. I thought he was tired, and asked him what he'd been doing.

"Nothing very much," he said. "I went out after tiffin to shoot pigeon."

"Did you have any luck?" I asked.

"Oh, I got half a dozen. They were very shy."

But now he said: "If Reggie got back late, I daresay he thought it wasn't worth while to come here. I expect he's had a bath, and when we get in we shall find him asleep in his chair."

"It's a good long ride from Kabulong," said the doctor's wife.

"He doesn't take the road, you know," Mrs. Bronson explained. "He takes the short cut through the jungle."

"Can he get along on his bicycle?" I asked.

"Oh yes; it's a very good track. It saves about a couple of miles."

We had just started another rubber when the bar-boy came in and said that there was a police-sergeant outside who wanted to speak to me.

"What does he want?" I asked.

The boy said he didn't know, but he had two coolies with him.

"Curse him," I said. "I'll give that sergeant hell if I find he's disturbed me for nothing."

I told the boy I'd come, and I finished playing the hand. Then I got up.

"I won't be a minute," I said. "Deal for me, will you?" I added to Cartwright.

I went out and found the sergeant with two Malays waiting for me on the steps. I asked him what the devil he wanted. You can imagine my consternation when he told me that the Malays had come to the police-station and said there was a white man lying dead on the path that led through the jungle to Kabulong. I immediately thought of Bronson.

"Dead?" I cried.

"Yes, shot. Shot through the head. A white man with red hair."

Then I knew it could only be Reggie Bronson, and indeed, one of them, naming his estate, said he had recognized him as the *tuan*. It was an awful shock, and there was Mrs. Bronson in the card-room waiting impatiently for me to sort my cards and make a bid. For a moment I really didn't know what to do. I was frightfully upset. It was dreadful to give her such a terrible and unexpected blow without a word of preparation, but I found myself quite unable to think of any way to soften it. I told the sergeant and the coolies to wait, and went back into the club. I tried to pull myself together. As I entered the card-room Mrs. Bronson said: "You've been an awful long time." Then she caught sight of my face. "Is anything the matter?" I saw her clench her fists and go white. You'd have thought she had a presentiment of evil.

"Something dreadful has happened," I said, and my throat was all closed up so that my voice sounded even to me hoarse and uncanny. "There's been an accident. Your husband's been wounded."

She gave a long gasp. It was not exactly a scream; it reminded me oddly of a piece of silk torn in two.

"Wounded?"

She leapt to her feet with her eyes starting from her head, and stared at Cartwright. The effect on him was ghastly. He fell back in his chair and went as white as death.

"Very, very badly, I'm afraid," I added.

I knew that I must tell her the truth, and tell it then, but I couldn't bring myself to tell it all at once.

"Is he"—her lips trembled so that she could hardly form the words—"is he—conscious?"

I looked at her for a moment without answering. I'd have given a thousand pounds not to have to.

"No, I'm afraid he isn't."

Mrs. Bronson stared at me as though she were trying to see right into my brain.

"Is he dead?"

I thought the only thing was to get it out and have done with it.

"Yes, he was dead when they found him."

Mrs. Bronson collapsed into her chair and burst into tears.

"Oh, my God!" she muttered. "Oh, my God!"

The doctor's wife went to her and put her arms round her. Mrs. Bronson, with her face in her hands, swayed to and fro, weeping hysterically. Cartwright, with that livid face, sat quite still, his mouth open, and stared at her. You might have thought he was turned to stone.

"Oh, my dear, my dear," said the doctor's wife, "you must try and pull yourself together." Then, turning to me: "Get her a glass of water and fetch Harry."

Harry was her husband, and he was playing billiards. I went in and told him what had happened.

"A glass of water be damned," he said. "What she wants is a good long peg of brandy."

We took it in to her and forced her to drink it, and gradually the violence of her emotion exhausted itself. In a few minutes the doctor's wife was able to take her into the ladies' lavatory so that she might wash her face. I had made up my mind now what had better be done. I could see that Cartwright wasn't good for much; he was all to pieces. I could understand that it was a fearful shock to him, for, after all, Bronson was his greatest friend, and had done everything in the world for him.

"You look as though you'd be all the better for a drop of brandy yourself, old man," I said to him.

He made an effort.

"It's shaken me, you know," he said. "I . . . I didn't. . . ." He stopped as though his mind was wandering; he was still fearfully pale. He took out a packet of cigarettes and struck a match, but his hand was shaking so that he could hardly manage it.

"Yes, I'll have a brandy."

"Boy," I shouted, and then to Cartwright: "Now, are you fit to take Mrs. Bronson home?"

"Oh yes," he answered.

"That's good. The doctor and I will go along with the coolies and some police to where the body is."

"Will you bring him to the bungalow?" asked Cartwright.

"I think he'd better be taken straight to the mortuary," said the doctor before I could answer. "I shall have to do a P.M."

When Mrs. Bronson, now so much calmer that I was amazed, came back, I told her what I suggested. The doctor's wife, kind woman, offered to go with her and spend the night at the bungalow, but Mrs. Bronson would not hear of it. She said she would be perfectly all right, and when the doctor's wife insisted—you know how bent some people are on forcing their kindness on those in trouble—she turned on her almost fiercely.

"No, no; I must be alone," she said. "I really must. And Theo will be there."

They got into the trap. Theo took the reins and they drove off. We started after them, the doctor and I, while the sergeant and the coolies followed. I had sent my *seis* to the police-station with instructions to send two men to the place where the body was lying. We soon passed Mrs. Bronson and Cartwright.

"All right?" I called.

"Yes," he answered.

We had to drive along the road that passed Bronson's estate and two miles further before we came to the short cut to Kabulong, along which poor Bronson had been killed. The Malays had been coming back from Kabulong when they found him. Fortunately the moon was full, and it was almost as light as day. For some time the doctor and I drove without saying a word; we were both of us deeply shocked. I was worried as well. Somehow or other I'd got to find the murderers, and I foresaw that it would be no easy matter.

"Do you suppose it was gang robbery?" said the doctor at last. He might have been reading my thoughts.

"I don't think there's a doubt of it," I answered. "They knew he'd gone into Kabulong to get the wages, and lay in wait for him on the way back. Of course, he should never have come alone through the jungle when everyone knew he had a large sum with him."

"He'd done it for years," said the doctor. "And he's not the only one."

"I know. The question is, how we're going to get hold of the fellows that did it."

"You don't think the two coolies who say they found him could have had anything to do with it?"

"No. They wouldn't have the nerve. I think a pair of Chinks might think out a trick like that, but I don't believe Malays would. They'd be much too frightened. Of course, we'll keep an eye on them. We shall see if they fling money about."

"It's awful for Mrs. Bronson," said the doctor. "It would have been bad enough at any time, but now she's going to have a baby . . ."

"I didn't know that," I said, interrupting him.

"No, for some reason she wanted to keep it dark. She was rather funny about it, I thought."

I recollected then that little passage between Mrs. Bronson and the doctor's wife. I understood why that good woman had been so anxious that Mrs. Bronson should not overtire herself.

"It's strange her having a baby after being married so many years."

"It happens, you know. But it was a surprise to her. When first she came to see me and I told her what was the matter, she fainted, and then she began to cry. I should have thought she'd be as pleased as Punch. She told me that Bronson didn't like children, and he'd be awfully bored at the idea, and she made me promise to say nothing about it till she had had a chance of breaking it to him gradually."

I reflected for a moment.

He was the kind of breezy, hearty cove whom you'd expect to be as keen as mustard on having kids.

"You never can tell. Some people are very selfish, and just don't want the bother."

"Well, how did he take it when she did tell him? Wasn't he rather bucked?"

"I don't know that she ever told him. Though she could not have waited much longer; unless I'm very much mistaken she ought to be confined in about five months."

"Poor devil," I said. "You know, I've got a notion that he'd have been most awfully pleased to know."

We drove in silence for the rest of the way, and at last came to the point at which Bronson, riding along the path, should have found the road. Here we stopped, and in a minute or two my trap, in which were the police-sergeant and the two Malays, came up. We took the headlamps to light us on our way. I left the doctor's *seis* to look after the ponies, and told him that when the policemen came they were to follow the path till they found us. The two coolies, carrying the lamps, walked ahead, and we followed them. It was a fairly broad track, wide enough for a small cart to pass, and before the road was built it had been the highway between Kabulong and Alor Lipis. It was firm to the foot and good walking. The surface here and there was sandy, and in places you could see quite plainly the trace of Bronson's bicycle that he had left on his way into Kabulong early in the day.

We walked twenty minutes, I should think, in single file, and on a sudden the coolies, with a cry, stopped sharply. The sight had come upon them so abruptly that, notwithstanding they were expecting it, they were startled. There, in the middle of the pathway, lit fitfully by the lamps the coolies carried, lay Bronson. He had fallen over his bicycle, and lay across it in an ungainly heap. I was too shocked to speak, and I think the doctor was, too. But in our silence the din of the jungle was deafening; those damned cicadas and the bull-frogs were making enough row to wake the dead. Even under ordinary circumstances the noise of the jungle at night always seems to me uncanny; because you feel that at that hour there should be an utter silence, it has an odd effect on you, that ceaseless and invisible uproar that beats upon your nerves. It surrounds you and hems you in. But just then, believe me, it was terrifying. That poor fellow lay dead, and all round him the restless life of the jungle pursued its indifferent and ferocious course.

He was lying face downwards. The sergeant and the coolies looked at me as though awaiting an order. I was a young fellow then, and I'm afraid I felt a little frightened. Though I could not see the face, I had no doubt that it was Bronson, but I felt that I ought to turn the body over to make sure. I suppose we all have our little squeamishnesses; you know I've always had a horrible distaste for touching dead bodies. I've had to do it fairly often, but it still makes me feel slightly sick.

" It's Bronson all right," I said.

The doctor—by George, it was lucky for me he was there—the doctor bent down and turned the head. The sergeant directed the lamp on the dead face.

" My God, half his head's been shot away," I cried.

" Yes."

The doctor stood up straight and wiped his hands on the leaves of a tree that grew beside the path.

" Is he quite dead?" I asked.

" Oh, yes. Death must have been instantaneous. Whoever shot him must have fired at pretty close range."

" How long has he been dead, d'you think?"

" Oh, I don't know—several hours."

" He would have passed here about five o'clock, I suppose, if he was expecting to get to the club for a rubber at six."

" There's no sign of any struggle," said the doctor.

" No, there wouldn't be. He was shot as he was riding along."

I looked at the body for a little while. I couldn't help thinking how short a time ago it was since Bronson, noisy and loud-voiced, had been so full of hearty life.

" You haven't forgotten that he had the coolies' wages on him," said the doctor.

" No; we had better search him."

" Shall we turn him over?"

" Wait a minute. Let us just have a look at the ground first."

I took the lamp and as carefully as I could looked all about me. Just where he had fallen the sandy pathway was trodden and confused; there were our footprints and the footprints of the coolies who had just found him. I walked back two or three paces, and then saw quite clearly the mark of his bicycle wheels; he had been riding straight and steadily. I followed it to the spot where he had fallen, to just before that, rather, and there saw very distinctly the prints, on each side of the wheels, of his heavy boots. He had evidently stopped there and put his feet to the ground. Then he'd started off again, there was a great wobble of the wheel, and he'd crashed.

"Now let's search him," I said.

The doctor and the sergeant turned the body over, and one of the coolies dragged the bicycle away. They laid Bronson on his back. I supposed he would have had the money partly in notes and partly in silver. The silver would have been in a bag attached to the bicycle, and a hasty glance told me that it was not there. The notes he would have put in a wallet. It would have been a good thick bundle. I felt him all over, but there was nothing. Then I turned out the pockets. They were all empty except the right trousers pocket, in which there was a little small change.

"Didn't he always wear a watch?" asked the doctor.

"Yes, of course he did."

I remembered that he wore the chain through the buttonhole in the lapel of his coat, and the watch and some seals and things in his handkerchief pocket. But watch and chain were gone.

"Well, there's not much doubt now, is there?" I said. It was clear that he had been attacked by gang robbers who knew he had a good sum of money on him, and after killing him they had stripped him of everything. I suddenly remembered the footprints that proved that for a moment he had stood still. I saw exactly how it had been done. One of them had stopped him on some pretext, and then, just as he started off again, another, slipping out of the jungle behind him, had emptied the two barrels of a gun into his head.

"Well," I said to the doctor, "it's up to me to catch them, and I'll tell you what—it'll be a real pleasure to me to see them hanged."

Of course, there was an inquest. Mrs. Bronson gave evidence, but she had nothing to say that we did not know already. Bronson had left the bungalow about eleven. He was to have tiffin at Kabulong, and was to be back between five and six. He asked her not to wait for him. He said he would just put the money into the safe and come straight to the club. Cartwright confirmed this. He had lunched alone with Mrs. Bronson, and after a smoke had gone out with a gun to shoot pigeon. He had got in about five—a little before, perhaps—had a bath, and changed to play tennis.

He was shooting not far from the place where Bronson was killed but never heard a shot. That, of course, meant nothing; what with a cicadas and frogs and the other sounds of the jungle, he would have had to be very near to hear anything; and besides Cartwright was probably back in the bungalow before Bronson was killed. We traced Bronson's movements. He had lunched at the club, he had got money at the bank just before it closed, had gone back to the club, and had one more drink, and then started off on his bicycle. He had crossed the river by the ferry. The ferryman remembered distinctly seeing him, but was positive that no one else with a bicycle had crossed. That looked as though the murderers were not following, but lying in wait for him. He rode along the main road for a couple of miles, and then took the path which was a short cut to his bungalow.

It looked as though he had been killed by men who knew his habits, and suspicion, of course, fell immediately on the coolies of his estate. We examined them all—pretty carefully—but there was not a scrap of evidence to connect any of them with the crime. In fact, most of them were able satisfactorily to account for their actions, and those who couldn't seemed to me for one reason and another out of the running. There were a few bad characters among the Chinese of Alor Lipis, and I had them looked up. But somehow I didn't think it was the work of the Chinese. I had a feeling that Chinese would have used revolvers and not a shot-gun. Anyhow, I could find out nothing there. So then we offered a reward of a thousand dollars to anyone who could put us in the way of discovering the murderers. I thought there were a good many people to whom it would appeal to do a public service and at the same time earn a tidy sum. But I knew that an informer would take no risks; he wouldn't want to tell what he knew till he knew he could tell it safely, and I armed myself with patience. The reward had brightened the interest of my police, and I knew they would use every means they had to bring the criminals to trial. In a case like this they could do more than I.

But it was strange, nothing happened; the reward seemed to tempt no one. I cast my net a little wider. There were two or three *kampongs* along the road, and I wondered if the murderers were there; I saw the headmen, but got no help from them. It was not that they would tell me nothing; I was sure that they had nothing to tell. I talked to the bad hats, but there was absolutely nothing to connect them with the murder. There was not the shadow of a clue.

"Very well, my lads," I said to myself, as I drove back to

Alor Lipis, "there's no hurry; the rope won't spoil by keeping."

The scoundrels had got away with a considerable sum, but money is no good unless you spend it. I felt I knew the native temperament well enough to be sure that the possession of it was a constant temptation. The Malays are an extravagant race, and a race of gamblers, and the Chinese are gamblers, too. Sooner or later someone would start flinging his money about, and then I should want to know where it came from. With a few well-directed questions I thought I could put the fear of God into the fellow, and then, if I knew my business, it should not be hard to get a full confession.

The only thing now was to sit down and wait till the hue and cry had died down and the murderers thought the affair was forgotten. The itch to spend those ill-gotten dollars would grow more and more intolerable, till at last it could be resisted no longer. I would go about my business, but I meant never to relax my watch, and one day, sooner or later, my time must come.

Cartwright took Mrs. Bronson down to Singapore. The company Bronson had worked for asked him if he would care to take Bronson's place, but he said, very naturally, that he didn't like the idea of it; so they put another man in, and told Cartwright that he could have the job that Bronson's successor had vacated. It was the management of the estate that Cartwright lives on now. He moved in at once. Four months after this Olive was born at Singapore, and a few months later, when Bronson had been dead just over a year, Cartwright and Mrs. Bronson were married. I was surprised; but on thinking it over I couldn't help confessing that it was very natural. After the trouble, Mrs. Bronson had leant much on Cartwright, and he had arranged everything for her. She must have been lonely and rather lost, and I daresay she was grateful for his kindness. He did behave like a brick; and so far as he was concerned I imagined he was sorry for her. It was a dreadful position for a woman; she had nowhere to go, and all they'd gone through must have been a tie between them. There was every reason for them to marry, and it was probably the best thing for them both.

It looked as though Bronson's murderers would never be caught, for that plan of mine did not work. There was no one in the district who spent more money than he could account for, and if anyone had that hoard buried away under his floor, he was showing a self-control that was superhuman. A year had passed, and to all intents and purposes the thing was forgotten. Could anyone be so prudent as after so long not to let a little money dribble out? It was incredible. I began to think that Bronson had been killed by a couple of wandering Chinese, who had got away to Singapore, perhaps, where there would be small chance of catching them. At last I gave it up. If you come to think of it, as a rule, it is just those crimes—crimes of robbery—in which there is least chance of getting the culprit, for there is nothing to attach suspicion to him, and if he is caught it can only be by his own carelessness. It is different with crimes of passion or vengeance; then you can find out who had a motive to put the victim out of the way.

It's no use grizzling over one's failures; and, bringing my common sense to bear, I did my best to put the matter out of my mind. No one likes to be beaten, but beaten I was, and I had to put as good a face on it as I could.

And then a Chinaman was caught trying to pawn poor Bronson's watch.

I told you that Bronson's watch and chain had been taken, and of course Mrs. Bronson was able to give us a fairly accurate description of it. It was a half-hunter, by Benson; there was a gold chain, three or four seals, and a sovereign purse. The pawnbroker was an astute fellow, and when the Chinaman brought the watch in he recognized it at once. On some pretext he kept the man waiting and sent for a policeman. The man was arrested and immediately brought to me. I greeted him like a long-lost brother. I was never so pleased to see anyone in my life. I have no feeling about criminals, you know. I'm rather sorry for them, because they're playing a game in which their opponents hold all the aces and kings; but when I catch one it gives me a little thrill of satisfaction, like bringing off a neat finesse at bridge. At last the mystery was going to be cleared up, for if the Chinaman had not committed the murder himself, we were pretty sure through him to trace the murderers. I beamed on him.

I asked him to account for his possession of the watch. He said he had bought it from a man he did not know. That was very thin. I explained the circumstances briefly, and told him he would be charged with murder. I meant to frighten him, and I did. He said then that he'd found the watch.

"Found it?" I said. "Fancy that! Where?"

His answer staggered me. He said he'd found it in the jungle. I laughed at him. I asked him if he thought watches were likely to be left lying about in the jungle. Then he said he'd been coming along the pathway that led from Kabulong to Alor Lipis, and had gone into the jungle, and had caught sight of something gleaming, and there was the watch. That was odd. Why should he have said he'd found the watch just there? It was either true or excessively astute. I asked him where the chain and the seals were, and he produced them immediately. I'd got him scared, and he was pale and shaking. He was a knock-kneed little fellow, and I should have been a fool not to see that I hadn't got hold of the murderer there. But his terror suggested that he knew something.

I asked him when he'd found the watch.

" Yesterday," he said.

I asked him what he was doing on the short cut from Kabulong to Alor Lipis. He said that he'd been working in Singapore and had gone to Kabulong because his father was ill, and now was come to Alor Lipis to work. A friend of his father, a carpenter by trade, had given him a job. He gave me the name of the man with whom he had worked in Singapore and the name of the man who had engaged him at Alor Lipis. All he said seemed plausible, and could so easily be verified that it was hardly likely to be false. Of course it occurred to me that if he had found the watch as he said it must have been lying in the jungle for more than a year. It could hardly be in very good condition. I tried to open it, but could not. The pawnbroker had come to the police-station, and was waiting in the next room. Luckily he was also something of a watchmaker. I sent for him, and asked him to look at the watch. When he opened it he gave a little whistle—the works were thick with rust.

" This watch no good," he said, shaking his head. " Him never go now."

I asked him what had put it in such a state, and without a word from me he said that it had been long exposed to wet. For the moral effect I had the prisoner put in a cell, and I sent for his employer. I also sent a wire to Kabulong and to Singapore. While I waited I did my best to put two and two together. I was inclined to believe the man's story true; his fear might be ascribed to no more guilt than consisted in his having found something and tried to sell it. Even quite innocent persons are apt to be nervous and lose their heads when they are in the hands of the police. I don't know what there is about a policeman; people are never very much at their ease in his company. But if he really had found the watch where he said, someone had thrown it there. Now that was a funny thing to do. Even if the murderers had thought the watch a dangerous thing to possess, one would have expected them to melt down the gold case. That would be a very simple thing for any native to do; and the chain was of so ordinary a pattern they could hardly have thought it possible to trace that. There were chains like it in every jeweller's shop in the country. Of course, there was the possibility that they had plunged into the jungle and, having dropped the watch in their hurry, had been afraid to go back and look for it. I did not think that very likely; the Malays are used to keeping things tucked away in their *sarongs,* and the Chinese have pockets in their coats. Besides, the moment they got into the jungle they knew there was no hurry. They probably waited and divided the swag then and there.

In a few minutes the man I had sent for came to the police-station and confirmed what the prisoner had said; and in an hour I got an answer from Kabulong. The police had seen his father, who told them that the boy had gone to Alor Lipis to get a job with a carpenter. So far everything he had said seemed true. I had him brought in again, and told him I was going to take him to the place where he said he had found the watch, and he must show me the exact spot. I handcuffed him to a policeman—though it was hardly necessary, for the poor devil was shaking with fright—and took a couple of men besides. We drove out to where the track joined the road and walked along it. Within five yards of the place where Bronson was killed the Chinaman stopped.

"Here," he said.

He pointed to the jungle, and we followed him in. We went in about ten yards, and he pointed to a chink between two large boulders, and said that he found the watch there. It could only have been by the merest chance that he had noticed it, and if he really had found it there, it looked very much as though someone had put it there to hide it.

Gaze stopped and gave me a reflective look.

"What would you have thought then?" he asked.

"I don't know," I answered.

"Well, I'll tell you what I thought. I thought that if the watch was there the money might be there too. It seemed worth while having a look. Of course, to look for something in the jungle makes looking for a needle in a bundle of hay a drawing-room pastime. I couldn't help that. I released the Chinaman—I wanted all the help I could get—and set him to work. I set my three men to work, and I started in myself. We made a line—there were five of us—and we searched from the road. For fifty yards on each side of the place at which Bronson was murdered and for a hundred yards in we went over the ground foot by foot. We routed among dead leaves and peered in bushes; we looked inside boulders and in the hollows of trees. I knew it was a foolish thing to do, for the chances against us were a thousand to one. My only hope was that anyone who had just committed a murder would be rattled, and if he wanted to hide anything would hide it quickly; he would choose the first obvious hiding-place that offered itself. That is what he had done when he hid the watch.

My only reason for looking in so circumscribed an area was that, as the watch had been found so near the road, the person who wanted to get rid of the things must have wanted to get rid of them quickly.

"We worked on. I began to grow tired and cross. We were sweating like pigs. At last I came to the conclusion that we must give it up as a bad job, for that day at least, when suddenly the Chinaman—he must have had sharp eyes, that young man—uttered a guttural cry. He stooped down and from under the winding root of a tree drew out a messy, mouldering, stinking thing. It was a pocket-book that had been out in the rain for a year, that had been eaten by ants and beetles and God knows what, that was sodden and foul, but it was a pocket-book all right, Bronson's, and inside were the shapeless, mushed-up, fetid remains of the Singapore notes he had got from the bank at Kabulong. There was still the silver, and I was convinced that it was hidden somewhere about, but I was not going to bother about that. I had found out something very important: whoever had murdered Bronson had made no money out of it.

"Do you remember my telling you that I had noticed the print of Bronson's feet on each side of the broad line of the pneumatic tyre, where he had stopped, and presumably spoken to someone? He was a heavy man and the prints were well marked. He hadn't just put his feet on the soft sand and taken them off, but must have stopped at least for a minute or two. My explanation was that he had stopped to chat with a Malay or a Chinaman, but the more I thought of it the less I liked it. Why the devil should he? Bronson wanted to get home, and though a jovial chap, he certainly was not hail-fellow-well-met with the natives. His relations towards them were those of master and servants. Those footprints had always puzzled me. And now the truth flashed across me. Whoever had murdered Bronson hadn't murdered him to rob. I knew at last who the murderer was."

I have always thought the detective story a most diverting and ingenious variety of fiction, and have regretted that I never had the skill to write one, but I have read a good many, and I flatter myself it is rarely that I have not solved the mystery before it was disclosed to me; and now for some time I had foreseen what Gaze was going to say, but when at last he said it I confess that it gave me, notwithstanding, somewhat of a shock.

"The man he met was Cartwright. Cartwright was pigeon-shooting. He stopped and asked him what sport he had had, and as he rode on Cartwright raised his gun and discharged both barrels into his head. Cartwright took the money and the watch in order to make it look like the work of gang robbers and hurriedly hid them in the jungle, then made his way along the edge till he got to the road, went back to the bungalow, changed into his tennis things and drove with Mrs. Bronson to the club.

"I remembered how badly he'd played tennis, and how he'd collapsed when, in order to break the news more gently to Mrs. Bronson, I said Bronson was wounded and not dead. If he was only wounded he might have been able to speak. By George! I bet that was a bad moment. The child was Cartwright's. Look at Olive: why, you saw the likeness yourself. The doctor said that Mrs. Bronson was upset when he told her she was going to have a baby, and made him promise not to tell Bronson. Why? Because Bronson knew that he couldn't be the father of the child."

"Do you think that Mrs. Bronson knew what Cartwright had done?" I asked.

"I'm sure of it. When I look back on her behaviour that evening at the club I am convinced of it. She was upset, but not because Bronson was killed; she was upset because I told her he was wounded. When I confessed that he was dead when they found him she burst out crying, but from relief. I know that woman. Look at that square chin of hers and tell me that she hasn't got the courage of the devil. She has a will of iron. She made Cartwright do it. She planned every detail and every move. He was completely under her influence; he is now."

"But do you mean to tell me that neither you nor anyone else ever suspected that there was anything between them?"

"Never. Never."

"If they were in love with one another and knew that she was going to have a baby, why didn't they just bolt?"

"How could they? It was Bronson who had the money; she hadn't a bean and neither had Cartwright. He was out of a job. Do you think he would have got another with that story round his neck? Bronson had taken him in when he was starving and he'd stolen his wife from him. They wouldn't have a dog's chance."

"They might have thrown themselves on his mercy."

"Yes, but I think they were too ashamed. He'd been so good to them, he was such a decent chap, I don't think they had the heart to tell him the truth. They preferred to kill him."

There was a moment's silence while I reflected over what Gaze said.

"Well, what did you do about it?" I asked.

"Nothing. What was there to do? What was the evidence? That the watch and notes had been found? They might easily have been hidden by someone who was afterwards afraid to come and get them. The murderer might have been quite content to get away with the silver. The footprints? Bronson might have stopped to light a cigarette or there might have been a tree-trunk across the path and he waited while the coolies he met there by chance moved it away. Who could prove that the child that a perfectly decent, respectable woman had had four months after her husband's death was not his child? No jury would have convicted Cartwright. I held my tongue and the Bronson murder was forgotten."

"I don't suppose the Cartwrights have forgotten," I suggested.

"I shouldn't be surprised. Human memory is astonishingly short, and if you want my professional opinion I don't mind telling you that I don't believe remorse for a crime ever sits very heavily on a man when he's absolutely sure he'll never be found out."

I thought once more of the pair I had met that afternoon: the thin, elderly, bald man with gold-rimmed spectacles, and that white-haired, untidy woman with her frank speech and kindly, caustic smile. It was almost impossible to imagine that in the distant past they had been swayed by so turbulent a passion, for that alone had made their behaviour explicable, that it had brought them in the end to such a pass that they could see no other issue than a cruel and cold-blooded murder.

"Doesn't it make you feel a little uncomfortable to be with them?" I asked Gaze. "For without wishing to be censorious I'm bound to say that I don't think they can be very nice people."

"That's where you're wrong. They are very nice people; they're about the pleasantest people here. Mrs. Cartwright is a thoroughly good sort and a very amusing woman. It's my business to prevent crime and to catch the culprit when crime is committed, but I've known far too many criminals to think that on the whole they're worse than anybody else. A perfectly decent fellow may be driven by circumstances to commit a crime, and if he s found out he's punished; but he may very well remain a perfectly decent fellow. Of course, society punishes him if he breaks its laws, and it's quite right, but it's not always his actions that indicate the essential man. If you'd been a policeman as long as I have, you'd know it's not what people do that really matters, it's what they are. Luckily, a policeman has nothing to do with their thoughts, only with their deeds."

Gaze flicked the ash from his cheroot and gave me his wry, sardonic, but agreeable smile.

"I'll tell you what, there's one job I shouldn't like," he said.

"What is that?" I asked.

"God's, at the Judgment Day," said Gaze. "No, sir."

THE FRILL

By

PEARL S. BUCK

"MY dear, the only way to manage these native tailors is to be firm!"

Mrs. Lowe, the postmaster's wife, settled herself with some difficulty into the wicker rocking-chair upon the wide veranda of her house. She was a large woman, red-faced from more food than necessary and little exercise over the ten-odd years she had spent in a port town on the China coast. Now as she looked at her caller and thus spoke, her square hard-fleshed face grew a little redder. Beside her stood a Chinese man-servant who had just announced in a mild voice:

"Tailor have come, missy."

Little Mrs. Newman looked at her hostess with vague admiration.

"I'm sure I wish I had your way with them, Adeline," she murmured, fanning herself slowly with a palm-leaf fan. She went on in a plaintive complaining way: "Sometimes I think it is scarcely worth while to bother with new clothes, although they are so cheap here, especially if you buy the native silks. But it is so much trouble to have them made, and these tailors say—my dear, my tailor promises me faithfully he will make a dress in three days and then he doesn't come for a week or two!" Her weak voice dwindled and ended in a sigh, and she fanned herself a trifle more quickly.

"Watch me, now," said Mrs. Lowe commandingly. She had a deep, firm voice, and round, hard, grey eyes set a little near together beneath closely-waved dead brown hair. She turned these eyes upon the Chinese manservant as he stood looking decorously down to the floor, his head drooping slightly, and said, "Boy, talkee tailor come this side!"

"Yes, missy," murmured the servant and disappeared.

Almost instantly there was the sound of soft, steady footsteps through the open doors, and from the back of the house through the hall following the manservant there came the tailor. He was a tall man, taller than the servant, middle-aged, his face quiet with a sort of closed tranquillity. He wore a long robe of faded blue grasscloth, patched neatly at the elbows and very clean.

Under his arm he carried a bundle wrapped in a white cloth. He bowed to the two white women and then, squatting down, put this bundle upon the floor of the veranda and untied its knots. Inside was a worn and frayed fashion book from some American company and a half-finished dress of a spotted blue and white silk. This dress he shook out carefully and held up for Mrs. Lowe to see. From its generous proportions it could be seen that it was made for her. She surveyed it coldly and with hostility, searching its details.

Suddenly she spoke in a loud voice: "No wantchee that collar, tailor! I have talkie you wantchee frill—see, so fashion!" She turned the pages of the book rapidly to a section devoted to garments for ample women. "See, all same fashion this lady. What for you makee flat collar? No wantchee—no wantchee—take it away!"

Upon the tailor's calm, patient face a perspiration broke forth. "Yes, missy," he said faintly. And then he pressed his lips together slightly and took a breath and began: "Missy, you first talkee frill, then you say no frill. Other day you say wantchee flat collar, frill too fat."

He looked imploringly at the white woman. But Mrs. Lowe waved him away with a fat, ringed hand.

"No, you talkee lie, tailor," she cried sternly. "I know how I talkee. I never say I wantchee flat collar—never! No lady have flat collar now. What for you talkee so fashion?"

"Yes, missy," said the tailor. Then brightening somewhat he suggested, "Have more cloth, missy. Suppose I makee frill, never mind."

But Mrs. Lowe was not to be thus easily appeased. "Yes, never mind you, but you have spoil so much my cloth. What you think, I buy this cloth no money? Plenty money you make me lose." She turned to her guest. "I have been counting on that dress, Minnie, and now look at it! I wanted to wear it to the garden party at the consulate day after tomorrow. I told him a frill—just look at that silly collar!"

"Yes, I know. It's just what I was saying," said Mrs. Newman in her tired peevish voice. "What I want to know is how will you manage it?"

"Oh, I'll manage it," replied Mrs. Lowe grimly.

She ignored the tailor for a while and stared out over her trim garden. In the hot sunshine a blue-coated coolie squatted over a border of zinnias, glittering in the September noon. A narrow sanded path ran about a square of green lawn. She said nothing, and the tailor stood acutely uncomfortable, the dress still held delicately by the shoulders. A small trickle of perspiration ran down each side of his face. He moistened his lips and began in a trembling voice:

"Missy wantchee try?"

"No, I do not," snapped Mrs. Lowe. "What for wantchee try? All wrong—collar all wrong—what for try?" She continued to stare out into the shining garden.

"Can makee all same frill," said the tailor eagerly, persuasively. "Yes, yes, missy, I makee all same you say. What time you want?"

"I want it tomorrow," replied the white woman. "You bring tomorrow, twelve o'clock. Suppose you no bring, then I no pay—savee? All time you talkee what time you bring and you never bring."

"Can do, missy," said the tailor, quietly. He squatted gracefully, folded the dress into the cloth again, and tied it tenderly, careful to crush nothing. Then he rose and stood waiting, upon his face some agony of supplication. His whole soul rose in this silent supplication, so that it was written upon his quiet, high-cheeked face, upon his close-set lips. Sweat broke out upon him afresh. Even Mrs. Lowe could feel dimly that imploring soul. She paused in her rocking and looked up.

"What is it?" she asked, sharply. "What more thing?"

The tailor wetted his lips again and spoke in a faint voice. "Missy, can you give me litty money?—one dollar, two dollar——" Before her outraged look his voice dropped yet lower. "My brother's son he die today, I think—he have three piecee baby, one woman—no money buy coffin—no nothing—he very ill today——"

Mrs. Lowe looked at her caller. "Well, of all the nerve!" she breathed, genuinely aghast. Mrs. Newman answered her look.

"It's just what I said," she replied. "They are more trouble than they are worth—and the way they cut—and then they think about nothing but money!"

Mrs. Lowe turned her rolling grey eyes upon the tailor. He did not look up, but he wiped his lip furtively with his sleeve. She stared at him an instant, and then her voice came forth filled with righteous anger.

"No," she said. "No. You finish dress all proper with frill, I pay you. No finish dress, no pay. Never. You savee, tailor?"

"Yes, missy," sighed the tailor. All vestige of hope had now disappeared from his face like a curtain. "I finish tomorrow twelve o'clock, missy," he said, and turned away.

"See that you do," shouted Mrs. Lowe triumphantly after

him, and she watched his figure with contempt as it disappeared into the hall. Then she turned to her caller. "If I say tomorrow," she explained, "perhaps it will be ready by the day after." She thought of something and reaching forward in her chair pressed a bell firmly. The servant appeared.

"Boy," she said, "look see tailor—see he no takee something."

Her loud voice penetrated into the house, and the tailor's body, still visible at the end of the hall, straightened itself somewhat and then passed out of sight.

"You never can tell," said Mrs. Lowe. "You can't tell whether they are making up these stories or not. If they need money—but they always do need money. I never saw such people. They must make a lot, though, sewing for all these foreigners here in the port. But this tailor is worse than most. He is for ever wanting money before his work is done. Three separate times he has come and said a child was dying or something. I don't believe a word of it. Probably smokes opium or gambles. They all gamble—you can't believe a word they say!"

"Oh, I know——" sighed Mrs. Newman, rising to depart. Mrs. Lowe rose also.

"After all, one simply has to be firm," she said again.

Outside the big white foreign house the tailor went silently and swiftly through the hot street. Well, he had asked her, and she would not give him anything. After all his dread and fear of her refusal, all his summoning of courage, she would not give him anything. The dress was more than half done, except for the frill, too. She had given him the silk two days ago, and he had been glad because it would bring him in a few dollars for this nephew of his, who was like his own son now that the gods had taken away his own little children, three of them.

He had, therefore, clung the more to this only son of his dead younger brother, a young man apprenticed to an iron-smith, and he had three little children now, too. Such a strong young man—who could have thought he would have been seized for death like this? Two months ago it was that the long piece of red-hot iron he was beating into the shape of a ploughshare had slipped somehow from his pincers and had fallen upon his leg and foot and seared the flesh away almost to the bone. It had fallen on his naked flesh, for it was summer and the little shop was hot, and he had only his thin cotton trousers on, rolled to his thighs.

Well, and they had tried every sort of ointment, but what ointment will grow sound flesh again, and what balm is there for such a wound? The whole leg had swollen, and now on this hot day in the ninth moon the young man lay dying. There were black plasters on his leg from hip to foot, but they were of no avail.

Yes, the tailor had seen that for himself this morning when he went to see his nephew—he had seen death there plainly. The young wife sat weeping in the doorway of the one room that was their home, and the two elder children stared at her gravely, too stricken for play. The third was but a babe she held in her bosom.

The tailor turned down an alleyway and into a door in a wall.

Above his head were stretched bamboo poles upon which were hung ragged garments washed in too scanty water and without any soap. Here about these courts a family lived in every room and poured its waste into the court, so that even though it was a dry day—and the days had been dry for a moon or more—yet the court was slimy and running with waste water.

But he did not notice this. He passed through three more courts like the first and turned to an open door at the right and went into the dark, windowless room. There was a different odour here. It was the odour of dying, rotten flesh. The sound of a woman's wailing rose from beside the curtained bed, and thither the tailor went; his face had not changed from the look it had borne away from the white woman's house. The young wife did not look up at his coming. She sat crouched on the ground beside the bed and her face was wet with tears. Her long black hair had come uncoiled and stretched over her shoulder and hung to the earth. Over and over she moaned: "Oh, my husband—oh, my man—I am left alone—oh, my husband——"

The babe lay on the ground beside her, crying feebly now and again. The two elder children sat close to their mother, each of them holding fast to a corner of her coat. They had been weeping, too, but now were silent, their streaked faces upturned to look at their uncle.

But the tailor paid no heed to them now. He looked into the hempen curtains of the bed, and said gently:

"Are you still living, my son?"

The dying man turned his eyes with difficulty. He was horribly swollen, his hands, his naked upper body, his neck, his face. But these were nothing to the immense log-like swelling of his burned leg. It lay there so huge it seemed he was attached to it, rather than it to him. His glazed eyes fixed themselves upon his uncle. He opened his puffed lips and, after a long time and a mighty effort of concentration, his voice came forth in a hoarse whisper:

"These children——"

The tailor's face was suddenly convulsed with suffering. He

sat down upon the edge of the bed and began to speak earnestly:

"You need not grieve for your children, my son. Die peacefully. Your wife and your children shall come to my house. They shall take the place of my own three. Your wife shall be daughter to me and to my wife, and your children shall be our grandchildren. Are you not my own brother's son? And he dead, too, and only I left now."

He began to weep quietly, and it could be seen that the lines upon his face were set there by other hours of this repressed silent weeping, for as he wept his face hardly changed at all, only the tears rolled down his cheeks.

After a long time the dying man's voice came again with the same rending effort, as though he tore himself out of some heavy stupor to say what must be said:

"You—are poor—too——"

But the uncle answered quickly, bending toward the dying man, for the swollen eyes were now closed and he could not be sure he was heard: "You're not to worry. Rest your heart. I have work—these white women are always wanting new dresses. I have a silk dress now nearly finished for the postmaster's wife—nearly done, except for a frill, and then she will give me money for it and perhaps more sewing. We shall do very well——"

But the young man made no further reply. He had gone into that stupor for ever, and he could rouse himself no more.

Nevertheless, he still breathed slightly throughout that long hot day. The tailor rose once to place his bundle in a corner and to remove his robe, and then he took his place again beside the dying man and remained immovable through the hours. The woman wailed on, but at last was exhausted.

But the children grew used to it. They grew used even to their father's dying, and they ran out into the court to play.

So the hot day drew on at last to its end and when twilight came the young man ceased breathing and was dead.

Only then did the tailor rise. He rose and put on his gown and took his bundle and he said to the crouching woman, "He is dead. Have you any money at all?"

Then the young woman rose also and looked at him anxiously, smoothing the hair back from her face. It could now be seen that she was still very young—not more than twenty years of age—a young common creature such as may be seen anywhere on any street in any day, neither pretty nor ugly, slight, and somewhat slovenly even on ordinary occasions, and now unwashed for many days.

Her grimy face was round, the mouth full and projecting, the eyes a little stupid. It was clear that she had lived from day to day, never foreseeing the catastrophe that had now befallen her.

"We have nothing left," she said. "I pawned his clothes and my winter clothes and the table and stools, and we have only the bed on which he lies."

The look of despair deepened on the man's face. "Is there anyone of whom you might borrow?" he asked.

She shook her head. "I don't know anyone except these people in the court. And what have they?" Then as the full terror of her position came upon her she cried out shrilly, "Uncle, we have no one but you in the world!"

"I know," he said simply. He looked once more at the bed. "Cover him," he said, in a low voice. "Cover him against the flies."

He passed through the courts quickly then, and went through the gate into the street and turned to the west where his own home was.

It seemed to him that this was the hottest day of that whole summer. So is the ninth moon hot sometimes, and so does summer often pass burning fiercely into autumn. The evening had brought no coolness, and thunderous clouds towered over the city. The streets were filled with half-naked men and with women in thinnest garb, sitting upon little low bamboo couches they had moved out of their houses. Some lay flat upon the street on mats of reed or strips of woven matting. Children wailed everywhere, and mothers fanned their babes wearily, dreading the night.

Through this crowd the tailor passed swiftly, his head bent down. He was now very weary, but still not hungry, although he had fasted the whole day. He could not eat—no, not even when he reached the one room in a court which was his home, and he could not eat even when his poor, stupid old wife, who could not keep her babies alive, came shuffling out of the street and placed a bowl of cold rice gruel on the table for him to eat.

There was that smell about his clothes—it filled his nostrils still. He thought suddenly of the silk dress. Suppose the white woman noticed the odour there! He rose suddenly and opened the bundle and shook out the dress, and, turning it carefully inside-out, he hung it to air upon a decrepit dressmaker's form that stood by the bed.

But it could not hang there long. He must finish it and have the money. He took off his robe and undershirt and his shoes and stockings, and sat in his trousers. He must be careful in this heat that his sweat did not stain the dress. He found a grey towel and wrapped it about his head to catch the drops of sweat, and put a rag upon the table on which to wipe his hands.

While he sewed swiftly, not daring to hasten beyond what he was able to do well, lest she be not pleased, he pondered on what he could do. He had had one apprentice last year, but the times were so evil he had had to let the lad go; and so had now but his own ten fingers to use.

But that was not altogether ill, because the lad had made so many mistakes and the white women said insistently. "You must makee yourself, tailor—no give small boy makee spoil." Yes, but with just these ten fingers of his could he hope to make another dress in three days—suppose she had another silk dress—that would be ten dollars for the two. He could buy a coffin for ten dollars down and the promise of more later.

But supposing she had no more work to give him now—then what could he do? What indeed, but to go to a usurer?

And yet that he did not dare to do. A man was lost if he went to a usurer, for the interest ran faster than a tiger upon him—in a few months double and triple what he had borrowed. Then when the coffin was buried he must bring the young wife and the three babies here. There was only this one room for them all, too. His heart warmed somewhat at the thought of the babies and then stopped in terror at the thought that he must feed them.

Midnight drew on, and he was not finished. There was the worst of all yet to be made—the frill. He fetched his fashion book and pored over it beneath the flickering light of the small tin kerosene lamp. So the frill went, here it turned, a long wide frill, closely pleated. He folded the small pleats, his hands trembling with fatigue. His wife lay snoring in the bed now. Nothing would wake her, not even the rackety, noisy sewing machine with which he set fast the carefully basted frill.

At dawn there remained the edge to whip by hand and the irons to heat on the charcoal brazier. Well, he would sleep a little and rest his aching eyes and then get up to finish it.

But not for long could he sleep. At seven he rose and went to his work again and worked until nearly noon, stopping only for a mouthful of the food he could not eat the night before. Then he was finished. It had taken him longer than he hoped it would. He squinted up at the sun. Yes, he could just get to the house by noon. He must hasten. He must not make her angry so that she would perhaps refuse him the other dress. No, somehow he must have the other dress. Then if he sewed this afternoon and tonight he could finish it in another day. He smelled the finished dress anxiously. A little odour, perhaps—would she notice it?

But fortunately she did not notice it. She was sitting in that strange moving chair she had on the veranda, and she looked at the dress critically.

"All finish?" she asked in her loud, sudden way.

"Yes, missy," he answered humbly.

"All right, I go try."

She had gone into her room then, and he held his breath, waiting. Perhaps there was some odour to it yet? But she came back wearing the dress, a satisfied look upon her face; but not too satisfied.

"How much?" she said abruptly.

He hesitated. "Five dollar, missy, please." Then, seeing her angry eyes, he added hastily: "Silk dress, five dollar, please, missy. Any tailor five dollar."

"Too much—too much," she declared. "You spoil my cloth, too!" But she paid the money to him grudgingly, and he took it from her delicately, careful not to touch her hand.

"Thank you, missy," he said gently.

He dropped to his heels and began to tie up his bundle, his fingers trembling. He must ask her now. But how could he? What would he do if she refused? He gathered his courage together desperately.

"Missy." he said, looking up humbly but avoiding her eyes. "You have more dress I can do?"

He waited, hanging on her answer, staring into the shining garden. But she had already turned to go into the house again to take off the dress. She called back to him carelessly:

"No—no more! You makee too muchee trouble. You spoil my cloth—plenty more tailor more cheap and not so muchee trouble!"

The next day at the garden party she met little Mrs. Newman, sitting languidly in a wicker chair, watching white figures move about the lawn intent upon a game of croquet. Mrs. Newman's faded blue eyes brightened somewhat at the sight of the new dress.

"You really did get your dress after all," she said with faint interest. "I didn't think you really would. He did that frill nicely, didn't he?"

Mrs. Lowe looked down upon her large bosom. There the frill lay, beautifully pleated, perfectly ironed. She said with satisfaction: "Yes, it is nice, isn't it? I am glad I decided to have the frill, after all. And so cheap! My dear, with all this frill the dress cost only five dollars to be made—that's less than two dollars at home! . . . What's that—oh, yes, he brought it punctually at twelve, as I told him he must. It's as I said—you simply have to be firm with these native tailors!"

THE SWORD OF RIDICULE

By

HENRY PETERSON

CONDEMNED to death, Peh Ming, famous scholar and ex-mandarin, waited in his cell with little hope of the Viceroy's reprieve.

He was found by the police beside his murdered wife, a dagger at his feet, his hands and sleeves smeared with blood.

But the executioner's sword could have got rusty while Canton waited for the old man's decision. Rumour had it that he could not bring himself to execute one who had once served under him, and who besides had married his niece.

Then one morning a notice appeared at the viceregal gates. Not only the Prefect of Police but eighty odd serving mandarins had been summoned to hear the unfortunate man's fate.

In dark-blue full ceremonial robes, peacock's feathers trailing from upturned satin hats, the dignified figures trooped into the long reception hall, and all degrees of rank were present, as could be seen from the nine different animals embroidered in their natural colours on the front and back of tunics, and the nine kinds of buttons crowning the hats, from ruby through sapphire and plain gold to worked silver.

It was a severely blended scene, for from the four lofty walls hung only six silk tapestries, and around them stood only six monochrome vases of Sung porcelain.

At one end the Viceroy sat alone, a calm, wrinkled man of seventy-five with thin moustaches, his whispy beard just touching the head of an embroidered Manchurian crane, while the button on his hat gleamed fiery. It was of ruby, and rubies shone, too, from the jade clasp of his silk girdle.

To right and left of his marble-faced chair mandarins of the second rank seated themselves, eight on each side, with red coral button, embroidered golden pheasant and girdle clasp of gold studded with small rubies.

Behind them stood the juniors, the emblems on their chests moving up and down with their breathing, from peacock through silver pheasant to long-tailed jay.

At the other end, with red coral button, sat the Prefect of Police, who had personally conducted the prosecution and wrung the death sentence from the chief magistrate. His fixed, arrogant stare and heavy jowl contrasted with the refined features of his chief.

"I have sent for so many of you," the old man began in his silvery voice, "for two reasons—to encourage the righteous and as a warning to the unrighteous." He threw a glance at the Prefect of Police, who rose as if amused.

"Your excellency, before you give your decision—which I can guess—I, too, would like to teach these juniors something. Just to remind them that though a Viceroy has power of life and death in his own province, there is a power higher even than his—the Throne's. That is all." He sat down with studied ease.

"So much is this the case," agreed the Viceroy, "that I am forwarding to the Throne a memorial the honourable Prefect of Police has submitted." He held up a document. "Here it is. It charges me with protecting a convicted murderer. I am going further in this breach of duty. I am setting the prisoner free."

The Prefect of Police laughed.

"I will go still further. I give you back your memorial, and ask you to bring it up to date, to include your censure of my decision."

There was a rustle of silk as neighbours exchanged incredulous glances. A servant took the document to the Prefect of Police while another brought him a small writing table.

"An imperial messenger is at this moment waiting to return to the capital. He will take your completed memorial as well as mine. But note carefully what is in my memorial. It gives not only a report of this case up to the prisoner's release, but what will happen in this hall in the next twenty minutes." The writer stayed his quick brush. "Yes, what will happen in this hall in the next twenty minutes. I do not wish to hurry you, but the imperial messenger must leave in ten minutes' time to catch the tide. I know you will not need ten minutes to complete your indictment against me,"

The writer answered with a sneer. In the dramatic silence the imperial messenger came forward, with a large tin tube in his hand, and a servant bowed him into a chair set before a table. As he laid on it a bar of soft solder, a soldering iron and a wick lamp, the Viceroy's secretary brought him the usual bundle of official documents, which he at once slipped into the tube.

The Prefect of Police now handed his refreshed memorial back to the waiting servant. His chief carefully read the addition before putting his vermilion seal below the prefect's. Then he passed it over to the imperial messenger with his own.

Deftly the metropolitan official made room for them in the

tin tube, slid the cover over and soldered together the join. Then spreading out the soft metal in two places he put the imperial seal on one, and took the tube to the Viceroy who put his seal on the other.

"Your excellency, I take my departure so that the imperial ear shall ever remain open."

"Your excellency, fair winds and good roads!"

Giving three deep bows, the imperial messenger left the hall. There was now no recalling those memorials to a throne that did not tolerate mistakes.

The Prefect of the Police arose.

"I have not finished," said the old man. "Pray resume your seat while I tell a tale."

"Your excellency, I have my duties awaiting me."

"No, you have no more official duties to perform. When you leave this room you will go as a prisoner. Sit and hear why you will yourself be standing your trial tomorrow."

"My trial?"

"At which I shall be the chief witness—for murder."

"For murder!" The Prefect of Police laughed very loud.

"It is all down in my memorial."

"What!"

"Perhaps now you may care to listen to my tale."

The old man sat back, and the eighty mandarins craned forward.

"Twenty years ago, when I was chief magistrate of this city, I had under me two subordinates who belonged to the two poles of human character. One was vain, ambitious and ruthless; the other, seven years younger, scholarly and charming.

"Then both received promotion into the Revenue Department. At once note one thing. The brilliant younger man was senior in office. That rankled with the brutal man. Besides that, the scholar could never resist the pleasure of thrusting with his witty tongue at his thin-skinned, bull-headed colleague. I never saw two men hate each other more.

"Five years later a serious misappropriation of funds was discovered. The senior's books showed he had stolen the money. As chief magistrate I tried him. My instinct was against the evidence, not because he had married my niece, but because I knew this humorous, deep scholar to be a true Confucian. And much though I disliked the tactics of the then Prefect of Police, who happened to be the junior's uncle, I had to administer the law.

"The prisoner received ten years' prison. Four years later, when I became viceroy, I set him free. Not one cent had been traced to him. You all know who they are."

"There is only one thing missing from your tale, your excellency," said the man opposite. "Why don't you openly accuse me of having stolen the money?"

"I have no need to, for I shall be having your head off within this week."

A great, contemptuous laugh again filled the hall.

The Viceroy lifted a hand. The Prefect of Police heard a noise behind him and saw four armed men advancing on him. His hand dived under his robe, but they had sprung forward and wrenched his pistol from him before he could pull it out. He sat back heavily and glared across at the smiling old man.

"To continue my tale—in this better atmosphere—the brilliant man, broken by injustice, took to opium. The other continued to rise in office.

"Eight years went by, then the scholar's bitterness found voice. He began writing epigrams and allegorical lampoons ridiculing a high official, pricking his pomposity and monstrous vanity. The Prefect of Police chose to regard them as pointing at himself. He is sitting opposite me. As you all know, a bully is the weakest of men, for he has no sense of humour. In his yamen he raged like a man demented as these catchy rhymes and witty lampoons continued month after month, year after year, for three years. Often he was heard to swear vengeance and destruction to his enemy.

"At last, two months ago, his opportunity came. The unfortunate man was found with blood on his hands beside his murdered wife.

"Now, you future viceroys, I want you to listen very closely to what is coming. Again my instinct told me the truth. Instinct! If you have it, trust it. The first time I could not protect an innocent man. This time I was in a position to do so. I knew so grand a scholar would not murder a wife he loved.

"Yet publicly I appeared helpless, for the Prefect of Police successfully obtained his verdict from the chief magistrate just on one point. He made the chief magistrate agree that it was not necessary to establish motive with an opium addict. His exact words were: 'In one of his trances the ex-swindler, not knowing what he was doing, stabbed his wife to death. And to invalidate this excuse in the future I demand the death penalty.'

"Well, my experience was that alcohol produces violence. Opium never—just the opposite, gentleness and peace. But I could not override the chief magistrate's sentence, for in point of evidence blood is blood, and the remote possibility of a man murdering in a trance cannot be discounted in law. So I began my inquiries.

"But it has taken me, with all my resources, these two months to complete the last link in the true evidence—the last ring. Remember *ring*.

"Yet I must ask you to bear in mind one other thing—that the Prefect of Police alone has control of all police and execution arrangements, which can give him a power of illegal manipulation denied any other official. For myself, knowing a policeman's trust in cunning, I sought for many coils of the serpent. At once one wriggled.

"The very next morning after the murder it so happened that fourteen pirates were executed." He waved his delicate hand across the hall. "See that fixed stare? I have touched a coil. That is how a serpent wriggles in public—by overdoing stillness."

"I protest!" shouted the Prefect of Police. Two of the guards pulled him down.

"Just observe—accuse him of murder and he laughs, but touch his vanity and he shouts." A chuckle rippled through the hall. "Well, it is a weekly affair, the execution of pirates in Canton. But these loyal wretches always die like brave men. That morning one struggled violently at sight of the executioner's sword shouting that he was not a pirate. That night I had all fourteen heads dug up and preserved.

"Now we go back a day, to the night of the murder. The prosecutor made great play of the circumstance that no suspicious character had been seen that night near the house of the murdered woman. But my subsequent inquiries showed that there had been such a suspicious character—a well-known burglar. That protesting pirate was that well-known burglar.

"You see, that burglar had to be got rid of because he was the murderer of the dead woman. From that moment two other persons had also to be killed, for this is a tale of very skilful destruction of evidence.

"First, there was the pirate who had not been executed. How was he disposed of? He was sent back to the pirate chief with a letter. You will hear its brilliant contents later.

"Next on the list was, of course, the detective who had arrested the burglar.... The moment he arrived back with the easily-found man, the Prefect of Police kept him in his own room. To instruct him in a special mission. Do you see the dramatic scene? Here was a pirate in the cells his chief had spared. Why? So that a reliable detective could follow him and track down the pirate lair!

"Puffed up with flattery, the innocent detective at once set off on this gift of a trail, and the next day, when he was hot on the letter-bearer's heels, the letter was in the pirate-chief's hands. Made up of words cut from a book or newspaper, it contained two interesting items for the pirate-chief. One, a description of the detective's disguise; and, two, that the bearer had given away secrets under torture.

"The messenger died a minute after delivering the letter, and the detective the next day. That completes the three murders.

"But I know that all this time there is an unsatisfied thought in most of your minds. In spite of all I have said of the prisoner's character, you are still asking yourselves this incredible question: How did a man in his high position come to do so stupid a thing as to commit murder after murder merely to achieve the death of an innocent man? The answer is simple. Twice before in my life I have seen this same violent animal reaction. . . . The sword of ridicule had nicked this vain man. That is all. Such men stand the rack better than wit."

"Prove it! Prove it! Prove all you've said!" cried the man held so skilfully in a vice.

"Why should you get so excited? I've written all this in my memorial. If I can't prove such serious charges, it is my head that will come off."

"And it will, even if you are in your dotage!"

"Perhaps I am in my dotage, so let me tell you what else is in my memorial. . . . You also made very impressive play at the trial of the circumstances that there had been no proved robbery. But you will remember that the prisoner maintained that his wife had a gold pin through the bun at the back of her head, the last bit of jewellery she possessed. No gold pin was found on the dead woman. I believed that one had been stolen from her.

"I know you laughed very much when I gave orders to my men to look for that pin in the pawn-shops, among a million such in Canton. But shall I tell you something now?

"They were searching the pawn-shops for something else, something that was stolen not from the dead woman—but from the prisoner." The Viceroy leaned forward. "Well may you blink so hard. This you did not know. And it is this that will fetch your head off on the execution ground. The head you removed, that preserved head of the burglar, was identified by the pawn-broker to whom he sold the stolen article. No laugh?"

"Childish talk!"

"Well, is this childish talk? The prisoner, being an ex-magistrate and familiar with your methods, said nothing about what had been stolen from him, except to the investigator that I had at oncc sent to his cell."

"What is this article? Your most honourable excellency, I am all ears!"

"A jade ring taken from his finger while he was in an opium stupor, a ring seen by the murderer while in the act of smearing his hands and sleeves with blood, after having stabbed his awakened wife to death."

The Prefect of Police narrowed his eyes with a sneer.

"Your excellency, you may insult my intelligence because you hate me, or even the throne's because you are a viceroy. But spare eighty grown-up men the rest of your fantasy. They are not in a position to laugh at you."

The Viceroy put the tips of his fingers together, tranquil as a Tang figurene. Everyone felt the threat of the still posture.

"A ring I gave him myself eleven years ago when he came out of prison."

"A ring you gave him yourself! Please quickly assure me that you told this to the throne!"

"I did. So did the jeweller who made that ring, in a sworn statement attached to my memorial."

The old man took a jade ring from his pocket and held it up.

"Look well at this ring, I ask all of you. You see how it is set? The stone is not set solid into the gold. You can look right through it. And this stone isn't just one stone. It is two stones cemented together." The gentle voice snapped out: "Hold his hands!"

Two of the guards bent back the prisoner's arms, and the secretary held up the ring for him against the light of a window. The Prefect of Police stared through the jade, and his heavy jaw dropped.

"Shall I read what you read?" the silvery voice asked. "'From Chao Hung Li to Peh Ming.' I think the throne knows that the first is my unworthy name, and the second that of the scholar who has killed you with his wit. Take him below!"

As the violent man was dragged out, eighty scholars burst into mocking laughter.

THE VICTOR

By

DALE COLLINS

ARCHIPELAGO RUBBER, with the best intentions in the world, sent all its brightest young men to the East to study production on the plantations. When these bright young men returned they knew a great deal about the business and other things, and were of increased value to the Company. When they did not return the East had taken them, but Archipelago Rubber did not understand that.

In accordance with the dispensation of his board, Peter Burney had stepped ashore at Maccalengleng three hours before, and as he walked between the grey-blue trees he told Sam Reid, the plantation manager, many things with the candour and confidence of twenty-two years. He talked of a girl with blue eyes as blue as the sea, of England, of system, of big business, of his dad, and of the East.

"The way I size up the East is it needs waking up and some life put into it," said Peter Burney. "There's labour in any quantity—cheap and good; the natural conditions are fine; there's any amount of room for increased production. The only catch is that the East's grown dull and sleepy through the centuries. It's like a worn-out old man—wants a dose of monkey gland, I'd say."

Sam Reid—grizzled, slovenly and drink-warped—heard him and gave a snort. He was not impressed. This was another of the bright young men. They left him cold, after a quarter of a century in the East. They came out full of this kind of stuff, and presently they went away again and he stayed on at Maccalengleng, where every mosquito carried fever and every bottle a more perilous disease. They came and went—these smart young men—but he remained, like part of the plantation, absorbed by it, as if the rubber had congealed about him. And they held him in contempt because he was of the East and didn't care what they thought, and knew them for young fools. Also, they didn't like him because he had forgotten how to part his hair and how to be polite and tactful and make pretty speeches.

But he got the rubber out of Maccalengleng, and that was more than they could have done.

"So——!" said Reid, and shrugged contemptuously.

This talk riled him, as did the cocksure young man, who was weak as a babe. Well, the fool would learn presently. With grim and bitter satisfaction the elder man looked forward into the long months of disillusionment.

And Peter Burney said his say with youth's cheerful arrogance, seeing Sam Reid as a wreck who didn't amount to anything.

Presently they went up to the veranda, where Reid drank a gin and Burney a lime-squash, the one sprawled out and comatose, the other alert and upright.

Before their eyes the grey-blue rows of rubber-trees marched down to the glassy sea, flanked on either hand by the living jungle. Two Malays drowsed in the shadow of the house; insects burred; lizards stared with jewelled eyes; the sun blazed down upon the world with intense, palpitating light.

"It fairly gets my goat, this East!" said Burney. "It's numb and lifeless and crusted with age. For all its fertility it's barren. Nothing happens here. Life doesn't get along. If a man were big enough he could shake up this East."

Reid took another gin.

"Yes," he said dryly, "if he was big enough!"

A flush stole into Burney's smooth face, his amiable mouth hardened and his eyes were aglow with the reflections of youth's dreams. He was vaguely aware of conflict with an intangible but powerful presence, and he rejoiced in the sensation. In a flaccid and exhausted world, too occupied with birth and decay to live, he, at least, was vigorous and virile.

The night was heavy on Maccalengleng, the darkness being so deep and thick that it had a substantial quality. A flare on a drifting sampan out on the unseen water gained the effect of burning in the heart of solid gloom. It was very quiet because the noises of the jungle seemed to weave into the silence and become part of it, so that the ear was not conscious of any sound at all. The stars were as holes in the night's mass, letting in hints of glory from a place beyond.

For two years and eleven months in the evening Peter Burney and Sam Reid had sat in their chairs on either side of the table on the veranda, and in that time nothing had happened—nothing of which they were actively conscious, nothing that had borne the appearance of importance. Through the days they had worked in broiling heat, slept after luncheon, risen and worked again, bathed and had the evening meal. Reid had been following this routine for as long as he could remember, and he had not changed. The sea, the rubber-trees, the jungle, the sweep of sky, and the steaming heat had not changed either; the Malays and the stone gods looking down on the village had not changed. But Peter Burney had.

He spoke no more of putting life into the East, nor of England, nor of the girl with eyes like the sea, nor of his dad. He had come to the knowledge that letter writing was a trial when the sweating arms stuck to the table. He did not drink lime-squash. Youth's dreams and enthusiasms and appetites had been his enemies and had betrayed him into the grasp of the East.

Reid had the satisfaction of seeing that he had been right on that first day when he had snorted. The degeneration had been rapid. Without lifting a hand he had been avenged upon the young man whose first quick glance had judged him to be a waster and good-for-nothing, and with justice.

Burney lifted his glass, lapped at the gin, shivered because there was still fever in him, and spoke, his mouth softer now and weaker, less likeable.

"Hell, why should I go back?" he asked, continuing their discussion. "There's something in all this gets a man." He waved his hand out at the mystery of the night. "There's colour and glamour in this—it's the life I was cut out for. They told me I'd be glad enough to get home! Rot! This is the little place I've been looking for—out here, out East! A man lives out here, takes his time, dreams along. It's warm here—like hell at times—but I don't know—it's a miracle. Supposing I went home to an office desk—could I stick it after this? Sleet and cold and snow—motor-cars, hustle—I wasn't planned for that. Out here a man's a king over subjects—back home I'd be a slave! I'd be chased round and on the run every day and all day just to earn a crust. It isn't worth it, Sam, and that's God's truth."

The manager made no comment beyond smiling darkly while he gloated over the completeness of his vindication. But Burney did not need an answer. He was thinking aloud. How the old wreck judged things did not matter.

"Go home——?" he swept on. "Go home to what? To slave, to moil, to strive to kill myself! And out here I've got everything I want—peace, quiet, prosperity, power. A man could live to be a hundred out here, and never know what the misery of life meant after he'd beaten the fever. A little bit of trading or planting—I've got enough of that—and he could live in luxury. To the devil with Archipelago Rubber! Why should I kill myself for them?"

"That's right," Reid agreed carelessly, "why should you?"

"Let's have a drink on it!"

Burney tipped the bottle dexterously, despite the fact that his hand trembled. His faced flushed, for he had had more gin than was good for him—more that night and more on previous nights. The tropics had sapped him, the monotony had blunted him. He was not the same young man who had landed at Maccalengleng. There were moments when he was dimly aware of this, but consolation and a means of quietening these qualms were available in the bottles on the store-room shelves.

"Well, you'll have to be sure positive before three weeks are up and the steamer comes," said the man who did not care, triumphing over his critic of yester-year.

"I'm all that now," was the answer.

They lay in silence which was broken only by the drumming of Burney's fingers upon the arm of his chair. Reid was inert, being twenty, twenty-five years past that stage.

"You were over at Njo-Angat's kampona again today?" he questioned at last.

The younger man stretched with elaborate unconcern.

"What if I was?" he countered, and then abruptly, because it was lonely on Maccalengleng and a man had to have a confidant, the truth came stumbling out in a torrent: "Tell you, Sam, I've fallen for that daughter of his, Sali. Yes, she's wonderful! She's like a little golden saint. She doesn't seem coloured. I put no account to coloured girls, but this one—well, she's different. All said and done, her skin's no darker than yours, and her heart's clear white. She's—oh, hell! what's the use of trying to express these things?—she's the living symbol of all that's fascinating in the East. She's calm and grave and quiet and polished; she's incomprehensible; she's the lovely riddle of all women; she's still and sweet and soft. I want that girl like I never wanted anything before." He broke off, panting. "She loves me," he resumed, his voice falling into an odd sing-song, "and I'm going over to Panjoeng with her when my time's up here, and I'm going to trade there, and we'll be happy and forget the world, forget everything except our joy. There's no escape from these things. They happen. It would be folly, and worse than folly, to run away. It is fate!"

He made a gesture of acceptance, which was Oriental in its resignation. Burney had gone East when he was young and fluid, and his soul had been easily shaped by his environment.

"That's so," Reid agreed, sucking his moustache, and then: "You'll be happy at Panjoeng, eh?"

"Yes!" said Burney, and swore, to emphasize the statement, for he had experienced a sudden twinge of doubt before the dry question as if he were sliding down an inclined plane to he knew not what and yet was powerless to stop his descent, and careless of its consequences. Memories flooded to him, and fears assailed him.

To clear his brain and steady his nerves he took a stiff gin. The effect was magical. Doubt died. He saw with crystal clarity that he was right and that it was a mercy of fate that had shown him his path. There was no sense in fighting and struggling. Life was a stream, and humanity no more than troubled flotsam upon its surface.

He thought of Sali, and she was as a star—distant, unreadable, almost beyond attainment, and yet brought within his grasp by this magical chance of love which broke down barriers of race and creed. He felt exhilarated, and was possessed by the fancy that he was one with the whole living night.

The man on the other side of the table drank again, and smiled bitterly, and yet as he looked out at the East a strange expression passed across his face, a look of respect and dread.

The triumph was so complete, so easily gained.

Thought was not a good occupation for Sam Reid. He was nearing fifty and had nothing much to look back on, and nothing to which he could look forward. And yet he found thought hard to escape from, and it was for this reason that he was devoting his concentrated attention to the liquid contents of the store-room.

Reid was often drunk, but he went on a proper spree about once in twelve months, and always when he was thinking. These debauches of his were lonely and terrible festivities, embarked upon deliberately and viciously, not enjoyed but terribly thorough.

He stood in the dimly-lit store-room, wearing only his pyjama trousers. A lantern flung upon the wall a shadow caricature of the caricature of a man. His grey moustache, his grey hair, emphasized the pity of him. Swaying, he drank from a bottle and flung it to one side. It struck the wall and shattered into tinkling fragments. What remained of its contents made a dark smudge on the split-bamboo floor.

Sam Reid swung about and faced out through the open door which gave on to the veranda. With the stupid dignity of a drunken man he raised a thin fist and shook it at the night.

"You——!" he snarled. "You——!"

Wrath, hatred and fear were in his eyes.

Reeling away from whatever he saw in the darkness, and spitting oaths, he dragged down another bottle. Two more fell with it, and his feet were wet with liquor. To and fro he swayed, a ghastly figure of licence, with his black shadow for company and his mind swamped in a sea of spirits. He sang, he shouted, he danced—now out on the veranda, now in the store-room.

The sensation of escape filled him with pride in his strength. He smashed and kicked and wrought havoc in a paroxysm of destruction, as if seeking to accomplish the ruination of his surroundings that they might match himself.

Two hours later Peter Burney returned from the kampong of Njo-Angat, where no white man should have been. He was surprised to see that the veranda was in darkness, and as he drew nearer he became aware of an atmosphere of calamity and collapse, so that his heart throbbed uneasily beneath the fingers of foreboding.

"Reid," he called, "Reid!" and broke into a run. There was no answer, and the black house crouched against the stars like a sulky monster.

At the head of the steps leading up to the veranda he struck a match. The light blazed brightly in the still air, revealing, with impish delight, the aftermath of Sam Reid's party. The manager lay at full length upon the floor, and about him was scattered an amazing array of bottles, some broken though still uncorked, but all empty. The boards were dark with stains, and the air reeked. Reid lay like a dead man, his arms flung out above his head, and each hand clutching a bottle.

For a second Burney stood aghast, an oath taking shape on his lips, and then he realized that Reid was not dead but drunk, for his shoulders were moving in the heavy breathing of intoxication.

A wave of wrath swept the younger man. Falling on his knees he gripped the manager with rough hands, and shook him this way and that, maddened by the thought of the reckless waste which had been involved in the orgy.

The sharp motion brought Reid to his senses, and he sat upright in the darkness.

"Here—here——" he mumbled. "What you mean, heh?—wake me up middle of night——!"

"I'll wake you up, you hog! What have you been doing? Tell me that, will you?"

Reid coughed and snorted, and then answered with dignity: "Certainly, m'boy, I tell you, yesh! I've helped meself to party while you were out courting—every man hish own amusement! I like the liquor, yesh! I've drunk and I've drunk, and I'd be drinking still if there was so much as another drop to drink in thish house!"

"What?" gasped Burney, astounded and appalled.

But having made his announcement, Reid collapsed again.

The other rose to his feet, his hands clenched and the blood pumping through his head. He wanted to break things, and most of all to break the head of the greedy old sot. Drink—that vital part of the East's life!—there wasn't a drop of drink left, and there he was marooned on Maccalengleng with no prospect of getting any more. The thought was unbearable and murder was in his heart. He had been pillaged, plundered, and the thief lay before him too drunken to fight.

"You——!" said Peter Burney, and expressed his candid opinion of Reid. But Reid did not hear him, being deep in heavy slumber.

"In the morning—boss or no boss—I'll punch you into jelly!" vowed the young man.

For the first night in more than two years Peter Burney drank plain water, and it failed lamentably to quench his thirst. His nerves missed the accustomed stimulant, and he lay wide awake for hours on his bed looking out through the mosquito netting at the great stars. No one, he argued with himself, could say that he was a drunkard—not like that swine Reid—but a man got into the way of taking alcohol in the East, and it hurt to be without it. He was wretched. The sentinel palms against the sky maddened him, the drone of the mosquitoes was like the chanting of fiends, and the glamour of the tropical night was not for him.

Sam Reid had not dwelt twenty-five years in the archipelago without acquiring certain powers, and one of these was the capacity for making a rapid recovery. With dawn stealing over the Eastern sea he was astir, and the first thing he saw by the pink and pearl light was that he had gained his junior's hatred. This did not trouble him—for the hatred of one held in contempt is a slight thing—but he had no desire to have life made uncomfortable. Accordingly he was busy.

His task was accomplished and he was toying with a breakfast of a mangosteen and a banana when Burney appeared on the veranda.

The young man's face was grim, and there was no greeting on his lips for the touselled, untidy wreck who sat at the table. Reid met his angry eyes calmly.

"I got off the chain last night," he said. "I suppose you figure I shouldn't have been so liberal with myself?"

Burney's face portended the coming storm.

"You're sober now, and I'm going to make you pay for last night."

But Reid sat at ease in his chair after one quick movement—a movement which resulted in the appearance of an automatic pistol, the chilly eye of which regarded Burney with cold disfavour. Beneath its scrutiny his advance was checked.

"If I hadn't been twenty years in the East I'd fight you with my fists," said Reid with a little gesture of apology, "but as I have been, I'm not much of a man and so I've got to windward of you.

I've cleansed the house of firearms this morning—all save this one. You'd better behave yourself, or I'll fill you that full of lead you'll sink into the ground. I'm a peaceful man, but I'm tired of you. For three years I've stuck it, but I'll not stand it any more. I'll have no jumped-up kid talking to me. I'm boss here, and I'll drink as much as I want. Twenty-five years I've been on Maccalengleng, and what's life got for me if I can't have a burst when I feel so inclined? I tell you, I forgot the empty misery of life last night, and that's a relief I'll not forgo out of consideration for you or anyone. When you've been East as long as me maybe you'll understand!"

He spoke with an air of finality, and Burney knew that he was mastered by reason of the weapon and the bitter experience which was the lot of his opponent.

His anger was displaced by an unanalysable feeling of hopelessness and despair. The night had sapped his energies, and the morning reviver which he needed so badly was not to be had. A shiver ran through him as he looked at Reid and understood how little life meant to him.

Burney was nauseated by Reid's presence, hating him because he was a wreck, a waster, a drunkard and a thief of other men's rights.

And Reid looked at him with open dislike, because he was a smart young man out from the home office and no stronger than a kitten.

For twenty days and twenty nights the two lonely men dwelt on the raw edge of hatred, speaking but little and brooding in the company of their own thoughts. The danger of violence had passed, for the heat and the absence of stimulants had left them without energy, so that all they wished to do was to avoid each other.

In Burney's heart remained gnawing anger which spread like a canker worm, so that the peace went out of his life and the lotus was bitter in his mouth. He found himself at war with everything in the sunny world, from the suave Malays to the green things of the jungle. There was nothing to which he could turn for aid to recapture that rosy glow which once had dimmed his eyes to the fact that he was a stranger in a strange land of which he was a little afraid. His eyes, seeing clearly now, discovered the truth, and he sickened for home. Even Sali seemed less delicious

But when the steamer came in it would be all right, he told himself. The steamer would replenish the store-room, and the dream would be resumed, effortless and soothing.

Upon the evening of the twentieth day, with the steamer due

upon the morrow, calamity overtook Peter Burney in the form of a second act of baser pillage by the man who hated him because he was young and better educated and had not learnt the East at the cost of twenty-five years of life.

Having broken the nose of the grave Njo-Angat, who told him the news of this event, Peter Burney set out for the plantation house to slay his boss.

But as he tramped back between the hot walls of jungle, with the calm stars looking down on him, and the presence of Asia breathing from the purple hills and from the purple sea—something snapped in his brain. He felt suddenly helpless and hopeless, cold and lost; he felt like a child that has strayed into a dark place and is beset by the knowledge of evil.

The beauty of the night disgusted him, as the beauty of something diseased and unclean. He was miserable and disillusioned, but even while he blamed Reid for his state he walked the more swiftly, fearing lest his just wrath should be swallowed up in other emotions, the causes of which he did not comprehend.

The manager sat upon the veranda, but he rose as his junior entered, for he saw by the whiteness of his face that he had discovered the position. Reid's hand rested on the pistol butt, and he smiled beneath his draggled moustache because now his victory was finally won, and the jeerer had been reduced to an object pitiable and to be mocked by all the world; the man who had failed in love.

"If I said what I think of you," said Burney, crouched on the topmost step, "it'd burn you up! You—you call yourself a man—and you'd go behind my back and steal the heart of the girl you know I love—you——!"

But the night was hot and the elder had no desire for a scene or prolonged argument.

"I'm boss here," he said, "because I know the East. I want to tell you something—I've got that girl because she's the cutest Malay I've ever seen, and there's not much in life for me. But I don't make the mistake you did—I didn't figure I've got her heart. I've bought her—that's all. She was going to the highest bidder; one white man or another meant nothing to her. She's a low caste Malay. Great stars, man, you don't think you're dealing with something white? I know the East, I tell you, and I know how much of her love Sali is going to give to me, to you, or to any other *tuan*. As there's not much in life for me, I shall be content!"

He broke off, sucking his moustache, and Burney, who had intended to be so fierce, stood silent, because he saw Reid as a poor prisoner in a dark jail—in a jail to which he clamoured to be admitted, insanely and without understanding.

"You're young," Reid said slowly, "but me— I've been twenty-five years out here, and I'm entitled to all I can get!"

He taunted the young man who was his enemy because he saw that the pride had gone out of him and that he was in the dust. He smiled, but although Burney saw all this he found no protest because he was broken.

Reid shouted the girl's name, and she came out of the night from around the corner of the veranda, and at a word from him in her own language sat down beside him cross-legged upon the floor, not looking at the boy who had been her lover, not looking at her master, not looking at anything their eyes could see, but at something in the night invisible to them.

Peter Burney stared at her, and for the first time noticed the flatness of her features, the childish smallness of her body, and the brownness of her feet. But his most vital discovery was that he saw her as if she sat a long way off in another world in which he had no existence.

A flush of shame and chagrin stole into his tanned cheeks, and he hastily averted his eyes. Then a savage laugh choked his throat, and his hands opened limply.

"Take her—Reid—take her!" he cried, and went unsteadily across the veranda to his room like a man who had been stunned and suffers all the pains of re-birth. And after an interval there came from within the sound of trunks being dragged about.

Sam Reid nodded his grizzled head as he gloated on the vanquishing of the self-righteous.

"That's taught the puppy!" he said to his pipe.

The big Dutch steamer lying off Maccalengleng flung up a plume of steam against the sunset sky, and a breath later a grunting hoot reached the beach, urging the boat to be quick since darkness stalked the world and there was a channel to be negotiated before the highway of the sea was reached.

"Now, sir!" said the officer in the stern.

Peter Burney hesitated, and suddenly extended his hand to his late manager.

"No ill-feeling, Sam," he said, jerkily. "I guess I'm not much fitted for this life out here." His face darkened. "I'm glad to see the last of the vile place!" With one comprehensive glance he swept the rising slopes.

"I know," said Sam Reid without emotion. "I been here twenty-five years!"

Their hands clasped, and a moment later the boat was clear of the beach, and Burney had started on his long voyage home to the offices of Archipelago Rubber. Every fibre of his being was a-thrill with relief, joy and anticipation, as if he went out to high adventure. His mind—freed from the oppression which had been upon it—was working clearly now, and the first effect of this was to cause him to strike his knee and shout an oath. The boat was a hundred yards from the shore, and the light was fading.

"Say, I've got another word to speak to Mr. Reid," he cried. "I've got to go back. I've got to thank him!" His voice rose excitedly.

But the phlegmatic Hollander in charge shook his head.

"It is not possible," he grunted.

Burney sprang to his feet and looked back over the stern. Along the beach the shrunken, white figure was receding into the shadows.

"Sam—I understand now—I see it now, Sam!" Burney yelled. "They won't let me come back to tell you, but thanks! thanks! thanks!"

The cry was heavily burdened with feeling, but the distance between boat and shore had widened, and it seemed that the lonely figure on the beach had not heard. And yet Burney fancied that he had seen a hand raised in acknowledgment, though he could not be certain, because, for some reason, his eyes had misted over and his head was spinning. He continued to shout his gratitude, and the boat went on.

Sam Reid had heard right enough.

"What's he understand?—nothing, the puppy!" he snorted.

The quick night had come before he reached the house. On the veranda sat Sali and her father. Reid nodded to the old Malay, and passing into the office returned with a roll of guilder notes, which he handed to him.

"Take her away, O Father," he said in Malay, "and marry her to one of thine own people!"

Njo-Angat rose obediently, his daughter's hand in his, and mumbled that the *tuan* was great and wise and good, that the peace of Allah would be upon him, and that there was no other god.

Sam Reid paid no attention, but when he was alone he raised his clenched fist and shook it at the night of the East which possessed the world with wanton witchery.

"Bah!" he cried. "Bah! That time I beat you—just that time I beat you!"

A smile of triumph was born on his face, and he stood erect, a proud man, a victor though for twenty-five years he had been enslaved.

THE LAGOON

By

JOSEPH CONRAD

THE white man, leaning with both arms over the roof of the little house in the stern of the boat, said to the steersman—"We will pass the night in Arsat's clearing. It is late."

The Malay only grunted, and went on looking fixedly at the river. The white man rested his chin on his crossed arms and gazed at the wake of the boat. At the end of the straight avenue of forests cut by the intense glitter of the river, the sun appeared unclouded and dazzling, poised low over the water that shone smoothly like a band of metal. The forests, sombre and dull, stood motionless and silent on each side of the broad stream. At the foot of big, towering trees, trunkless nipa palms rose from the mud of the bank, in bunches of leaves enormous and heavy, that hung unstirring over the brown swirl of eddies. In the stillness of the air every tree, every leaf, every bough, every tendril of creeper and every petal of minute blossoms seemed to have been bewitched into an immobility perfect and final. Nothing moved on the river but the eight paddles that rose flashing regularly, dipped together with a single splash; while the steersman swept right and left with a periodic and sudden flourish of his blade describing a glinting semicircle above his head. The churned-up water frothed alongside with a confused murmur. And the white man's canoe, advancing up stream in the short-lived disturbance of its own making, seemed to enter the portals of a land from which the very memory of motion had for ever departed.

The white man, turning his back upon the setting sun, looked along the empty and broad expanse of the sea-reach. For the last three miles of its course the wandering, hesitating river, as if enticed irresistibly by the freedom of an open horizon, flows straight into the sea, flows straight to the east—to the east that harbours both light and darkness. Astern of the boat the repeated call of some bird, a cry discordant and feeble, skipped along over the smooth water and lost itself, before it could reach the other shore, in the breathless silence of the world.

The steersman dug his paddle into the stream, and held hard with stiffened arms, his body thrown forward. The water gurgled aloud; and suddenly the long straight reach seemed to pivot on its centre, the forests swung in a semicircle, and the slanting beams of sunset touched the broadside of the canoe with a fiery glow, throwing the slender and distorted shadows of its crew upon the streaked glitter of the river. The white man turned to look ahead. The course of the boat had been altered at right-angles to the stream, and the carved dragon-head of its prow was pointing now at a gap in the fringing bushes of the bank. It glided through, brushing the overhanging twigs, and disappeared from the river like some slim and amphibious creature leaving the water for its lair in the forests.

The narrow creek was like a ditch: tortuous, fabulously deep; filled with gloom under the thin strip of pure and shining blue of the heaven. Immense trees soared up, invisible behind the festooned draperies of creepers. Here and there, near the glistening blackness of the water, a twisted root of some tall tree showed amongst the tracery of small ferns, black and dull, writhing and motionless, like an arrested snake. The short words of the paddlers reverberated loudly between the thick and sombre walls of vegetation. Darkness oozed out from between the trees, through the tangled maze of the creepers, from behind the great fantastic and unstirring leaves; the darkness, mysterious and invincible; the darkness scented and poisonous of impenetrable forests.

The men poled in the shoaling water. The creek broadened, opening out into a wide sweep of a stagnant lagoon. The forests receded from the marshy bank, leaving a level strip of bright green, reedy grass to frame the reflected blueness of the sky. A fleecy pink cloud drifted high above, trailing the delicate colouring of its image under the floating leaves and the silvery blossoms of the lotus. A little house, perched on high piles, appeared black in the distance. Near it, two tall nibong palms, that seemed to have come out of the forests in the background, leaned slightly over the ragged roof, with a suggestion of sad tenderness and care in the droop of their leafy and soaring heads.

The steersman, pointing with his paddle, said, "Arsat is there. I see his canoe fast between the piles."

The polers ran along the sides of the boat glancing over their shoulders at the end of the day's journey. They would have preferred to spend the night somewhere else than on this lagoon of weird aspect and ghostly reputation. Moreover, they disliked Arsat, first as a stranger, and also because he who repairs a ruined house, and dwells in it, proclaims that he is not afraid to live amongst the spirits that haunt the places abandoned by mankind. Such a man can disturb the course of fate by glances or words; while his familiar ghosts are not easy to propitiate by wayfarers upon whom they long to wreak the malice of their human master. White men care not for such things, being unbelievers and in league with the Father of Evil, who leads them unharmed through the invisible dangers of this world. To the warnings of the righteous they oppose an offensive pretence of disbelief. What is there to be done?

So they thought, throwing their weight on the end of their long poles. The big canoe glided on swiftly, noiselessly, and smoothly, towards Arsat's clearing, till, in a great rattling of poles thrown down, and the loud murmurs of "Allah be praised!" it came with a gentle knock against the crooked piles below the house.

The boatmen with uplifted faces shouted discordantly, "Arsat! O Arsat!" Nobody came. The white man began to climb the rude ladder giving access to the bamboo platform before the house. The juragan of the boat said sulkily, "We will cook in the sampan, and sleep on the water."

"Pass my blankets and basket," said the white man curtly.

He knelt on the edge of the platform to receive the bundle. Then the boat shoved off, and the white man, standing up, confronted Arsat, who had come out through the low door of his hut. He was a young man, powerful, with a broad chest and muscular arms. He had nothing on but his sarong. His head was bare. His big, soft eyes stared eagerly at the white man, but his voice and demeanour were composed as he asked, without any words of greeting—

"Have you medicine, Tuan?"

"No," said the visitor in a startled tone. "No. Why? Is there sickness in the house?"

"Enter and see," replied Arsat, in the same calm manner, and turning short round, passed again through the small doorway. The white man, dropping his bundles, followed.

In the dim light of the dwelling he made out on a couch of bamboos a woman stretched on her back under a broad sheet of red cotton cloth. She lay still, as if dead; but her big eyes, wide open, glittered in the gloom, staring upwards at the slender rafters, motionless and unseeing. She was in a high fever, and evidently unconscious. Her cheeks were sunk slightly, her lips were partly open, and on the young face there was the ominous and fixed expression—the absorbed, contemplating expression—of the unconscious who are going to die. The two men stood looking at her in silence.

"Has she been long ill?" asked the traveller.

"I have not slept for five nights," answered the Malay, in a deliberate tone. " At first she heard voices calling her from the water and struggled against me who held her. But since the sun of today rose she hears nothing—she hears not me. She sees nothing. She sees not me—me!"

He remained silent for a minute, then asked softly—

" Tuan, will she die?"

" I fear so," said the white man sorrowfully. He had known Arsat years ago, in a far country in times of trouble and danger, when no friendship is to be despised. And since his Malay friend had come unexpectedly to dwell in the hut on the lagoon with a strange woman, he had slept many times there, in his journeys up and down the river. He liked the man who knew how to keep faith in council and how to fight without fear by the side of his white friend. He liked him—not so much perhaps as a man likes his favourite dog—but still he liked him well enough to help and ask no questions, to think sometimes vaguely and hazily in the midst of his own pursuits, about the lonely man and the long-haired woman with audacious face and triumphant eyes, who lived together hidden by the forests—alone and feared.

The white man came out of the hut in time to see the enormous conflagration of sunset put out by the swift and stealthy shadows that, rising like a black and impalpable vapour above the tree-tops, spread over the heaven, extinguishing the crimson glow of floating clouds and the red brilliance of departing daylight. In a few moments all the stars came out above the intense blackness of the earth, and the great lagoon gleaming suddenly with reflected lights resembled an oval patch of night sky flung down in the hopeless and abysmal night of the wilderness. The white man had some supper out of the basket, then collecting a few sticks that lay about the platform, made up a small fire, not for warmth, but for the sake of the smoke, which would keep off the mosquitoes. He wrapped himself in his blankets and sat with his back against the reed wall of the house, smoking thoughtfully.

Arsat came through the doorway with noiseless steps and squatted down by the fire. The white man moved his outstretched legs a little.

" She breathes," said Arsat in a low voice, anticipating the expected question. " She breathes and burns as if with a great fire. She speaks not; she hears not—and burns!"

He paused for a moment, then asked in a quiet, incurious tone—

" Tuan . . . will she die?"

The white man moved his shoulders uneasily, and muttered in a hesitating manner—

" If such is her fate."

"No, Tuan," said Arsat calmly. "If such is my fate. I hear, I see, I wait. I remember . . . Tuan, do you remember the old days? Do you remember my brother?"

"Yes," said the white man. The Malay rose suddenly and went in. The other, sitting still outside, could hear the voice in the hut. Arsat said: "Hear me! Speak!" His words were succeeded by a complete silence. "O Diamelen!" he cried suddenly. After that cry there was a deep sigh. Arsat came out and sank down again in his old place.

They sat in silence before the fire. There was no sound within the house, there was no sound near them; but far away on the lagoon they could hear the voices of the boatmen ringing fitful and distinct on the calm water. The fire in the bows of the sampan shone faintly in the distance with a hazy red glow. Then it died out. The voices ceased. The land and the water slept invisible, unstirring and mute. It was as though there had been nothing left in the world but the glitter of stars streaming, ceaseless and vain, through the black stillness of the night.

The white man gazed straight before him into the darkness with wide-open eyes. The fear and fascination, the inspiration and the wonder of death—of death near, unavoidable, and unseen—soothed the unrest of his race and stirred the most indistinct, the most intimate of his thoughts. The ever-ready suspicion of evil, the gnawing suspicion that lurks in our hearts, flowed out into the stillness round him—into the stillness profound and dumb, and made it appear untrustworthy and infamous, like the placid and impenetrable mask of an unjustifiable violence. In that fleeting and powerful disturbance of his being the earth enfolded in the starlight peace became a shadowy country of inhuman strife, a battlefield of phantoms terrible and charming, august or ignoble, struggling ardently for the possession of our helpless hearts. An unquiet and mysterious country of inextinguishable desires and fears.

A plaintive murmur rose in the night; a murmur saddening and startling, as if the great solitudes of surrounding woods had tried to whisper into his ear the wisdom of their immense and lofty indifference. Sounds hesitating and vague floated in the air round him, shaped themselves slowly into words; and at last flowed on gently in murmuring stream of soft and monotonous sentences. He stirred like a man waking up and changed his position slightly. Arsat, motionless and shadowy, sitting with bowed head under the stars, was speaking in a low and dreamy tone—

". . . for where can we lay down the heaviness of our trouble but in a friend's heart? A man must speak of war and of love. You, Tuan, know what war is, and you have seen me in time of danger seek death as other men seek life! A writing may be lost; a lie may be written; but what the eye has seen is truth and remains in the mind!"

"I remember," said the white man quietly. Arsat went on with mournful composure—

"Therefore I shall speak to you of love. Speak in the night. Speak before both night and love are gone—and the eyes of day look upon my sorrow and my shame; upon my blackened face; upon my burnt-up heart."

A sigh, short and faint, marked an almost imperceptible pause, and then his words flowed on, without a stir, without a gesture.

"After the time of trouble and war was over and you went away from my country in the pursuit of your desires, which we, men of the islands, cannot understand, I and my brother became again, as we had been before, the sword-bearers of the Ruler. You know we were men of family, belonging to a ruling race, and more fit than any to carry on our right shoulder the emblem of power. And in the time of prosperity Si Dendring showed us favour, as we, in time of sorrow, had showed to him the faithfulness of our courage. It was a time of peace. A time of deer-hunts and cock-fights; of idle talks and foolish squabbles between men whose bellies are full and weapons are rusty. But the sower watched the young rice-shoots grow up without fear, and the traders came and went, departed lean and returned fat into the river of peace. They brought news, too. Brought lies and truth mixed together, so that no man knew when to rejoice and when to be sorry. We heard from them about you also. They had seen you here and had seen you there. And I was glad to hear, for I remembered the stirring times, and I always remembered you, Tuan, till the time came when my eyes could see nothing in the past, because they had looked upon the one who is dying there—in the house."

He stopped to exclaim in an intense whisper, "O Mara bahia! O Calamity!" then went on speaking a little louder.

"There's no worse enemy and no better friend than a brother, Tuan, for one brother knows another, and in perfect knowledge is strength for good or evil. I loved my brother. I went to him and told him that I could see nothing but one face, hear nothing but one voice. He told me: 'Open your heart so that she can see what is in it—and wait. Patience is wisdom. Inchi Midah may die or our Ruler may throw off his fear of a woman!' . . . I waited! . . . You remember the lady with the veiled face, Tuan, and the fear of our Ruler before her cunning and temper. And if she wanted her servant, what could I do? But I fed the hunger of my heart on short glances and stealthy words. I loitered on the path to the bath-houses in the daytime, and when the sun had fallen behind the forest I crept along the jasmine hedges of the women's courtyard. Unseeing, we spoke to one another through the scent of flowers, through the veil of leaves, through the blades of long grass that stood still before our lips; so great was our prudence, so faint was the murmur of our great longing. The time passed swiftly . . . and there were whispers amongst women—and our enemies watched—my brother was gloomy, and I began to think of killing and of a fierce death. . . . We are of a people who take what they want—like you whites. There is a time when a man should forget loyalty and respect. Might and authority are given to rulers, but to all men is given love and strength and courage. My brother said, 'You shall take her from their midst. We are two who are like one.' And I answered, 'Let it be soon, for I find no warmth in sunlight that does not shine upon her.' Our time came when the Ruler and all the great people went to the mouth of the river to fish by torchlight. There were hundreds of boats, and on the white sand, between the water and the forests, dwellings of leaves were built for the households of the Rajahs. The smoke of cooking-fires was like a blue mist of the evening, and many voices rang in it joyfully. While they were making the boats ready to beat up the fish, my brother came to me and said, 'Tonight!' I looked to my weapons, and when the time came our canoe took its place in the circle of boats carrying the torches. The lights blazed on the water, but behind the boats there was darkness. When the shouting began and the excitement made them like mad, we dropped out. The water swallowed our fire, and we floated back to the shore that was dark with only here and there the glimmer of embers. We could hear the talk of slave-girls amongst the sheds. Then we found a place deserted and silent. We waited there. She came. She came running along the shore, rapid and leaving no trace, like a leaf driven by the wind into the sea. My brother said gloomily, 'Go and take her; carry her into our boat.' I lifted her in my arms. She panted. Her heart was beating against my breast. I said, 'I take you from those people. You came to the cry of my heart, but my arms take you into my boat against the will of the great!' 'It is right,' said my brother. 'We are men who take what we want and can hold it against many. We should have taken her in daylight.' I said, 'Let us be off'; for since she was in my boat I began to think of our Ruler's many men. 'Yes. Let us be off,' said my brother. 'We are cast out and this boat is our country now—the sea is our refuge.' He lingered with his foot on the shore, and I entreated him to hasten, for I remembered the strokes of her heart against my breast and thought that two men cannot withstand a hundred. We left, paddling downstream close to the bank; and as we passed by the creek where they were fishing, the great shouting had ceased, but the murmur of voices was loud like the humming of insects flying at noonday. The boats floated, clustered together, in the red light of torches, under a black roof of smoke, and the men talked of their sport. Men that boasted, and praised, and jeered—men that would have been our friends in the morning, but on that night we already were enemies. We paddled swiftly past. We had no more friends in the country of our birth. She sat in the middle of the canoe with covered face; silent as she is now; unseeing as she is now—and I had no regret at what I was leaving because I could hear her breathing close to me—as I can hear her now "

He paused, listened with his ear turned to the doorway, then shook his head and went on.

"My brother wanted to shout the cry of challenge—one cry only—to let the people know we were freeborn robbers who trusted our arms and the great sea. And again I begged him in the name of our love to be silent. Could I not hear her breathing close to me? I knew the pursuit would come quick enough. My brother loved me. He dipped his paddle without a splash. He only said, 'There is half a man in you now—the other half is in that woman. I can wait. When you are a whole man again, you will come back with me here to shout defiance. We are sons of the same mother.' I made no answer. All my strength and all my spirit were in my hands that held the paddle—for I longed to be with her in a safe place beyond the reach of men's anger and of women's spite. My love was so great, that I thought it could guide me to a country where death was unknown, if I could only escape from Inchi Midah's fury and from our Ruler's sword. We paddled with haste, breathing through our teeth. The blades bit deep into the smooth water. We passed out of the river; we flew in clear channels amongst the shallows. We skirted the black coast; we skirted the sand beaches where the sea speaks in whispers to the land; and the gleam of white sand flashed back past our boat, so swiftly she ran upon the water. We spoke not. Only once I said, 'Sleep, Diamelen, for soon you may want all your strength.' I heard the sweetness of her voice but I never turned my head. The sun rose and still we went on. Water fell from my face like rain from a cloud. We flew in the light and heat. I never looked back, but I knew that my brother's eyes, behind me, were looking steadily ahead, for the boat went as straight as a bushman's dart, when it leaves the end of the sumpitan. There was no better paddler, no better steersman than my brother. Many times, together, we had won races in that canoe. But we never had put out our strength as we did then—then, when for the last time we paddled together! There was no braver or stronger man in our country than my brother. I could not spare the strength to turn my head and look at him, but every moment I heard the hiss of his breath getting louder behind me. Still he did not speak. The sun was high. The heat clung to my back like the flame of fire. My ribs were ready to burst, but I could no longer get enough air into my chest. And then I felt I must cry out with my last breath, 'Let us rest!' . . . 'Good!' he answered; and his voice was firm. He was strong. He was brave. He knew not fear and no fatigue. . . . My brother!"

A murmur powerful and gentle, a murmur vast and faint; the murmur of trembling leaves, of stirring boughs, ran through the tangled depths of the forests, ran over the starry smoothness of the lagoon, and the water between the piles lapped the slimy timber once with a sudden splash. A breath of warm air touched the two men's faces and passed on with a mournful sound—a breath loud and short like an uneasy sigh of the dreaming earth.

Arsat went on in an even, low voice.

"We ran our canoe on the white beach of a little bay close to a long tongue of land that seemed to bar our road; a long, wooded cape going far into the sea. My brother knew that place. Beyond the cape a river has its entrance, and through the jungle of that land there is a narrow path. We made a fire and cooked rice. Then we lay down to sleep on the soft sand in the shade of our canoe, while she watched. No sooner had I closed my eyes than I heard her cry of alarm. We leaped up. The sun was halfway down the sky already, and coming in sight in the opening of the bay we saw a prau manned by many paddlers. We knew 't at once: it was one of our Rajah's praus. They were watching the shore, and saw us. They beat the gong, and turned the head of the prau into the bay I felt my heart become weak within my breast. Diemelen sat on the sand and covered her face. There was no escape by sea. My brother laughed. He had the gun you had given him, Tuan, before you went away, but there was only a handful of powder. He spoke to me quickly: 'Run with her along the path. I shall keep them back, for they have no firearms, and landing in the face of a man with a gun is certain death for some. Run with her. On the other side of that wood there is a fisherman's house—and a canoe. When I have fired all the shots, I will follow. I am a great runner, and before they can come up we shall be gone. I will hold out as long as I can, for she is but a woman—that can neither run nor fight, but she has your heart in her weak hands.' He dropped behind the canoe. The prau was coming. She and I ran, and as we rushed along the path I heard shots. My brother fired—once—twice—and the booming of the gong ceased. There was silence behind us. That neck of land is narrow. Before I heard my brother fire the third shot I saw the shelving shore, and I saw the water again: the mouth of a broad river. We crossed a glassy glade. We ran down to the water. I saw a low hut above the black mud, and a small canoe hauled up. I heard another shot behind me. I thought, 'That is his last charge.' We rushed down to the canoe; a man came running from the hut, but I leaped on him, and we rolled together in the mud. Then I got up, and he lay still at my feet. I don't know whether I had killed him or not. I and Diamelen pushed the canoe afloat. I heard yells behind me, and I saw my brother run across the glade. Many men were bounding after him. I took her in my arms and threw her into the boat, then leaped in myself. When I looked back I saw that my brother had fallen. He fell and was up again, but the men were closing round him. He shouted, 'I am coming!' The men were close to him. I looked. Many men. Then I looked at her. Tuan, I pushed the canoe! I pushed it into deep water. She was kneeling forward looking at me, and I said, 'Take your paddle,' while I struck the water with mine. Tuan, I heard him cry. I heard him cry my name twice; and I heard voices shouting, 'Kill! Strike!' I never turned back. I heard him calling my name again with a great shriek, as when life is going out together with the voice—and I never turned my head. My own name! . . . My brother! Three times he called—but I was not afraid of life. Was she not there in that canoe? And could I not with her find a country where death is forgotten—where death is unknown!"

The white man sat up. Arsat rose and stood, an indistinct and silent figure above the dying embers of the fire. Over the lagoon a mist drifting and low had crept, erasing slowly the glittering images of the stars. And now a great expanse of white vapour covered the land: it flowed cold and grey in the darkness, eddied in noiseless whirls round the tree-trunks and about the platform of the house, which seemed to float upon a restless and impalpable illusion of a sea. Only far away the tops of the trees stood outlined on the twinkle of heaven, like a sombre and forbidding shore—a coast deceptive, pitiless and black.

Arsat's voice vibrated loudly in the profound peace.

"I had her there! I had her! To get her I would have faced all mankind. But I had her—and——"

His words went out ringing into the empty distances. He

I heard him calling my name again with a great shriek, as when life is going out together with the voice—and I never turned my head. . . . My own name! . . . . My brother!

paused, and seemed to listen to them dying away very far—beyond help and beyond recall. Then he said quietly—

" Tuan, I loved my brother."

A breath of wind made him shiver. High above his head, high above the silent sea of mist the drooping leaves of the palms rattled together with a mournful and expiring sound. The white man stretched his legs. His chin rested on his chest, and he murmured sadly without lifting his head——

" We all love our brothers."

Arsat burst out with an intense whispering violence—

" What did I care who died? I wanted peace in my own heart."

He seemed to hear a stir in the house—listened—then stepped in noiselessly. The white man stood up. A breeze was coming in fitful puffs. The stars shone paler as if they had retreated into the frozen depths of immense space. After a chill gust of wind there were a few seconds of perfect calm and absolute silence. Then from behind the black and wavy line of the forests a column of golden light shot up into the heavens and spread over the semi-circle of the eastern horizon. The sun had risen. The mist lifted, broke into drifting patches, vanished into thin flying wreaths; and the unveiled lagoon lay, polished and black, in the heavy shadows at the foot of the wall of trees. A white eagle rose over it with a slanting and ponderous flight, reached the clear sunshine and appeared dazzlingly brilliant for a moment, then soaring higher, became a dark and motionless speck before it vanished into the blue as if it had left the earth for ever. The white man, standing gazing upwards before the doorway, heard in the hut a confused and broken murmur of distracted words ending with a loud groan. Suddenly Arsat stumbled out with outstretched hands, shivered, and stood still for some time with fixed eyes. Then he said—

" She burns no more."

Before his face the sun showed its edge upon the tree-tops, rising steadily. The breeze freshened; a great brilliance burst upon the lagoon, sparkled on the rippling water. The forests came out of the clear shadows of the morning, became distinct, as if they had rushed nearer—to stop short in a great stir of leaves, of nodding boughs, of swaying branches. In the merciless sunshine the whisper of unconscious life grew louder, speaking in an incomprehensible voice round the dumb darkness of that human sorrow. Arsat's eyes wandered slowly, then stared at the rising sun.

"I can see nothing," he said half aloud to himself.

" There is nothing," said the white man, moving to the edge

of the platform and waving his hand to his boat. A shout came faintly over the lagoon and the sampan began to glide towards the abode of the friend of ghosts.

"If you want to come with me, I will wait all the morning," said the white man, looking away upon the water.

"No, Tuan," said Arsat softly. "I shall not eat or sleep in this house, but I must first see my road. Now I can see nothing—see nothing! There is no light and no peace in the world; but there is death—death for many. We were sons of the same mother—and I left him in the midst of enemies; but I am going back now."

He drew a long breath and went on in a dreamy tone.

"In a little while I shall see clear enough to strike—to strike. But she has died, and . . . now . . . darkness."

He flung his arms wide open, let them fall along his body then stood still with unmoved face and stony eyes, staring at the sun. The white man got down into his canoe. The polers ran smartly along the sides of the boat, looking over their shoulders at the beginning of a weary journey. High in the stern, his head muffled up in white rags, the juragan sat moody, letting his paddle trail in the water. The white man, leaning with both arms over the grass roof of the little cabin, looked back at the shining ripple of the boat's wake. Before the sampan passed out of the lagoon into the creek he lifted his eyes. Arsat had not moved. He stood lonely in the searching sunshine; and he looked beyond the great light of a cloudless day into the darkness of a world of illusions.

KIN YEN, THE PICTURE MAKER

By

ERNEST BRAMAH

THERE are moments in the life of a person when the saying of the wise Ni-Hyu that " Misfortune comes to all men and to most women " is endowed with double force. At such times the faithful child of the Sun is a prey to the whitest and most funereal thoughts, and even the inspired wisdom of his illustrious ancestors seems more than doubtful, while the continued inactivity of the Sacred Dragon appears for the time to give colour to the scoffs of the Western barbarian.

The name of the despicable person who here sets forth his immature story is Kin Yen, and he is a native of Kia-Lu in the Province of Che-Kiang. Having purchased from a very aged man the position of Hereditary Instructor in the Art of Drawing Birds and Flowers, he gave lessons in these accomplishments until he had saved sufficient money to journey to Pekin. Here it was his presumptuous intention to learn the art of drawing figures in order that he might illustrate printed leaves of a more distinguished class than those which would accept what true politeness compels him to call his exceedingly unsymmetrical pictures of birds and flowers. Accordingly, when the time arrived, he disposed of his Hereditary Instructorship, having first ascertained in the interests of his pupils that his successor was a person of refined morals and great filial piety.

Alas! it is well written, " The road to eminence lies through the cheap and exceedingly uninviting eating-houses." In spite of this person's great economy, and of his having begged his way from Kia-Lu to Pekin in the guise of a pilgrim, journeying to burn incense in the sacred Temple of Truth near that city, when once within the latter place his taels melted away like the smile of a person of low class when he discovers that the mandarin's stern words were not intended as a jest. Moreover, he found that the story-makers of Pekin, receiving higher rewards than those at Kia-Lu, considered themselves bound to introduce living characters into all their tales, and in consequence the very ornamental drawings of birds and flowers which he had entwined into a legend, entitled " The Last Flight of the Heaven-sent Tcheng "—a story which had been entrusted to him for illustration as a test of his skill—were returned to him with the communication in which the writer conveyed his real meaning by stating contrary facts. It therefore became necessary that he should become competent in the art of drawing figures without delay, and with this object he called at the picture-room of Tieng Lin, a person whose experience was so great that he could, without discomfort to himself, draw men and women of all classes, both good and bad. When the person who is setting forth this narrative revealed to Tieng Lin the utmost amount of money he could afford to give for instruction in the art of drawing living figures, Tieng Lin's face became as overcast as the sky immediately before the Great Rains, for in his ignorance of this incapable person's poverty he had treated him with equality and courtesy, nor had he kept him waiting in the mean room on the plea that he was at that moment closeted with the Sacred Emperor. However, upon receiving an assurance that a rumour would be spread in which the number of taels should be multiplied by ten, and that the sum itself should be brought in advance, Tieng Lin promised to instruct this person in the art of drawing five characters, which, he said, would be sufficient to illustrate all stories except those by the most expensive and highly rewarded story-tellers—men who have become so proficient that they not infrequently introduce a score or more of living persons into their tales without confusion.

After considerable deliberation this unassuming person selected the following characters, judging them to be the most useful, and the most readily applicable to all phases and situations of life:

1. A bad person, wearing a long dark pigtail and smoking an opium pipe. His arms to be folded, and his clothes new and very expensive.

2. A woman of low class. One who removes dust and useless things from the rooms of the over-fastidious and of those who have long nails; she to be carrying her trade-signs.

3. A person from Pe-ling, endowed with qualities which cause the beholder to be amused. This character to be especially designed to go with the short sayings which remove gravity.

4. One who, having incurred the displeasure of the sublime Emperor, has been decapitated in consequence.

5. An ordinary person of no striking or distinguished appearance. One who can be safely introduced in all places and circumstances without great fear of detection.

After many months spent in constant practice and in taking measurements, this unenviable person attained a very high degree of proficiency, and could draw any of the five characters without hesitation. With renewed hope, therefore, he again approached those who sit in easy-chairs, and concealing his identity (for they are stiff at bending, and when once a picture-maker is classed as "of no good" he remains so to the end, in spite of change), he succeeded in getting entrusted with a story by the elegant and refined Kyen Tal. This writer, as he remembered with distrust, confines his distinguished efforts entirely to the doings of sailors and of those connected with the sea, and this tale, indeed, he found upon reading to be the narrative of how a Hang-Chow junk and its crew, consisting mostly of aged persons, were beguiled out of their course by an exceedingly ill-disposed dragon, and wrecked upon an island of naked barbarians.

The sayings of the ancient philosopher Tai Loo are indeed very subtle, and the truth of his remark, "After being disturbed in one's dignity by a mandarin's foot it is no unusual occurrence to fall on the face in crossing a muddy street," was now apparent. Great as was the disadvantage owing to the nature of the five characters, this became as nothing when it presently appeared that the avaricious and clay-souled Tieng Lin, taking advantage of the blindness of this person's enthusiasm, had taught him the figures so that they all gazed in the same direction. In consequence of this it would have been impossible that two should be placed as in the act of conversing together had not the noble Kyen Tal been inspired to write that "his companions turned from him in horror." This incident the ingenious person who is recording these facts made the subject of three separate drawings, and having in one or two other places effected skilful changes in the writing, so similar in style to the strokes of the illustrious Kyen Tal as to be undetectable, he found little difficulty in making use of all his characters. The risks of the future, however, were too great to be run with impunity; therefore it was arranged, by means of money—for this person was fast becoming acquainted with the ways of Pekin—that an emissary from one who sat in an easy-chair should call upon him for a conference, which appeared in narrative form in the *Pekin Printed Leaves of Thrice-distilled Truth:*

"The brilliant and amiable young picture-maker Kin Yen, in spite of the immediate and universal success of his accomplished efforts, is still quite rotund in intellect, nor is he, if we may use a form of speaking affected by our friends across the Hoang Hai, 'suffering from swollen feet.' A person with no recognized position, but one who occasionally does inferior work of this nature for us, recently surprised Kin Yen without warning, and found him in his sumptuously appointed picture-room, busy with compasses and tracing-paper. From the conversation we can make it known that this versatile person will confine himself entirely to illustrations of processions, funerals, armies on the march, persons pursued by others, and kindred subjects which appeal strongly to his imagination. Kin Yen has severe emotions on the subject of individuality in art, and does not hesitate to express himself forcibly with reference to those who are content to degrade the names of their ancestors by turning out what he wittily describes as 'so much of varied mediocrity.'"

The prominence obtained by this pleasantly composed notice—for it was copied by others who were unaware of the circumstances of its origin—had the desired effect. In future, when one of those who sit in easy-chairs wished for a picture after the kind mentioned, he would say to his lesser one: "Oh, send to the graceful and versatile Kin Yen; he becomes inspired on the subject of funerals," or persons escaping from prison, or families walking to the temple, or whatever it might be. In that way this narrow-minded and illiterate person was soon both looked at and rich, so that it was his daily practice to be carried, in silk garments, past the houses of those who had known him in poverty.

True are the words written in the elegant and distinguished Book of Verses: "Beware lest when being kissed by the all-seeing Emperor, you step upon the elusive banana-peel." It was at the height of eminence in this altogether degraded person's career that he encountered the being who led him on to his present altogether too lamentable condition.

Tien Nung is the earthly name by which is known she who combines all the most illustrious attributes which have been possessed of women since the days of the divine Fou-Hy. Her father is a person of very gross habits, and lives by selling inferior merchandise covered with some of good quality. Upon past occasions, when under the direct influence of Tien, and in the hope of gaining some money benefit, this person may have spoken of him in terms of praise, and may even have recommended friends to entrust articles of value to him, or to procure goods on his advice. Now, however, he records it as his unalterable decision that the father of Tien Nung is by profession a person who obtains goods by stratagem, and that, moreover, it is impossible to gain an advantage over him on matters of exchange.

The events that have happened prove the deep wisdom of Li Pen when he exclaimed "The whitest of pigeons, no matter how excellent in the silk-hung chamber, is not to be followed on the field of battle." Tien herself was all that the most exacting of persons could demand, but her opinions on the subject of picture-making were not formed by heavy thought, and it would have been well if this had been borne in mind by this person. One morning he chanced to meet her while carrying open in his hands four sets of printed leaves containing his pictures.

"I have observed," said Tien, after the usual personal inquiries had been exchanged, "that the renowned Kin Yen, who is the object of the keenest envy among his brother picture-makers, so little regards the sacredness of his accomplished art that never by any chance does he depict persons of the very highest excellence. Let not the words of an impetuous maiden disarrange his digestive organs if they should seem too bold to the high-souled Kin Yen, but this matter has, since she has known him, troubled the eyelids of Tien. Here," she continued, taking from this person's hands one of the printed leaves which he was carrying, "in this illustration of persons returning from extinguishing a fire, is there one who appears to possess those qualities which appeal to all that is intellectual and competitive within one? Can it be that the immaculate Kin Yen is unacquainted with the subtle distinctions between the really select and the vastly ordinary? Ah, undiscriminating Kin Yen! are not the eyelashes of the person who is addressing you as threads of fine gold to junk's cables when compared with those of the extremely commonplace female who is here pictured in the act of carrying a bucket? Can the most refined lack of vanity hide from you the fact that your own person is infinitely rounder than this of the evilly intentioned looking individual with the opium pipe. O blind Kin Yen!"

Here she fled in honourable confusion, leaving this person standing in the street astounded, and a prey to the most distinguished emotions of a complicated nature.

"Oh, Tien," he cried at length, "inspired by those bright eyes, narrower than the most select of the three thousand and one possessed by the sublime Buddha, the almost fallen Kin Yen will yet prove himself worthy of your esteemed consideration. He will, without delay, learn to draw two new living persons, and will incorporate in them the likenesses which you have suggested."

Returning swiftly to his abode, he therefore inscribed and despatched this letter, in proof of his resolve:

"To the Heaven-sent human chrysanthemum, in whose body reside the Celestial Principles and the imprisoned colours of the rainbow.

"From the very offensive and self-opinionated picture-maker.

"Henceforth this person will take no rest, nor eat any but the commonest food, until he shall have carried out the wishes of his one Jade Star, she whose teeth he is not worthy to blacken.

"When Kin Yen has been entrusted with a story which contains a being in some degree reflecting the character of Tien, he will embellish it with her irreproachable profile, and come to hear her words. Till then he bids her farewell."

From that moment most of this person's time was necessarily spent in learning to draw the two new characters, and in consequence of this he lost much work, and, indeed, the greater part of the connection which he had been at such pains to form gradually slipped away from him. Many months passed before he was competent to reproduce persons resembling Tien and himself, for in this he was unassisted by Tien Lin, and his progress was slow.

At length, being satisfied, he called upon the least fierce of those who sit in easy-chairs, and requested that he might be entrusted with a story for picture-making.

"We should have been covered with honourable joy to set in operation the brush of the inspired Kin Yen," replied the other with agreeable condescension; "only at the moment it does not chance that we have before us any stories in which funerals, or beggars being driven from the city, form the chief incidents. Perhaps if the polished Kin Yen should happen to be passing this ill-constructed office in about six months' time——"

"The brush of Kin Yen will never again depict funerals, or labourers arranging themselves to receive pay or similar subjects," exclaimed this person impetuously; "for, as it is well said, 'The lightning discovers objects which the paper-lantern fails to reveal.' In future none but tales dealing with the most distinguished persons shall have his attention."

"If this be the true word of the dignified Kin Yen, it is possible that we may be able to animate his inspired faculties," was the response. "But in that case, as a new style must be in the nature of an experiment, and as our public has come to regard Kin Yen as the great exponent of Art Facing in One Direction, we cannot continue the exceedingly liberal payment with which we have been accustomed to reward his elegant exertions."

"Provided the story be suitable, that is a matter of less importance," replied this person.

"The story," said the one in the easy-chair, "is by the refined Tong-king, and it treats of the high-minded and conscientious doubts of one who would become a priest of Fo. When preparing for this distinguished office he discovers within himself leanings towards the religion of Lao-Tse. His illustrious scruples are enhanced by his affection for Wu Ping, who now appears in the story."

"And the ending?" inquired this person, for it was desirable that the two should marry happily.

"The inimitable stories of Tong-king never have any real ending, and this one, being in his most elevated style, has even less end than most of them. But the whole narrative is permeated with the odour of joss-sticks and honourable highmindedness, and the two characters are both of noble birth."

As it might be some time before another story so suitable should be offered, or one which would afford so good an opportunity of wafting incense to Tien, and of displaying her incomparable outline in dignified and magnanimous attitudes, this was eagerly accepted, and for the next week this obscure person spent all his days and nights in picturing the lovely Tien and his debased self in the characters of the nobly born young priest of Fo and Wu Ping. The pictures finished, he caused them to be carefully conveyed to the office, and then, sitting down, spent many hours in composing the following letter, to be sent to Tien, accompanying a copy of the printed leaves wherein the story and his drawings should appear:

"When the light has for a period been hidden from a person, it is no uncommon thing for him to be struck blind on gazing at the sun; therefore, if the sublime Tien values the eyes of Kin Yen, let her hide herself behind a gauze screen on his approach.

"The trembling words of Tien have sunk deep into the inside of Kin Yen and become part of his being. Never again can he depict persons of the quality and in the position he was wont to do.

"With this he sends his latest efforts. In each case he conceives his drawings to be the pictures to the written words; in the noble Tien's case it is undoubtedly so, in his own he aspires to it. Doubtless the unobtrusive Tien would make no claim to the character and manner of behaving of the one in the story, yet Kin Yen confidently asserts that she is to the other as the glove is to the hand, and he is filled with the most intelligent delight at being able to exhibit her in her true robes, by which she will be known to all who see her, in spite of her dignified protests. Kin Yen hopes; he will come this evening after sunset."

The week which passed between the finishing of the pictures and the appearance of the eminent printed leaves containing them was the longest in this near-sighted person's ill-spent life. But at length the day arrived, and going with exceedingly mean haste to the place of sale, he purchased a copy and sent it, together with the letter of his honourable intention, on which he had bestowed so much care, to Tien.

Not till then did it occur to this inconsiderable one that the impetuousness of his action was ill-judged; for might it not be that the pictures were evilly printed, or that the delicate and fragrant words painting the character of the one who now bore the features of Tien had undergone some change?

To satisfy himself, scarce as taels had become with him, he purchased another copy.

There are many exalted sayings of the wise and venerable Confucius constructed so as to be of service and consolation in moments of strong mental distress. These for the greater part recommend tranquillity of mind, a complete abnegation of the human passions and the like behaviour. The person who is here endeavouring to bring this badly-constructed account of his dishonourable career to a close pondered these for some moments after twice glancing through the matter in the printed leaves, and then, finding the faculties of speech and movement restored to him, procured a two-edged knife of distinguished brilliance and went forth to call upon the one who sits in an easy-chair.

"Behold," said the lesser one, insidiously stepping in between this person and the inner door, "my intellectual and all-knowing chief is not here today. May his entirely insufficient substitute offer words of congratulation to the inspired Kin Yen on his effective and striking pictures in this week's issue?"

"His altogether insufficient substitute," answered this person, with difficulty mastering his great rage, "may and shall offer words of explanation to the inspired Kin Yen, setting forth the reason of his pictures being used, not with the high-minded story of the elegant Tong-king for which they were executed, but accompanying exceeding base, foolish, and ungrammatical words written by Klan-hi, the Pekin remover of gravity—words which will evermore brand the dew-like Tien as a person of light speech and no refinement;" and in his agony this person struck the lacquered table several times with his elegant knife.

"O Kin Yen," exclaimed the lesser one, "this matter rests not here. It is a thing beyond the sphere of the individual who is addressing you. All he can tell is that the graceful Tong-king withdrew his exceedingly tedious story for some reason at the final moment, and as your eminent drawings had been paid for, my chief of the inner office decided to use them with this story of Klan-hi. But surely it cannot be that there is aught in the story to displease your illustrious personality?"

"Judge for yourself," this person said, "first understanding that the two immaculate characters figuring as the personages of the narrative are exact copies of this dishonoured person himself and of the willowy Tien, daughter of the vastly rich Pe-le-Chen, whom he was hopeful of marrying."

Selecting one of the least offensive of the passages in the work, this unhappy person read the following immature words:

"This well-satisfied writer of printed leaves had a highly

distinguished time last night. After Chow had departed to see about food, and the junk had been fastened up at the lock of Kilung, on the Yangtse-Kiang, he and the round-bodied Shang were journeying along the narrow path by the river-side when the right leg of the graceful and popular person who is narrating these events disappeared into the river. Suffering no apprehension in the dark but that the vanishing limb was the left leg of Shang, this intelligent writer allowed his impassiveness to melt away to an exaggerated degree; but at that moment the circumstance became plain to the round-bodied Shang, who was in consequence very grossly amused at the mishap and misapprehension of your good lord, the writer, at the same time pointing out the matter as it really was. Then it chanced that there came by one of the maidens who carry tea and jests for small sums of money to the sitters at the little tables with round white tops, at which this remarkable person, the confidant of many mandarins, ever desirous of displaying her priceless power of removing gravity, said to her:

" 'How much of gladness, Ning-Ning? By the Sacred Serpent this is plainly your night out."

'Perceiving the true facts of the predicament of this commendable writer, she replied:

" 'Suffer not your illustrious pigtail to be removed, venerable Wang; for in this maiden's estimation it is indeed your night in.'

"There are times when this valued person wonders whether his method of removing gravity be in reality very antique or quite new. On such occasions the world, with all its schools, and those who interfere in the concerns of others, continues to revolve around him. The wondrous sky-lanterns come out silently two by two like to the crystallized music of stringed woods. Then, in the mystery of no-noise, his head becomes greatly enlarged with celestial and highly profound thoughts; his groping hand seems to touch matter which may be written out in his impressive style and sold to those who print leaves, and he goes home to write out such."

When this person looked up after reading, with tears of shame in his eyes, he perceived that the lesser one had cautiously disappeared. Therefore, being unable to gain admittance to the inner office, he returned to his home.

Here the remark of the omniscient Tai Loo again fixes itself upon the attention. No sooner had this incapable person reached his house than he became aware that a parcel had arrived for him from the still adorable Tien. Retiring to a distance from it, he opened the accompanying letter and read:

"When a virtuous maiden has been made the victim of a heartless jest or a piece of coarse stupidity at a person's hands, it is no uncommon thing for him to be struck blind on meeting her father. Therefore, if the degraded and evil-minded Kin Yen values his eyes, ears, nose, pigtail, even his dishonourable breath, let him hide himself behind a fortified wall at Pe-li-Chen's approach.

"With this Tien returns everything she has ever accepted from Kin Yen. She even includes the brace of puppies which she received anonymously about a month ago, and which she did not eat, but kept for reasons of her own—reasons entirely unconnected with the vapid and exceedingly conceited Kin Yen."

As though this letter, and the puppies of which this person now heard for the first time, making him aware of the existence of a rival lover, were not enough, there almost immediately arrived a letter from Tien's father:

"This person has taken the advice of those skilled in extorting money by means of law forms, and he finds that Kin Yen has been guilty of a grave and highly expensive act. This is increased by the fact that Tien had conveyed his seemingly distinguished intentions to all her friends, before whom she now stands in an exceedingly ungraceful attitude. The machinery for depriving Kin Yen of all the necessaries of existence shall be put into operation at once."

At this point, the person who is now concluding his obscure and commonplace history, having spent his last piece of money on joss-sticks and incense paper: and being convinced of the presence of the spirits of his ancestors, is inspired to make the following prophecies:—That Tieng Lin, who imposed upon him in the matter of picture-teaching, shall come to a sudden end, accompanied by great internal pains, after suffering extreme poverty; that the one who sits in an easy-chair, together with his lesser one and all who make stories for them, shall, while sailing to a rice feast during the Festival of Flowers, be precipitated into the water and slowly devoured by sea monsters, Klan-hi in particular being tortured in the process; that Pe-li-Chen, the father of Tien, shall be seized with the dancing sickness when in the presence of the august Emperor, and being in consequence suspected of treachery, shall, to prove the truth of his denials, be submitted to the tests of boiling tar, red-hot swords, and of being dropped from a great height on to the Sacred Stone of Goodness and Badness, in each of which he shall fail to convince his judges or to establish his innocence, to the amusement of all beholders.

These are the true words of Kin Yen, the picture-maker, who, having unweighted his mind and exposed the avaricious villainy of certain persons, is now retiring by night to a very select and hidden spot in the Khingan Mountains.

THE HEAD

By

KATHLEEN WALLACE

In the outer courtyard of the temple the crowd surged, churning and muttering like waters that have burst their dam. They had waited there, gathering in greater numbers, since the first grey rift of earliest morning. Waiting for Chen Hsuei, the city magistrate, who had orders from Li, the war-lord, for a deed so dreadful that not a man in the crowd dared to lift his voice as he spoke of it, but muttered below his breath, his eyes sliding left and right with terror. It was nothing less than to destroy the great idol who sat alone in the silence of the inner hall of the temple, alone, as he had sat before any of them could remember, they, and their fathers and their fathers' fathers. Their own Ch'eng Huang Yeh, the god of the city moat. He whose temple was beset springtime after springtime by praying women in their thousands, eager for sons. Whose vast fair was held every year in the temple precincts under the rolling clouds of perfumed smoke shot through with the red glow of flames—the incense burnt in his honour. And now, he was to go. To be torn down from his dais, his sacred limbs hacked in pieces, his remains thrown into the cesspools, on to the dung-heaps outside the city. By order of the general, Li; the dictator, the absolute.

For Li was a ruthless innovator, a destroyer of what he held to be the old bonds that were paralysing the China he stood to save. A glib foreign journalist had interviewed him, and had headed his interview " The Mussolini of the East," in the slipshod but effective manner of certain newspaper folk. Li was a Mussolini only in his inexorable methods, his sheer domination. Not for him the old customs, crusted, cankered with usage. Shackles, he called them, and struck them off. Not realizing that limbs which have been shackled too long and too deeply are something worse than helpless before too swift and too complete a release. Under his rule, dealers in opium, smokers of the precious poppy-drug, could be shot down in their houses. Women who ventured to make their tottering way into the streets on their bound feet, were seized by Li's police and their bandages of a lifetime torn off. His people had already made away with some of the lesser gods of the district, but no one was found except Chen Hsuei himself, to dare such a frightful deed as the shattering of Ch'eng Huang Yeh.

Presently the rumour came wavering through the crowd, swaying them as corn is swayed by a wind passing through. There was a scuffle, a stampede, an outcry at the gate, as the magistrate's military guard forced their way in. And among them, his face livid and set, his eyes fixed only on the ground, the magistrate himself. The crowd closed in behind them like engulfing waters. They watched while the ladder was placed, and Chen climbed up, and with the axe in his palsied hands, struck at the idol's head. The axe-blade flew off and fell to the stone floor with a clatter. A woman's voice shrieked suddenly in the crowd, and then a silence more pregnant than any cries, fell upon the whole courtyard. They waited to see Chen fall dead before them. But instead, a tall guard fixed on the axe-head, handed it up again, and the magistrate turned to the idol once more. Another blow, and the great head rolled to the temple floor. The murmur of horror from the crowd swelled into a groan. Chen, as though some desperate force nerved him, hurled himself at the headless trunk and hacked until it lay on the ground in pieces, until even the disfigured block was splintered. The guards closed round him and bore rather than ushered him between the two sections of the crowd, which had shrunk back leaving a pathway, and out into the street. The people saw him lifted into the saddle. The guards parleyed a moment, then one of them advanced to the horse's head and spoke in an undertone to Chen. He made no sign of even hearing the man, but he turned his horse, and the procession moved down the street.

It did not make for the magistrate's compound. Instead, the motionless figure on the roan horse paced slowly through the city, surrounded by the guard, that all men might see that no harm had come to the man who was brave enough to obey the command of the general Li and make away with an ancient and powerless idol. But a coolie woman washing vegetables at a wayside gutter, stared after the figure on horseback and turned back to her neighbours.

"He's alive," she said shrilly. "But, *aie,* look at him! Look at his eyes! Ch'eng Huang Yeh may have spared his body, but he has set death upon him. It's in his face."

At the club, Mrs. Chester Burton got up from the mahjongg table, and dropped the two dollars and thirty cents of her winnings into her little bag of silver-chain mesh. A look of placid satisfaction was on her small, pink face as she powdered her nose, poked a mouse-coloured piece of hair into sight on each cheek, and thanked the Consul's wife for a lovely afternoon. The other three women looked after her idly and without particular interest as she

The magistrate turned to the idol once more. Another blow, and the great head rolled to the temple floor. The murmur of horror from the crowd swelled into a groan.

sauntered across the club veranda, and waved off with her pink sunshade the rickshaw coolies who came running up.

"*Buh yao hwambache—yao dzo-dzo!*" her shrill, small voice was heard explaining several times and with growing irritation. (I don't want a rickshaw. I wish to walk).

"Nellie Burton has the luck of the innocent," said one of the women, lighting a cigarette. "How she ever manages to win a hand—*what* a little fool!"

"'m—perhaps! But awfully harmless," demurred the Consul's wife who was a conscientious woman.

"Oh—harmless! I should say so! Do you know, she reminds me of nothing so much as the mouse in Sylvie and Bruno. What happened to it, Bruno? Nothing happened to it. It was too teeny-weeny. Coming, Mary? Can I give you a lift?"

Mrs. Chester Burton walked tranquilly down the white and dusty road beside the creek and its trailing willows, humming a little out of tune as she walked. She and Chester were dining at the B.A.T. mess; she would wear her pink organdie. The Consul's wife this afternoon had worn an imported frock—beige lace. She wondered whether Nung Wo, the tailor, could do one like it in fillet lace dyed flesh colour? Fillet is so cheap. On the table beside her bed at home was a box of chocolates, only half-empty. She would get it, and the new "Tatler" and "Bystander" and lie on the *chaise longue* on the veranda and have a nice read. Home papers always made her feel a little homesick when they arrived, but then——

At this moment a man came round the corner face to face with Mrs. Chester Burton. He was walking unsteadily, wavering from side to side as though he were drunk. But his face was not the face of a drunken man. Mrs. Burton got one ghastly sight of it, and it was the sight of that livid face with the open, panting mouth and staring eyes that made her give the one sharp scream she gave. Not the blade he suddenly flashed from beneath his long gown, for that she never saw. She never saw anything more. Her little body in its pink frock lay on the dusty path in a pool of blood, headless. And the man was tearing down the road at a long, lurching run, bearing in his arms the head of Mrs. Burton with its bobbed mouse-coloured curls.

Chester Burton was met, on his return from the office, by the Consul, whose face was a strange, grey hue, and whose teeth chattered oddly as he tried to speak. And presently, while the husband was left with that sheet-covered form on the upstairs bed, the Consul had the task of combing the city for the mutilated head of his friend's wife. It was midnight when he was met by one of his Chinese clerks and by two Chinese soldiers, who begged him to come immediately to the Governor's *yamen*—there was news, said the clerk vaguely and incoherently. The Consul, who had spent some four hours searching alleys, tea hovels, and latrines, came with them. He found in one of the stone cells, two guards leaning against the walls, stolidly eating peanuts and spitting the shells on to the filthy floor, while on the pallet crouched a figure with manacles on the clutching hands and a chain binding the writhing feet like the feet of an animal bought at the market. The Consul would have said that there could be no further shocks for him after the night's work from which he had just come; but his nerve-racked body did give one more leap, and a queer sound was forced from his lips, as he bent over the bed and made out that the thing which writhed and moaned there was indeed, or had been, the suave, cultured gentleman, Chen Hsuei, the city magistrate.

The Consul spoke hoarsely in mandarin.

"Chen Hsuei—Chen Hsuei—my poor friend, what does this mean? Speak to me——"

"He has spoken—but he will not know you, *Lin-sze* (Consul)," the clerk put in. "He is mad, you see. Quite mad."

Whether the thing on the bed ever did know him or not, the Consul could never decide. But Chen Hsuei raised himself, rolling over, and lifted his bound arms in some desperate entreaty, and spoke rapidly, his dreadful eyes darting hither and thither about the cell, mad, quite mad, with terror.

"He made me kill my god. He made me. And I did it. I cut off his head, and it rolled—it rolled. They carried it outside the walls, yes, to the cess-pool. My god, my god's head. What could I do? I saw her, the foreign woman, the thing of the West, the accursed West that has taught the new devil-ways. Her head, her white face, her yellow hair, her silly foreign head-dress with flowers on it. . . . I struck it off. Her head. I ran off with it. Yes. It is with his, my god's—in the cess-pool beyond the walls—he will pardon me now, Ch'eng Huang Yeh. He knows I was forced to it. And I have paid——"

So, at the second dawn, they dredged from the outer cess-pool, the maimed block of painted wood that had been the honoured head of the God of the City Moat; and also the unrecognizable and indescribable thing that had once been the head of Nellie Burton.

They were spared the problem of dealing with Chen Hsuei. When morning came, the drowsy guards found that his god had not forgotten him. He had managed to get his manacled hands and their fetters about his own throat. He was dead.

THE JUSTICE OF SUAN HLI

By

REGINALD CAMPBELL

SUAN HLI was old, older than memory. He was thin and bent, and his wizened features were a mass of criss-cross wrinkles. How long he had lived in his store in the town of Raheng no one seemed to know, but all the Loa-Siamese inhabitants of the district agreed that he must have dwelt there for many, many years.

Suan Hli himself could have told them, but he was not communicative. His store was his little world, and his hopes centred round a pagoda he one day hoped to build in the compound of the largest Chinese temple in Bangkok, the great capital that was situated some three hundred miles down-river to the south.

That pagoda! Suan Hli, sitting behind his counter, thought of it. It would be built as an everlasting tribute to his sacred ancestors, and it would be a worthy gift to them, for would it not cost him the whole of his life's savings?

Suan Hli, seeing the hour was late, rose stiffly to his feet, closed his store for the night, then slip-slopped into a little room at the back. There, placed on shelves, were rows and rows of boxes containing dirty, well-fingered one-tical notes to the grand total of nine thousand eight hundred. It was a large amount of money to have at the back of beyond, miles away from civilization and any possible aid of police; nevertheless he felt sure of its safety, for he had an amateur burglar-alarm system set up in his house; he had an automatic pistol at his side every night as he slept; and above all, by his long association with them, he had earned the respect of the majority of the simple-minded natives among whom he lived.

Suan Hli smiled like a little gnome, and stroked the boxes with loving hands. How they had grown in number during all these years! A tical here, a tical there, given him in return for the tinned meats, brooches, odd garments and finery that appealed to the simple souls of the district—these little contributions had gradually swelled to a mighty sum, and soon, say in four moons' time, the ten thousand tical mark would be reached, and then would he take his departure for distant Bangkok. Five days' journey through the forest would bring him to the nearest railway station, after which only a few hours' travel would lie between him and Siam's capital. Once there, he would hand the money over to his Chinese *kong see,* and that community would attend to the building of the pagoda.

And he? He would then lay down his bones and die, for he was tired; very, very tired. He was old, wracked with rheumatism, burnt out with fever, and would willingly die now but for the fact that he must get those many ticals safely down to Bangkok for the sake of the pagoda.

A frown of anxiety creased the already wrinkled forehead of Suan Hli as he thought of the journey before him. Pack-bullocks would bear the boxes of wealth, and he would hire some trustworthy Kamoo coolies to form an escort; but—what of the five days' travel through the jungle before he reached the safety of the railway? Jungle vultures there were, he knew, vultures that might come and, overpowering his coolies, slay him and steal the precious ticals.

Should he hire boats and journey the entire way down to Bangkok by the river that ran outside his store? No; there would be more danger than ever in that enterprise, for robbers could wait for him along the banks and, moreover, the period of danger would be extended from five days to several weeks.

Suan Hli thought long, then, rising, lit tapers before a niche in the wall and communed with his ancestors. The incense burned. Night cloaked the land. Silence was in the store. Suan Hli was alone with the dead.

The following morning, Mong Hpo, a Burmese, tied up his boats opposite Suan Hli's store. Mong Hpo had come up from Bangkok by water, and was now on his way to the far distant forests of the north, where he would trade in teak and elephants. Being short of provisions, and anxious to replenish his failing stock, he climbed up the bank and entered the shop. Suan Hli greeted him, and, being strangers to one another, they bowed low in many salaams before going into the Chinaman's inner room.

There tea was served, and the pair talked and drank until the sun blazed high in the sky, whereupon orders were given, and soon many were the cases of tinned foods and milk that were carried out of the store and placed in Mong Hpo's boats.

The Burmese then took his departure for the north, and as a result of his visit Suan Hli found himself the possessor of the required ten thousand ticals. So he immediately called his head coolie and gave him certain instructions; and the coolie, pleasantly intrigued, told a friend. The friend told another friend, so that by the time evening mellowed over the world the whole village was talking. In one month from now, when the rains would have cleared sufficiently to ensure pack-bullocks easy travel, old Suan Hli was leaving Raheng, never to return.

The dusky Laos and Siamese debated the matter with great interest, for the Chinaman had come to be looked on as part of the town itself. One and all of them showed much concern at his going, and none more so than a certain half-dozen evil-featured men who crouched in the attap-roofed shelter at the far end of the market-place.

"Without doubt," said one, "Suan Hli must have much money, for has he not been here these many years? Then will good fortune come to us."

"But may-be he will have a coolie escort," complained another.

"Pah! Kamoo coolies he may have, but will not we be six strong men, all armed with guns? *Leukarn,* his money is ours for sure."

"Nevertheless, will not all the district know of his departure?" grumbled the second speaker. "Perchance other men may conspire to get the money, even as we are doing. And these men might steal the money before we can."

Whereupon small, crafty Nai Deng spoke. "If we went as his protectors, then all would be well, since thus we would be certain of being in his presence from the start to the finish of the journey. That being the case, we could slay him when we liked."

Ten minutes later Nai Deng was salaaming in Suan Hli's store. "Great One," he said respectfully, "I would fain speak to you on a secret matter."

"So," answered Suan Hli, and he led the newcomer into a little room at the back.

Nai Deng crouched almost double on the floor, and his shifty eyes glanced sideways at certain boxes that were placed row upon row on the shelves.

"Great One," he whispered, "it is said in the market-place that in one moon you are leaving for the railway. Now, Great One, it is also said that much money has come to you during your sojourn with us, wherefore it seems to me that many evil men will be plotting for this money."

"That thought has occurred to me also," said Suan Hli gently, and his little face smiled.

"Lord and Great One, I, Nai Deng, have five friends. They are big men and to be trusted. Moreover, they have guns, every one of them, and souls that have no fear. If they could form your escort, then would no harm come to you; though should you travel with Kamoo coolies, I very much fear for your Honour, since Kamoos are timid men."

Nai Deng paused significantly.

"Nai Deng and his friends would require a reward for this service?" Suan Hli asked in Siamese.

"They would," answered Nai Deng decidedly.

"How much?"

"Lord, we desire one hundred ticals for each of us."

"It is too much. I give only eighty."

There followed much bargaining, but eventually an agreement was reached at ninety ticals, the money to be paid after the Chinaman's safe arrival at the railway station.

Nai Deng then rose to depart, but Suan Hli restrained him. "Though I know of no evil against thee, Nai Deng," he said smoothly, "yet have I no knowledge of good. Now I would fain have proof that thou canst be trusted."

"Lord," answered the Siamese earnestly, "if such is in your power, it would gladden my heart to have a proof whereby to earn your Honour's trust."

Suan Hli thought awhile. His slanting eyes gazed vacantly into space as if he had forgotten his companion, and not until a full ten minutes had elapsed did he speak.

"Nai Deng, I have a coat," said he. "It is a rich coat, made of much fine cloth and woven gold. Now this coat I wish to send to my *kong see* in Bangkok, so that it may come as a present to them and as a token of my goodwill before I myself arrive to join their company. If tomorrow Nai Deng would take this coat to the railway station, deliver it to the booking-clerk, and bring back the receipt for it to me in safety, then will I trust him."

"Lord, this will I do," answered Nai Deng, "though, owing to the distance, it will be eight—nine—ten days before I get back to Raheng again."

"It matters not," the Chinaman told him, "since I, Suan Hli, will not start forth till one moon from now. So Nai Deng will go?"

"He will go."

"Then come tomorrow morning, and I will give thee the coat."

Punctually the next morning Nai Deng arrived at the Chinaman's store. He was shown into the inner room, and there on the table lay the coat, which was a rich coat, even as Suan Hli had said. The Chinaman took up the garment, rolled it into a bundle, wrapped it in brown paper, and made a neat parcel of it. The parcel he then addressed in Siamese writing to his *kong see* in Bangkok, after which he handed it, together with the postage money, to the expectant Nai Deng.

"Now go, Nai Deng, and may good luck attend thee on the journey. And see that thou dost not forget to bring back the booking-clerk's receipt."

The man vanished, and Suan Hli turned to a niche in the wall. He lighted tapers, and the pungent smell of incense wafted through the room. Suan Hli was with his ancestors again.

Nine days elapsed, and at noon on the tenth Nai Deng re-appeared in the store, bringing the treasured receipt with him. The parcel was now safely posted to Bangkok, but the journey to and from the railway had been no light undertaking. He had had to cross mountainous paths, still wet and slippery from the rains; he had been obliged to endure heat, cold, fever and weariness for nine successive days, but at last his trial was ended and the proof of his good faith to hand.

"Thou hast done well," said Suan Hli, after carefully examining his receipt. "And now, since Suan Hli is just, here are ten ticals for thy services, also an agreement engaging thee and thy men as his escort to the railway station."

"And when will the Great One be pleased to start?" asked Nai Deng, as he pocketed the money and agreement.

"In two weeks from now, provided the weather favours. Meanwhile see that your guns are cleaned and ready for use if need be."

"Great One, we will see to that," said Nai Deng fervently.

Exactly a fortnight later the Chinaman moved off with his escort. His thin, frail body, wracked more than ever with pain, was balanced on a quiet old pony. Behind the pony four patient pack-bullocks trod meekly, carrying their loads of square wooden boxes in baskets suspended on each side of their meagre flanks. Ahead and astern of the animals there strode three stalwart guards, each heavily armed.

The party passed through the market-place of the town, where the villagers, one and all, salaamed a last good-bye to the little Chinaman. Suan Hli smiled a gnome-like farewell to them, and soon their chattering faded in the distance and the towering walls of the jungle rose up in solid sheets of green to left and right of the path that led to the distant railway.

Mile after mile slid by, until, when evening came, the party found itself in the very heart of the forest. Here camp was made and a shelter of bamboo fronds was prepared for Suan Hli. When the old man was at rest, the boxes were taken from off the bullocks' backs and placed all round him; fires were lit and the evening meal of rice cooked and eaten. Then the guards squatted in a circle outside the shelter, and silence descended on the dark forest.

Suan Hli lay very still, listening to that silence. His body was sore stricken, for the unaccustomed ride had brought him added suffering; nevertheless that wistful smile still lingered on his features, for through the fronds above him he could see the stars. They were age-old, those stars, and invested with certain great truths upon which Suan Hli had pondered much. Truth, truth begat philosophy, and Suan Hli was a philosopher—wherefore in spite of his pain he smiled.

The night wore on, and presently the old man was aware of a sound outside his shelter. He withdrew his gaze from the heavens, and beheld his guards grouped round the entrance. Foremost was Nai Deng.

"Death comes to thee, Oh, Chinaman," said Nai Deng, raising his gun.

Suan Hli stood upright and folded his hands crosswise in his loose sleeves. "Nai Deng is well skilled in the use of his gun?" he asked the murderer.

"He is well skilled," echoed Nai Deng, and fired.

The little Chinaman fell, and lay upon his back, quite still. He was smiling as never before, as if he were happy to be free from his pain, as indeed he was.

The robbers stooped and, after examining the motionless form, sprang upon the boxes. Shouting in greedy eagerness they prised them open with their jungle-knives, then they drew back aghast. For, jammed tightly in each of the boxes, were, not tical notes, but ball upon ball of worthless packing paper.

Some three months later a Burmese named Mong Hpo, having recently returned by rail to Bangkok after an exhaustive tour of the north, had occasion to visit a certain wealthy Chinese merchant. The pair conversed for a time on trade matters, and then——

"Ah Fong," said the Burmese to the Chinaman sitting before him, "on my visit up north I was helped greatly on one occasion by a man of your race."

"This is pleasant talk to hear," murmured Ah Fong politely.

"The person was one Suan Hli, who lives at Raheng," continued Mong Hpo. "Now I, Mong Hpo, had been guilty of great foolishness in that I had travelled by water from Bangkok with ten notes to the value of one thousand ticals each as my only means of buying the wherewithal to live. As I said, this was great foolishness, for of what use is a one-thousand tical note in the wilderness?"

"Of what use, indeed?" echoed Ah Fong gravely.

"I reach Raheng, where I see Suan Hli's store. I need provisions, also I think he may be able to change one may-be two of my notes. I enter that store, and speak to Suan Hli privately. He sell me all the goods I require, and, what did please me more, he gave me one-tical notes to the total value of nine thousand eight hundred ticals. For these, together with the food I bought, did I then give him my ten one-thousand-tical notes in exchange and thus did I benefit greatly."

Mong Hpo paused, spat betel-nut into a large lacquer bowl on the floor, then continued:

"I think Suan Hli a clever man," said he, "for he not let me take those one-tical notes in their boxes to my boats. No, instead he make me put them in empty milk cases, for he say that if the populace see much money going out of the store, may-be evil men will hear of the matter and attack me for the sake of my wealth. This did I do, with much profit to myself, since I had my notes of small value which were easy to circulate, and yet was I safe from attack. Wherefore, O Ah Fong, Suan Hli did perform me a great service, and I would fain see him again one day."

"That," answered Ah Fong, "will Mong Hpo never do, for Suan Hli is dead."

The Burmese was distressed. He spread his hands and made sympathetic enquiries. The Chinaman explained:

"Three and a half moons ago, my *kong see* did receive a parcel," he said gravely. "The parcel was from Suan Hli, and it contained a coat. Sewn in the coat were ten notes to the value of one thousand ticals each. There was also a letter from Suan Hli which explained that the money was for the building of a pagoda in our temple compound here in Bangkok. This letter stated in addition that he was leaving Raheng shortly for the railway, but that robbers might attack him on the way. If, so he wrote, he did not arrive in Bangkok by a certain date, we were to inform the police and state, amongst other things, that a certain Nai Deng might be suspected of the murder."

"Huh," breathed the Burmese, deeply interested.

"I will end this tale," said Ah Fong, "by saying that yesterday, following a trial, Nai Deng was executed, and five other robbers were sentenced to imprisonment for life."

"Which was all exceeding just," murmured Mong Hpo, after he had digested the information.

"It was just," agreed the other. "Moreover, it was strange,

for we found out that it was Nai Deng himself who delivered the parcel to the railway clerk."

"*Meh,*" exclaimed Mong Hpo in surprise. "Then this Nai Deng not only delivered the money to safety, but he also took his own death warrant."

"He did," said Ah Fong. "Of a truth, Nai Deng helped our good friend greatly, and I think the greatest service of all was the last he performed."

"Meaning the killing?"

"Meaning even that; for had Suan Hli wished to live, why should he have taken decoy cases through the jungle, as we now know well he did?"

Mong Hpo spat again. "Suan Hli wished to die, of that we can be sure," he told his companion. "The money was safe, and he—he was old and in great pain, and of what then is the use of life?"

"Of no use at all," said Ah Fong, and sipped his tea.

ONE—NOT TWO

By

ACHMED ABDULLAH

On her way to the Mission Chapel, Miss Rutter met Bill Devoy, detective in charge of the Chinatown beat of opium and sewer gas, and yellow man and white and almost-white.

"Mr. Devoy," she asked him, and there was a certain triumph in her wheezy old voice, "do you recall the trouble some years ago, between Lee Fong and Han Mok?"

"Sure. Lee Fong swiped all Han Mok's kale and . . ."

"No, no. They had a business disagreement."

"He did him in the eye—that's wot he done."

"Put it that way if you prefer." Miss Rutter permitted herself the rare luxury of a smile. "But," she continued fervently, "he has repented. He'll see to it that, in the future, Han Mok suffers no want. Han Mok came out of Bellevue to-day—cured."

"A Chink hop-head—cured? Wot're yer givin' me?"

"You *are* a doubting Thomas."

"It's my business—as a cop. Well—mebbe he'll stay cured." He laughed. "But I hope he won't trust Lee Fong. Why—if that hard-boiled Mongol egg has toined over a new leaf, then there's hope for the Devil."

"You're doing him an injustice," said Miss Rutter severely. "He is ready and eager to atone . . ."

"Ah—wot the h——!"

Then Devoy saw the woman's thin, pathetic, ineffectual face. He remembered the rather hysterical idealism which hid from her mind the world of crass Chinatown realities; and so he changed the oath to a cough and walked away on an apocryphal errand, while Miss Rutter turned toward the Mission Chapel which was her life.

Lonely and drab the small brownstone building seemed here amidst the warm reek of grease and spice and sandalwood; waging a brave, losing fight against the huge Buddha who, in the joss temple across the way, squatted on his carved lotus pedestal, on his painted lips the tenuous, sardonic smile of the centuries. Oh, yes—lonely and drab the little church! Stale, musty, dusty. Yet glorious and sweet to the middle-aged woman in black satin who knelt before the altar and poured out her soul to her Maker:

"I thank Thee, dear Lord, because, in Thy mercy, Thou hast caused my beloved brother Lee Fong to see the error of his ways and to clear his stubborn heart of sin!"

She was happy. She thought of Lee Fong and Han Mok. Friends for years; then enemies; now, once more, friends.

They had been children together in Canton. There Lee Fong's father had been a coolie, underpaid, underfed, and Han Mok's father something of a professional man—an acrobat, who had taught his son the tricks of his ancient trade. Feats of strength and skill with rope, pole and trapeze. But chiefly sword work: tossing the gleaming weapons from the distance with precision and speed, so that eight lengths of steel would cut through the air, swish unerringly between ten fingers, held trustingly apart like the sticks of a fan, and bury their sharp points in a wooden slab.

Han Mok was an apt pupil. Occasionally, still in his teens, when his father had smoked too much opium, he would take the latter's place; would earn the money for the evening rice, and be applauded by merchant and mandarin. But his rising fame made no difference in his affection for the coolie's son. They loved each other; confided in each other; spent pleasant hours discussing their dreams and hopes for the future.

Dreams, always, of high adventure, until with young manhood, came the eagerness to turn these dreams into facts. Therefore—the one tall and burly, the other so puny, the one versed in his father's craft, the other untrained, yet endowed with a stony resolve to clout his path to success—they went to America.

There was, of course, the Asiatic Exclusion Act, which closed the door of the New World to the Mongol emigrant. So they greased many crooked, rapacious hands—white hands and yellow hands—and suffered untold hardships before they reached their goal. But the hardships and dangers brought them even more closely together. And, shortly after their arrival in Pell Street, it became a saying in laundry shop and restaurant, in curio store and gambling club, that they were like the right and left wings of a bird, one useless without the other; that—according to Nag Hong Fah, the owner of the Place of Sweet Desire and Heavenly Entertainment—if you cut Lee Fong's wrist, Han Mok would bleed, and if you filled Han Mok's belly, Lee Fong would belch with satisfaction.

Han Mok's renown had preceded him. On Saturday nights, Chinatown's older generation would crowd the Place of Sweet Desire and Heavenly Entertainment, where he gave exhibitions of ancient sword-craft. They never tired of watching him. The flotsam and jetsam of Canton they were, unimportant measured with the Broadway or Wall Street yardsticks; but men at whose back stretched forty centuries of racial pride and achievement—thus dignified, conservative men who held that what had been good enough for their ancestors was good enough for them; who applauded Han Mok generously, rewarded him as generously. Besides, his services were in demand when Chinatown—noisily, with firecrackers and discordant music—celebrated wedding or birth or religious festival.

Lee Fong, on the other hand, earned merely a miserable pittance at the start. He would have known cold and hunger, might indeed have starved to death—for who, amongst his countrymen, would have cared if one more coolie's soul had leaped the dragon gate—had it not been for his friend, who said:

"Whatever I have is yours. How can it be else? We are one—not two . . ."

But, presently, relations changed, Chinatown's younger generation, New York bred, came more to the fore. They had no reverence for the hoary traditions—in philosophy and ethics no less than in sword-craft—of the dead dynasties of Sung and Ming. They jeered at these traditions, preferring American sports, American vaudeville and motion pictures.

So Han Mok's income began to shrink. He still gave his weekly performance at the Place of Sweet Desire and Heavenly Entertainment. But he was no longer in demand when Chinatown was on its festive occasions. He knew idle days and nights and—a weakness inherited from his father—smoked more opium than was good for him.

By this time Lee Fong, with his tough, slow-grinding brain, had learned America's golden potentialities and had fashioned them into a weapon for his own gain. He used this weapon efficiently, ruthlessly, accumulating the dollars with a selfishness that was sublimely shameless—until his, finally, became a name to conjure with in that slab of real estate which is pinched in between the Bowery and Mulberry Bend like a thin, ironic wedge of Asia, driving apart bartering, narrow-chested, whining Russian Hebrew and bartering, bull-necked, shrill Sicilian.

He fought them both. He pitted his Mongol wit against Latin cunning and Semite guile, daily putting new and amazing twists into his algebraic brain to meet the shabby competition of Europe's backstairs—greatly to the confusion of the latter and the enrichment of accounts carried by the soundest of New York banks under the picaresque ledger heading: "The Golden Phœnix Syndicate." For, on the advice of Jake Rosenblatt, the Bowery lawyer, he had incorporated his enterprise, taking into the firm a number of junior partners, handpicked for their wealth and keenness.

Han Mok was not wealthy. Nor was he keen in business matters. Yet he, too, became a partner—though a silent one—and invested all his small savings in the Golden Phœnix; Lee Fong, furthermore, presenting him with a considerable block of stock as a free gift, because:

"You fed me, clothed and sheltered me, when I was poor. It is as you said. We are one. Not two."

The other bowed.

"You are my brother, very old and very wise," he replied.

"We are more than brothers. We are friends. And, speaking as a friend, may I tell you what is on my mind?"

"Please do."

"It is not that I share the prejudices of the coarse-haired barbarians. The poppy—no doubt of it—is an elegant drug. But you smoke too much. Last Saturday, when you gave your exquisite performance, your right hand trembled—you dropped one of the swords—and . . ."

"I remember. There was laughter. I lost a great deal of face."

"Therefore—you will smoke less?"

"I shall try."

He did try and, in the end, succeeded. Not thanks to his own will-power. Thanks, rather, to Lee Fong who, when the craving was upon Han Mok, would sit by the side of his couch, arguing, imploring; who, at times, though he so frail and the other so burly, would attack him with all his feeble strength and smash the opium lay-out; and who—when Han Mok, maddened with desire, knocked him down brutally—even then, prone on the ground, hurt and bleeding, would continue to implore:

"Please. For my sake. Because we love each other. Because we are one—not two."

Friendship as hard as steel—and, in Pell Street's motley annals, this friendship, in the course of the years, assumed the character of something lyrical, something almost religious. It was spoken of with pride and faint envy. The tale of it drifted to the Pacific coast; and even in far China wise men mentioned it with a hush of reverence as they floated down the river on their painted house-boats in peach-blossom time.

"Ah"—they would smile—"blessed be the Buddha. They are one—not two!"

And then, suddenly, they were two, not one. Two who hated each other with a passion as strong as their love had been . . .

Bill Devoy heard of it and—there being always the danger of bloody Tong war or private feud—worried. He interviewed Theodore Roosevelt Fu, who was New York born and, by inclination as well as for reasons of self-defence, a stool-pigeon.

"Wot's the dope, Teddy?" Devoy demanded.

"Just a business row," the other answered. He pointed at the fact that Lee Fong had stripped Han Mok of all his small savings invested in the Golden Phœnix: had also taken away the block of stock presented to him as a free gift; had done it—for there was Jake Rosenblatt, well versed in the intricacies of the coarse-haired barbarians' laws—by strictly legal methods.

"I know," said the detective impatiently. "But I don't get it. Why—them two bozos have been side-kicks for years——"

"And now the kickin' is the other way about. Lee Fong kickin' Han Mok right in the pants."

"Well—how come?"

"One o' them things, chief."

"Oh, yeah? Wot's in the back of it?"

"No savvy," replied Theodore Roosevelt Fu—and lied. He savvied quite well—as all Chinatown savvied, rolling the scandal over thick tongues. But since the scandal was purely of Pell Street and could not affect the powers that be, either at police headquarters or at Tammany Hall, he had no intention of taking Devoy into his confidence. So he went on smoothly: "Y'know—we gotta sayin' in Chinkie——" He spluttered sing-song monosyllables; translated: "All things come to an end, except the beards of the beardless."

This, too, was the proverb quoted that evening, in the Place of Sweet Desire and Heavenly Entertainment, by Yu Ch'ang, the priest, who added:

"Yet even the beards of the beardless come to an end—at times."

"When?" inquired Li Ping-Yeng, the money-lender.

"When the beardless grow beards, and then——"

"Cut them off?"

"As these two did—Lee Fong and Han Mok. The fools. To cut off their honourable beards because of one grey hair."

"To cut off their honourable noses," chimed in Yung Long, the wholesale grocer, "because of one small pimple."

"One small pimple?" exclaimed Ho Ti, the tea merchant. "Not a very complimentary remark when applied to delightful Lin Hai." He smacked his lips. "I have seen her."

"So have I."

"And I."

" She is a polished emerald of beauty."

" A blending of poppy and jade."

" I would have made an offer to buy her," announced the tea merchant, " were it not for the fact that my esteemed wife has a mouth like a running tap."

Came laughter. And gossip—about Lee Fong and Han Mok and Lin Hai, not to forget Susie Wong, who dealt in living wares and who, under contract with the former's parents, had smuggled her in from Canton. Gossip of the bitter scene, one day, in the woman's Mott Street flat: Lee Fong entering, dressed in his black silk best—seeing there Han Mok seated between Lin Hai and Susie Wong—giving a start—and Han Mok rising, saying with a smile:

" Wish me happiness, O wise and older brother!"

" Happiness——?"

" Yes. You see, I love Lin Hai, and," smiling at the girl over his shoulder, " she loves me. Susie Wong has given her consent."

A silence. Then Lee Fong cried:

" No!"

" Eh——?"

" You cannot have her! *I* love her. *I!* And—I came here to——"

" I understand."

A longer silence—like a pall. They stared at one another, while Susie Wong smiled maliciously and figured potential profits, telling herself that, though she had reached an agreement with Han Mok, Lee Fong was ten times—no, twenty times—as rich as the former . . . ah—the richest man, the most powerful, in all Chinatown. And she looked at the two men who continued to stare at each other, their implacable eyes meeting, contending, like two blades equally choice of temper crossing in a duel of death.

Friends . . .?

Why—the same thought in both their brains—they had not reckoned with the terrible thing called love of woman; this dark force which had suddenly risen between them like a wall . . . and, with a mercilessly acute apprehension, they knew that their friendship was at an end—because of Lin Hai, sitting erect on her chair, like a small idol carved out of ivory and gold.

Lee Fong broke the silence.

" How much has Han Mok offered?" he asked Susie Wong.

" Seventeen thousand dollars."

" My all," Han Mok added. " And"—with a slow, queer smile—" one more thing."

" Oh——?"

"Marriage——"

"Marriage——?" Lee Fong echoed incredulously. He was shocked. And no wonder. Lin Hai—oh, yes—was beautiful. Modest she was and virtuous. Still—she was a *shuey-kee,* a "water-fowl" born and bred on a Canton river-boat. She was a slave-girl, a commodity which one bought and sold; and not even the lowest coolie could marry such a one without grave loss of face. He told Han Mok so, but mockingly: "I cannot permit you to bring this black disgrace upon your ancestors. Therefore," to Susie Wong, "I offer forty thousand dollars—without marriage."

"An excellent price," the woman replied. "I accept."

"How can you?" Han Mok was furious. "We made a deal——"

"The purchase papers have not yet been signed."

"The girl loves me. Don't you, Lin Hai? Don't you?"

"I do," in clear accents. "I shall always love you."

"Pah," Susie laughed, "love buys no tea. Forty thousand is the price. But listen, Han Mok, I am generous. Give me," with a wink at Lee Fong, "thirty-nine thousand and the girl is yours."

"How can I? I have offered my all——"

"And it seems," interrupted Lee Fong, "that your all is not enough. Ah"—cruelly perhaps, because, at that moment, he understood that Lin Hai would never love him—"maybe, when I am through with her, I shall give her to you as a present——"

Then, all at once, a crimson rage came upon Han Mok. He struck out without warning, his fist hitting Lee Fong square between the eyes. The other went down. Han Mok kicked him where he lay; kicked him with all his massive strength. He bent and picked him up; stood him upon his feet; knocked him down again, again kicked him, again pulled him up—over and over, as if it were some hideous game of hide-and-seek.

Drunk with fury. Insane. Seeing nothing. Hearing nothing. Only the vibrations in his own soul—surging up immensely, chokingly, echoing with a terrible rhythm:

"Kill! Kill! Kill!"

He would have killed, had not the noise of the savage fight drifted out into the street, slashing brutally through the pavement's tawdry Mongol symphony. And people hurrying up the stairs; bursting into the flat; pouncing upon Han Mok; dragging him away and out of the house; and, not long afterwards, the clank of an ambulance and Lee Fong taken to the hospital. . . .

Up in the room, Lin Hai wept as if her heart would break.

She stammered forth her unhappiness. Why—she loved Han Mok; could not live without him . . . "please, please!" imploringly to Susie Wong—and the latter's harsh rejoinder:

"Be quiet, O creature. You belong to me."

She continued more gently:

"Besides, consider your parents. They are poor. Only twice a month have they pork with their evening rice. And now—forty thousand dollars! Twenty thousand to me. The same to you. Out of your half you can send princely sums to them each month. Hereafter, they will be able to eat pork twice a day."

She left. Lin Hai was alone.

Typically Chinese in filial devotion, she told herself that, for her parents' sake, she must obey. She remembered what she had heard about American women: proud, free women, living as they listed. Well—she was not free. A slave she would be to Lee Fong, since a slave she was to China's stony traditions. And so she sat there, staring at nothing in particular, while tangled dreams and desires ran to and fro over the surface of her soul.

Dear Buddha, she sighed, it was her duty, her fate . . .

And her duty, her fate, a week later, robed in stiff brocade, her hair elaborately done, her cheeks painted stark red and white, to be awaiting the coming of her lord and master who, with his face still bandaged, was being escorted through Chinatown by his friends, congratulating him, strewing flowers, tossing fireworks.

Bang went the crackers. Swish went the rockets. Swizz went the squibs. The street rushed with lights, scarlet-hearted, blue-tipped, yellow-frayed.

"Ten thousand years!" yelled the crowd.

"Ten thousand times ten thousand years!"

"May she find your lips in spite of the bandages!" cried Ying Long, the wholesale grocer.

"Listen!" Susie Wong's shamelessly practical advice. "Musk mixed with sandalwood to rouse the waning passions! A drop behind the ear, O elegant dragon!"

Laughter. More shouts:

"Ten thousand times ten thousand years!"

The procession filed round the corner, the fireworks blending into the purple dome of night, their sparks of red and gold and green softening to a running play of rainbow hues, then dying altogether with a single high-light still glistening, like the blood-gleam in a black opal. "Ten thousand years——" very faintly from the distance—a mere memory of sound—while Han Mok, who had watched from the window of his room, went over to the table that held his opium lay-out. . . .

With shaking fingers he kneaded the brown cube. He roasted it; filled his pipe; emptied it at one deep inhalation.

The drug tasted sweet as summer rain. Again he smoked and again; seventeen pipes one after the other—and the poppy ghost drew swiftly about him with a wall of fragrant, gossamer clouds, suffusing his soul, hiding the world of facts.

These facts touched him no longer; hurt him no longer. They were untrue. They were not; had never existed.

He was happy. He stared at the rolling opium clouds. They seemed filled with a roaring sunset of colours, fox-brown and steel-blue and violet; like the colours of his past dreams blazing before him, changing into his future dreams. The poppy juice sizzled with a reedy song. There was no other sound. Even the hooting of the elevated, around the corner on Chatham Square, had died. The street cries had guttered out like spent candles.

He smoked again. . . .

On the fourth morning he found that the opium jar was empty. He left the room to buy more. Crossing Pell Street, he met Bill Devoy, who put a heavy hand on his shoulder.

"Say!" he exclaimed. "I don't want to pinch yer. Ye're a decent lad. I'm only gonna talk t'yer like a Dutch uncle—see——? Y'gotta cut out the hop—get me? Why—yer poor, heathen fish—" pushing Han Mok up against a well-polished shop window "—take a good squint at yerself! Yer look like hell hit with a brick! Yaller yer look—yaller even for a Chink! And all shaky and trembly! Y'gotta cut it out—or else——"

With the threat unfinished, he went on his way, while Han Mok stared into the window and saw the reflection of himself. Yellow—oh, yes—and shaky. A sick man, sick with the opium fumes in his brain, the despair in his soul; and—he discovered in the course of the day—a ruined man.

For Lee Fong had called on lawyer Rosenblatt. Mongol knavery and Semite craftiness had mingled; had robbed Han Mok of all his savings invested in the Golden Phœnix. Too, the bills he owed to tradesmen had been bought up by Lee Fong, who began to apply pressure, steadily, mercilessly; dragging the other to court; obtaining judgments; satisfying them by selling every one of Han Mok's modest possessions.

He did more.

A week later there was a feast day—the *Chung Ho* or "Festival of Flowers"—and so Pell Street's financial and social cream had foregathered in the Place of Sweet Desire and Heavenly Entertainment where they exchanged seasonal wishes with the polished and curiously insincere phraseology of their race.

Lee Fong entered; shook hands right and left; said casually:

"I am a rich man. A very rich man."

A pause. He pointed at people here and there, addressing them with stark directness:

"You, Ho Ti, have not yet paid me for the last shipment of cloudy-mountain tea. Your note for three thousand dollars, Li Ping-Yeng, falls due next month. You," turning to the priest, 'have asked me for a large contribution for your temple——"

Name after name he mentioned; debt after debt; favour received or expected. He went on:

"The Buddha has granted me power. It is my hope that Han Mok be no longer permitted to come here and entertain us with his sword tricks; that, furthermore, his services be no longer required when we celebrate wedding or birth or religious festival."

No answer was needed or given. The silence was heavy. No sound except the sizzling of the pipes, a sucking of boiling-hot tea sipped by thin lips, a street organ gurgling through the window with the tail-end of some cloying gutter-ballad. The assembled company carefully avoided looking at each other. Their faces were carved ivory masks. They knew that none would disobey. Lee Fong had the might.

So Han Mok's sources of income were cut off; and it was Yung Long who—for the sake of pity or, belike, of parsimony—gave Han Mok a job as porter, at a wage hardly large enough to keep body and soul together.

Still, as the months passed, Lee Fong's hate grew. It became a pathological obsession. For there was Lin Hai—whom he, the rich man, had bought—had not been able to buy. . . .

He was generous to her—as he understood it. He surrounded her with luxuries, Chinese as well as American. There was the fur coat which had cost him a thousand dollars, the expensive radio, the diamond ring. There were, in her room, Pekinese furnishings worthy of a coral-button mandarin: a dragon rug of taupe and tawny orange stretching underfoot; the door hidden by a great ebony-framed screen of pale lotus silk embroidered in silver and maroon; and, on table and tarboret, priceless pieces of porcelain, Kang-he beakers in aubergine and ox-blood, peachblow celadon and Fong-hoang emblems in ash-grey and apple-green.

All this because of his love, his desire—which was never able to conquer her love and desire.

She thanked him, politely, since it was her duty. She kept house for him, immaculately, since it was her duty. She submitted to his embraces, supinely, since it was her duty. But that was all—and Chinatown knew it, as it knew everything. The gossip of it filtered through skulking backyards and furtive, reticent corner entrances into every last little rickety, red-brick building. It was being cackled over by the women as they stirred the savoury stews of pork and water-chestnuts and bamboo sprouts against the return of their lords and masters and talked from window to window.

"Pah——" commented the wife of Ho Ti, the tea merchant—"the iron of passion has entered the buffalo's soul!"

"Indeed," agreed the wife of Kang Kee, the hatchetman, "he has placed his hand and his heart on the sill of the door of love. And she—ah—she spurns him."

"And what is she," exclaimed an elderly widow, "with all her airs and graces? What is she but a *shuey-kee*?"

"Aye!" The mother of Nag Hop Fat, the soothsayer, spat out her contempt through blackened teeth. "Nothing but a slave-girl!"

And that's what Lin Hai replied, on the same afternoon, when Lee Fong asked her for the twentieth time if she loved him.

"I am nothing but a slave girl. I belong to you as this rug belongs to you. The rug does not love you. Nor do I."

"You—" in a low voice—"you love Han Mok?"

"I do. I shall always love him."

Then he beat her—and the gossip of the beating, too, drifted through Chinatown. Han Mok heard of it; and, meeting the other near the joss temple, he attacked him, murder in his heart, though unable to carry out his bloody intent. For, these last months, he had spent almost all his miserable earnings on opium; had starved himself to pay for it. He was weak, was easily winded—and Lee Fong, while frail, was his match.

So they grappled. They rolled on the ground, got up again, each striving to batter down the other with feeble blows—and the Pell Street hoodlums, yellow and white, looking on and shouting coarse, ironic advice:

"Dat's de stuff, Chinkie!"

"Smack him on de kisser!"

"Hey! Bitin' ain't allowed, yer slit-eyed swine!"

For ten minutes they fought, out of breath, hysterical with pain and hate, until Policeman O'Malley ran up and mixed in the contest with democratic impartiality, kicking Lee Fong's feet from under him and bringing his night-stick down on Han Mok's head. And the latter arrested: charged with assault and battery; and Judge G. W. Lefkowitz saying:

"Thirty days! Next case——"

There was no opium in jail; opium which he craved, which

he must have. Therefore, a month later, when he was released, he was weaker than ever, sunk into himself, the skin on his throat loose and flabby, his eyes red-rimmed.

Bill Devoy saw him and took pity.

"Here y'are—" giving him a ten-dollar bill—"buy yerself a square feed."

He should have known better. Should have known that Han Mok would go straight to Yung Long's shop and exchange the money for a jar of potent Benares poppy. Then, in the windowless back room where the grocer permitted him to sleep amongst the packing-cases, he smoked. He smoked continuously.

The drug fumes whirled up, wreathing everything in floating vapours. The walls disappeared; the room; the house. And it seemed to him that he saw another house—the Pavilion of Exquisite Love it was called—that rose slowly from a garden of great, black poppies, curved fantastically into an upper storey framed by balconies, then raced away with spires and turrets and tinkling silver bells to a bright, pigeon-blue sky.

So he smoked again. The fragrant fumes, with the light of the tiny lamp playing upon them, laid a shining ribbon of gold from his heart to the pavilion. His feet stepped softly upon it. He reached the pavilion and entered.

Lin Hai was sitting erect on a chair of ebony and lacquer encrusted with rose-quartz. She rose when she saw him.

"Hayah! my bridegroom!" she said.

"Hayah! my bride!" he replied—and kowtowed three times.

Happy. So happy.

Then, on the sixth day, he awakened. He was cold. He shivered. The opium jar was empty. He tottered out into the street—and Bill Devoy saw him and cursed loudly and profanely.

"Wot a sucker I was—" he cried—"slippin' yer that ten-spot! Well—it's Bellevue for yer. Mebbe they'll cure yer—though I have my doubts."

And now, today, Han Mok had come out of Bellevue; and so there was Devoy, walking his beat, prey to pessimistic reflections; there was Miss Rutter, in the Mission Chapel, pouring out her soul to her Maker with optimistic and rather imbecile serenity, praying: "I thank Thee, dear Lord, because, in Thy mercy, Thou hast caused my beloved brother Lee Fong to see the error of his ways!" and—though this preceded Devoy's pessimism as well as Miss Rutter's optimism, being responsible for both—there was Lee Fong, staring down at Lin Hai who was cowering on her couch, her robe half torn from her body, her back criss-crossed by crimson welts

For a long time he was silent. His rage rose in waves. Then, all at once, he smiled.

"I have reconsidered," he told her. "I have thought left and thought right. It is not Han Mok's fault that you are nothing but a *shuey-kee*, ungrateful, obstinate. I shall reach out a helping hand to him. For once—ah—we were one, not two."

That evening, in the Place of Sweet Desire and Heavenly Entertainment, he spoke similar words:

"For years Han Mok and I were friends. I had almost forgotten. Now I remember."

"You mean"—asked the priest—"you will forgive?"

"More than forgive. I shall atone. I—I promise—shall see to it that he suffers no want. I might give him a monthly sum. But he hates me. He would not accept. Therefore, let him, as before, amuse us each Saturday with his sword tricks. We shall pay him a hundred dollars a week."

"Too much!" objected Li Ping-Yeng.

"Not too much when you consider that—unbeknown to him—I myself shall contribute ninety of the hundred."

"You are a man of pure heart," exclaimed the priest.

"I am indeed," replied Lee Fong.

He left; and Yung Long gave a little laugh.

"All honour to Lee Fong," he said in the manner of one who is weaving truth close to the loom of lies. "His heart—doubtless—is as pure as the spring wind, his promise as tight as the skin of the unripened lime. Still—looking at it now from the point of view of Han Mok—would a wise man keep meat on trust with a jackal, though the jackal give seventy time seventy promises?"

"Han Mok," chuckled Ho Ti, "has no meat. And has it not been remarked that a hungry stomach has neither ears with which to listen to the sounds of danger nor pride to stiffen his pride?"

And here in this home-spun coolie proverb, lay much of the secret of what was to follow.

A hungry stomach. A hundred dollars a week. Food it bought. Raiment. But, chiefly, opium—and Lee Fong seeing to it that the other got it cheaply. Opium which raddled his brain and sucked the marrow from his bones so that, Saturday after Saturday, a jittery wreck faced the company at the Place of Sweet Desire and Heavenly Entertainment, his eyes bleary, his hands shaky; therefore no longer skilled at throwing swords, and no longer greeted by applause but by shrill laughter.

For the men of Pell Street were amused after their Mongol

fashion—which meant Mongol humour, which meant Mongol cruelty. They would look at him standing on the platform at the farther wall of the room, trembling, perspiring, his face mottled and bluish, his fingers fumbling awkwardly. They would break into paroxysms of mirth when, occasionally, he dropped one of the blades and cut himself. Hayah—but it was fun!

Harrying him. Mocking him. Shouting sardonic encouragement. Slapping their thighs when, with his last remaining shred of pride, he tried again and again to master the ancient craft, to toss the eight swords in a gleaming arc; failed again and again; and Lee Fong laughing loudest of all—yelling:

"Ah—if Lin Hai could see you now, O straw man, O tiger!"

"Paper tiger!" cried Nag Hong Fah.

"Paper tiger with paper teeth!" chimed in Li Ping-Yeng.

Still, Saturday after Saturday, he played the mountebank, the tragic buffoon in cap and bells and motley—because of the money; the opium which it bought; and, at night in his shabby room, the ever-recurring poppy dreams of the Pavilion of Exquisite Love. And there Lin Hai awaiting him, her face like a small ivory flower beneath the great wedding-crown of paper-thin gold leaves, carved balls of moonstone swinging from the lobes of her ears, her finger-nails encased by pointed filigree of lapis lazuli studded with seed pearls.

Rising as he opened the door. Saying: "Hayah! my bridegroom!"

Happiness—and nothing separating them but the delicate threshold between fact and dream.

The end came on a Saturday in November. A cold evening with rain driving the people to warmth and shelter, and the Place of Sweet Desire and Heavenly Entertainment crowded with paunchy merchants who laughed at Han Mok's performance. Laughed a little less loudly because they were beginning to get bored with it; then Lee Fong entering; and—"ah!" a tense breath of amazement sucked in almost simultaneously by fifty thin lips—hands stopping in mid-air with a feathery tinkle—tinkle of tea cups—and Yung Long exclaiming "By the Buddha's toe-nails!"

For Lee Fong was not alone. Lin Hai was by his side.

Earlier in the day, she had kowtowed to him; had said:

"My lord, I had word from Canton."

"Indeed?"

"My parents have died. They have leaped the dragon gate."

"May they," he had mumbled ceremoniously, hypocritically, "find bliss at the yellow springs!"

"And so," she had continued, "there is no more need for me

to send the monthly allowances. Thus—if you will permit me to return my dower——"

"And set you free?"

"Yes, my lord."

"You still love Han Mok?"

"I shall always love him."

He had flushed with rage; had raised a fist to strike her. But, all at once, he had changed his mind, as, staring at her, the sudden knowledge had come to him that she was no longer young, or lovely or desirable. Wrinkled she was, her eyes lustreless, her face seamed with suffering. And he had smiled; had told her:

"Come!"

"Where?"

"To meet your lover"

So now, in the Place of Sweet Desire and Heavenly Entertainment, Lee Fong approached the platform where Han Mok was fumbling with his swords.

"Did I not tell you," he addressed him, "that, when I was through with Lin Hai, I would give her to you? Behold! I give her to you tonight. No,"—as the other was about to rush from the platform—"wait! I am a business man. There is the matter of the dower. You are poor. You cannot pay. Except——"

"Except——?" whispered Han Mok.

"By amusing us with an exhibition of your ancient craft. Ah!"—shrilly—"do your best tonight, O strong man, O tiger! Entertain us well—and entertain your bride!"

Came laughter, and, a moment later, fear.

For, as they watched, it seemed as if the drug-soaked wreck was regaining his power. His eyes seemed clear; his wrists supple; his accents steady as he exclaimed:

"So be it!"

He picked up his weapons; went on.

"Stand still, all of you! Stand very still! Here—if you move as little as an inch—is death!"

The next second, he launched the lengths of steel, left, right, with the utmost speed and precision. One swishing between Yung Long's left ear and his left hand held high in a gesture of terror. The second nailing one of Li Ping-Yeng's loose sleeves to the table. The third slicing off the button on Ho Ti's cap. The fourth tossed through the air; the fifth and sixth and seventh. And, finally, only one blade left; and, swinging it around his head in gleaming circles, he stepped from the platform and up to Lee Fong.

His features were a grinning, evil mask. He said mockingly:

" Now is the time for you to order shroud and coffin."

And then, as he was bringing down the sword, all at once, he let it drop. He stammered, in a thin whisper, heard only by Lee Fong:

" I—oh!—I cannot do this—this thing. For once we were one—not two——"

And his strength left him. He stumbled, fell, grovelled on the ground, again the drug-soaked wreck—and the merchants, their rage released as their fear ceased, were about to pounce on him, to make him pay for this fear to beat him to a pulp, when there was a sharp voice:

" Stop!"

It was Lee Fong who spoke. He stood there, shielding Han Mok with his body; and, as there were mutterings, threats, curses, he repeated:

" Stop!"

" But——"

" I am the rich man of Pell Street. I command."

Then, to Nag Hop Fat:

" Call a taxi!"

And to Lin Hai:

" What good are tears? Dry your eyes, O almost useless one, and lend a hand! Take your lover by the head—gently, gently—and I shall take him by the feet!"

And so, as years ago, there were evenings when Lee Fong sat by the side of Han Mok's couch, arguing, imploring—as Lin Hai would be arguing, imploring; when, at times, with the craving upon Han Mok, he attacked him with all his feeble strength and smashed the opium lay-out; when—as the other, maddened with desire, knocked him down brutally—even then, prone on the ground, hurt and bleeding, he continued to implore:

" Please! For my sake! Because we love each other! Because we are one—not two!"

And Lin Hai, smiling; saying softly:

" No, no! We are one—not three——"

CRESS

By

JOHN GRANT

"SOME more cress, George?" Fauthorpe paused with his hand upon the bell.

"Thanks very much. I will."

Fauthorpe summoned a club waiter and gave the order. Then he turned, smiling. "You seem partial to cress, George. You literally wolfed that first lot."

George grinned. "I love it," he said. "When it is there I always grab it."

"Your cress, sir."

"Like to hear a story about cress?" asked George, as he munched.

"One of those silly limericks?"

"No, a story."

"Fire away."

"It mainly concerns a village across the North-West Frontier," said George. "You know the kind of thing—a score or so of mud-walled houses, the usual stream, the tiny over-tilled rocky fields, primitive ploughs, a few goats, the Himalayan foothills all round, no squalor, but a general air of hard-uppishness and, of course, dozens of kids."

The principal figure in the village, both physically and in his own estimation, was Daulat Ram, the moneylender. He had been in the place for more than twenty-five years, and he had prospered.

It was easy money. All he had to do was to sit back and wait for the harvest. When the crops were garnered he would apportion out so much per head—just enough to keep these unfortunate people alive. The rest would be sold—on account of interest that would accrue.

When the sowing season came round the villagers, of course, would have no seed grain. There would be further loans on account of seed—and a little more on the mortgage—just to make doubly sure.

He had the best house in the village, and he was always adding to it. When he shoved on a new room or a new verandah, or bought something from Peshawar or Lahore, he would saunter majestically through the village, his immense paunch swaying round as he walked, and he would cotton on to a villager.

"Come and see my fine house," he would say, and the man would have to go whether he wanted to or not. When you owe a bloke like that money it behoves you to be careful. Up at the house Daulat Ram would proudly display his new acquisition, but here was the rub. He would chortle with glee, boisterously smack the chap on the back and say, with an evil leer: "You paid for that."

"Quite matey of him," interjected Fauthorpe.

Quite; but that was not the worst. He had the village constables, both of them, and the *naik* (N.C.O.) on his books—all were local men—and he could do pretty well what he liked. And he liked all kinds of things that he shouldn't.

Stories used to come down across the border, sometimes about women and all that, but nothing much came of them. The village police would be asked for a report, and they would say that there was nothing in it. What else could they do, poor devils?

Then, one day, Daulat Ram announced his intention of going to Delhi—a pretty hefty journey. He was anxious to pick up something luscious, however, and the thought of a week away from the village did not deter him. All the crops had been sown, it was just before the breaking of the monsoon, there was nothing doing in the fields—his fields—and a week did not matter so much. He went. That evening there was jubilation in the village. The mere removal of his presence lifted a great oppressive weight from the minds of the people. For once they were jubilant.

There was one who did not follow the Koran as he should, who had a little more brain than the others. By some means he had become possessed of some liquor. This, in the fastness of his own home, he proceeded to drink. When he came to join the village conclave round the evening fire his alert brain was working a few more 'revs' than usual. Also, he was inclined to be talkative. He squatted with the rest.

"Daulat Ram, the swine," he grunted. He spat expressively. The men of the village spat with him—copiously and in sympathy.

"Why do we tolerate him?" he demanded. "Why don't we see that he dies—and his books with him? There are many ways.

"Have the people of this village got any courage?" he cried aggressively. "Are we to remain here, always tightening our pyjama strings, while this son of a dog waxes fat at our expense? There is not one of us here who has not paid more than treble the amount that we have borrowed."

"But what can we do?" demanded one of his listeners, impatiently. "Haven't we debated the matter dozens of times?"

"What can we do?" echoed Din Mohammed. Once again he broke forth into rude laughter. "Is it not the time of the monsoon?" he choked. "Will not the rains be on us to-day or to-morrow? Look at the clouds. What say the greybeards?"

"Truly he has lost his wits," murmured the *naik*.

"Will the rains come or not?" Din Mohammed ignored the comment.

Several heads nodded.

"And Daulat Ram will be away for a week?"

Again the heads nodded.

"Then we can do it—if we have courage. It would be a great jest, too," he went on, in explanation, "and it would raise high the name of our village along the frontier."

"Tell us what is troubling your brain," the *naik* broke in, compassionately, for no frontier people will illtreat those who are deranged.

"We will muster the entire village," went on Din Mohammed, dramatically, "and we will pull down Daulat Ram's house."

"We will do what?"

"We will pull down Daulat Ram's house and convey the stones piecemeal to a distance. We will dig up the foundations, we will plough the ground, we will construct irrigation channels and we will sow the ground with *masthi*."

That, as you probably know, Fauthorpe, is the eastern equivalent of cress. It comes up in a night during the rains and quickly hides newly-turned soil.

There were bewildered mutterings from the village folk.

"But what good will that do?" asked one. "When Daulat Ram returns there will be trouble and we shall be worse off than ever."

"Not only will we destroy his house and plough his ground," Din Mohammed proceeded, with a grand gesture, "but we will burn his books and all his papers, and leave nothing that is his."

"Yes, but what then?"

"Then when he returns we will say that he does not live here—has never lived here—that we know him not—and that he has lost his wits."

A great shout of delighted laughter greeted this explanation. The *naik* looked serious, the two constables grinned. "We cannot do this," said the *naik* at length. "It would be against the law."

Din Mohammed made a rude face. "Is it the law that you

should pay this son of a dog for ever?" he shouted. "Is it the law that your land should pass out of your family? Is it the law that your sons should be beggars? And after you have repaid your loan many times over!"

The *naik* made a helpless gesture.

For six days the village toiled as it had never toiled before. On the seventh it waited the return of Daulat Ram with an impatience and an expectancy that were ill-concealed. Presently Daulat Ram was discerned in the distance, riding his heavy cob. He came to the outskirts of the village. He called loudly to one of the villagers. The man gazed up at him appraisingly. His accustomed salaaming obedience was absent.

The veins in Daulat Ram's neck swelled—he was not used to such insolence. He glared at the man and urged his cob towards him. "What is the meaning of this, Yakub?" he shouted. "Where are your manners?"

Still the man gazed at him with a blank expression.

"You know me, Yakub," spluttered the moneylender, beside himself with rage. "Have I changed so much in a week's absence?"

Still the man remained silent, an expression of astonishment on his face. Daulat Ram kicked at his cob and passed Yakub disdainfully. Further on Daulat Ram encountered the *naik*. He bustled his tired animal towards him. "What has come over the village, *naik-ji?*" he asked, his voice suffused with anger. "I go away for a week and all this happens. Even you," he added meaningly, "do not make the customary salutations."

The *naik* gazed at the moneylender with a blank expression.

"I hope you took good care of my property while I was away," Daulat Ram went on viciously. "It will go ill with your account if you did not."

"Your property?"

"Yes, my property, idiot. My fine house, your house, your fields, all the houses, all the fields."

"I am afraid I do not understand you, stranger."

"Stranger?" Daulat Ram reeled on his horse in his fury. "Stranger? What sorry jest is this?"

The *naik* raised a hand. His expression was sympathetic. "Stranger," he said, "the day has been hot, and the way has probably been long. Would you care to come and rest at my house for a while?"

Daulat Ram followed the speech with amazement. More than once he opened his lips to speak, but he could not. He rested weakly on his cob for a few moments, and then turned on the *naik*. "Your house!" he shrieked. "Your house! Why should I demean myself by entering your house when there is my own palatial home awaiting me? Tell me, have you all gone mad?"

The *naik,* who by this time had been joined by a number of other villagers, looked straight at Daulat Ram. "Perhaps the stranger would tell us," he said, "exactly where we may be expected to find this fine house?"

The moneylender made a gurgling noise. His exasperation almost overcame him. "You shall pay for this stupid effrontery," he mouthed. "Where is my house?" he choked. "Come, you poor things, I will show you." His podgy legs kicked at his cob.

The procession, reinforced by the rest of the villagers, made its way towards the recent scene of activity. Daulat Ram led the way, fuming. Behind him, came first the men, then the children, and some distance behind, encumbered by their purdah, the women, who refused to be left out of the excitement. As the procession neared the corner of the village, beyond which, ordinarily, the abode of Daulat Ram should have come into full view, a silence came on the villagers. All that could be heard were the mutterings of the moneylender.

The man pressed forward his horse, as if impatient to be done with the business, and he rounded the corner.

"Look, you fools," he began, and then his speech failed. He raised his hands and vigorously rubbed his eyes. Then he glared furiously into the distance. Where his house should have stood there was nothing except well-tilled fields. He fell, rather than alighted, from his horse, and with gasping little cries ran forward. The crowd followed him. He reached the site of his home and delved into the ground with his fingers, as if he hoped, thereby, to bring his house to light. Not a vestige of it remained. He stood there, stunned. Saliva streamed from his mouth, and his monstrous paunch heaved mightily with stertorous breathing. He gazed wildly round. He tore at his turban. He cast it to the ground. Suddenly he screamed a frightful, nerve-searing scream. "My house," he moaned. "My house. What has become of my house? These people are robbers; they are felons." He fell to the ground writhing.

The *naik* moved forward. He was authoritative. "Help me with this stranger," he said to the constables. "Obviously he is quite mad. He must be placed in the lock-up for his own protection. We must send for a doctor—a white doctor would be preferable—and then a report must go to the authorities." He had command of the situation.

Quite by chance it was a civilian doctor who was approached. He was called out late at night to attend to a man across the frontier. At first he demurred, but he was offered such a surprising fee that he changed his mind.

A night and a day in the seclusion of the jail had done something to calm the agitated Daulat Ram. In the hours of meditation which had been vouchsafed him he had guessed something of the scheme which was afoot and he was firmly resolved when the doctor did appear, that he would restrain his anger, and make a great effort to appear strictly rational.

When the doctor was ushered in he had a deep, satisfying feeling of relief. They were known to each other, for some years before Daulat Ram had consulted him when afflicted with a trifling ailment. His old, overbearing confidence returned with a rush. He could even afford to be rude to the *naik* in whose custody he was. "You will rue this," he said banefully. "The doctor sahib and I are known to each other. I have been a patient of his. He will tell all that I am Daulat Ram and that I am of this place."

The *naik* had the grace to look abashed. He saw the whole scheme falling to the ground.

"You know me doctor sahib, don't you?" went on the money-lender, confidently advancing across the room.

The Englishman looked at him squarely. "I am afraid that you are mistaken," he said shortly. "To the best of my knowledge I have never seen you before."

"Daulat Ram lost his aplomb. "But doctor sahib," he cried, "you have attended me. You have given me medicine."

The doctor glanced at the *naik*. "Will you please leave me alone with the patient while I make my examination?" he asked in entirely professional tones. The *naik* retired.

Durlat Ram rushed frenziedly forward. "Doctor, doctor," he gasped in his agitation, "surely you know me?"

The Englishman stared at the man for a moment. Then he nodded. "Yes, I know you," he agreed quietly.

"Then you will say that I am not mad. You will tell the authorities that I am the victim of an awful plot?" Daulat Ram was beseeching.

"I shall say that you are mad."

"But, sahib, I am not. You know that I am not."

"Yes, I know that."

"Then sahib?" Daulat Ram fell to his knees. He bent his head and rubbed his forehead on the Englishman's shoes. It was the lowliest form of obeisance. It signified that the Englishman was absolutely master and that he who knelt was slave.

"Listen!" The tone was curt and sharp. Daulat Ram rose to his feet. "Before you decided to concentrate your energies on this village—when you had been here about ten years, in fact, you had another establishment across the frontier."

Daulat Ram nodded a miserable acquiescence.

"A young subaltern came to see you. He was in difficulties. The polo funds of which he was in charge, were missing. He had been robbed."

"Sahib, there were many subalterns. I but seldom listened to their stories."

"This subaltern wanted one thousand rupees very badly and very quickly."

Daulat Ram was silent. He wrung his hands.

"You made him sign a bill for two thousand rupees and the interest which you charged was one anna in the rupee per month."

Still there was silence.

"You knew that a subaltern, unacquainted with the terms of usury, could never hope to redeem that bill out of his pay?"

Daulat Ram kept his eyes on the floor.

"That subaltern shot himself."

"Sahib, sahib, that is untrue. He was out riding and he fell into a disused well."

"He shot himself!"

"But the well?"

"That was the story that was told."

"But, sahib, I would never have pressed that young man. I was not responsible for what he did."

"Responsible!" The word positively dripped hatred.

"Responsible! Daulat Ram, that young man was my son."

Daulat Ram sank to the floor.

"Good heavens," muttered Fauthorpe, "what a story."

"It isn't quite finished yet," said his companion. "When the authorities gave orders for Daulat Ram's removal across for a final examination, he really was mad. There was no question of that. He was a disgusting sight."

"And that subaltern," queried Fauthorpe, "did he really shoot himself?"

"He did," answered the other, quietly. "He was my cousin. We were at Sandhurst together."

"Hence the cress, old man?"

"Hence the cress."

NO LADIES' MAN

By

DOROTHY BLACK

CAPTAIN DARLING lay back in his long chair. Over the valley the sun went down behind distant mountains, a gold penny posting itself into a dark box. At the sound of his coming, his servant brought a short whisky and a long soda. Ice tinkled alluringly in the glass.

Captain Darling raised it to his lips, and asked of life meantime nothing more. This was his glorious hour, and this his perfect rose—the knowledge of a good day's work behind him, the sun going down, and a long drink. Elephants in the jungle calling to the tame ones in the *keddah,* little bats flickering around in a friendly fashion, interested in the lamp.

Stretched out in his long chair, there seemed to be a good bit of him, and it was not entirely prepossessing. When alone in the jungle, Captain Darling grew a beard. Though his hair was coal black as his eye-brows and eye-lashes, his beard came red. He could do nothing to stop it. So he removed it whenever he went down to civilization, thinking, and rightly, that this, combined with his nose, which was singularly large, domineering, and masterful, was more than one man could carry off, in one life-time, with only one face.

In the jungle it did not matter. Burmans, who themselves cannot grow more than a few straggling hairs on their chins, unworthy of a goat, look on the ability to raise a beard of any kind, as inspired. To raise one a different shade from the hair, bordered on the god-like.

Without his beard, Captain Darling was well known in all ports of call between Pall Mall and Mandalay. But he was not greatly beloved. He had a dry and scholarly wit, and a rich fund of quotations from *Alice in Wonderland,* Edward Lear, and the classics. The official ladies, and the commercial ladies of the Empire's outpost, never understood any of them, and just thought he was being rude. This caused Captain Darling to become noted for the strength and duration of his silences, which were interpreted as ill as his remarks.

He felt he would never be a ladies' man. Candidly, he preferred elephants, who did not wear funny hats, squeeze themselves into odd and ever-changing shapes, coo at him, or when he quoted "Fat white woman who nobody loves," instantly take personal offence. If the gods were good, and ever sent him the woman of his dreams, he would have been glad to marry. But, meantime, on such occasions as duty took him to Bhamo, Rangoon, or Mandalay, he longed for his jungle fastness as marooned men long for beer.

So he lay back in his long chair, asking nothing else of life. Ice tinkled in his long glass, and all was well with the world until he sat up, and perceived with a start someone crawling up the steep and winding pathway that approached his bungalow from the rough landing-stage, where the mail boat paused to deposit his office baskets and his mails. It was a man in white, and he was followed by a coolie who bore on his head what appeared to be a coffin about suitable for a medium-sized baby.

Quietly as endearment, Captain Darling said "damn," and leaned out into the twilight. The man who presently emerged was young. He was sweating a good deal, wore jaded white ducks and brown suède shoes which would inevitably be the wrong brown when the dust was brushed off. He had horn-rimmed glasses and the personality that exuded a nice mixture of bounce and bonhomie that enabled Captain Darling to place him with a single glance.

"Salesman!"

The coolie, panting and exhausted, placed the baby's coffin on the ground and fell prone beside it, after the manner of a coolie intimating he had no intentions of going any farther that night. The young man came right in, sat right down, mopped his brow, and said:

"Hello, Beardie. That is certainly some climb you have up to your country home. I began to think we'd never make it before dark."

He laughed, and reminded Captain Darling uncomfortably of a horse.

"There were some queer noises, too," said the young man.

"Elephants are dangerous in the mating season."

The young man shivered.

"Well, I'm safe home now, anyway. I suppose you'll be a christian and give the poor traveller a bed?"

A salesman faced in the open had no terrors for Captain Darling. He could, and did, meet them on their own ground and they retired, vanquished. Itinerant vendors of brass gods, fox skins, carpets, patent medicines guaranteed to cure everything from corns to old age, passed his bungalow by. Even the Armenian who came on an ass, peddling shaving-soap, looked once at Captain Darling's beard, and did not call.

But a salesman parked on you for the night, bringing the full blast of his technique to bear over the dinner, and breakfast table! That was a different matter. Since he could hardly refuse the man a bed, Captain Darling gloomily faced the worst and wondered what he would do with the baby's coffin when he had got it. It wasn't a thing you could pass on lightly as a Christmas gift, or raffle at a mission, or present to one of the Burra Mem's on your way through Mandalay.

The young man cooled down, and cheered up.

"Well, I'll say this is a hard place to live. Right at the Empire's back door you certainly are. I'll warrant nobody has ever come right up here before, and spent two days and nights on that dog-gorn boat, just to give you the opportunity of purchasing our new model, self-oiling, ball-bearing, double-geared sewing-machine, with eighteen months' guarantee?"

So that was what it was. Captain Darling took another look at it. To the best of his knowledge it was the first time he had met a sewing-machine, and looked it in the face.

Very gravely he said:

"You are right. Nobody ever has."

"What did I say?" burst forth the young man. "Enterprise. That's what we as a nation lack. No one wants to leave the broken track. No one wants to adventure forth into the wide open spaces in commerce. We all, if I may say so, sir, hug the bank, whereon await us three hot meals a day. It's this lack of enterprise which does us down everywhere. . . . Why, look at the Germans. . . ."

Captain Darling said: "Won't you have a drink?"

The young man had one. It did not gag him. It acted as a refilling of his tank of inspiration. . . .

"And if there is one thing that must be entirely and absolutely obvious to anyone who cares to take the trouble to sit down and think, it is that here, far removed from the amenities of civilization, there must be a greater and more crying need for our new model, self-oiling, ball-bearing and double-geared sewing-machine, with guarantee, than in the more congested towns and cities, within reach of shops and bazaars, where those things a man wants—a man needs——"

Captain Darling said: "Quite."

"Just think of it, sir! Just think of it!" Damp with persuasion the young man leaned closer. "Consider the little things your good lady could run up for you in a brace of shakes—the dainty oddments for the home, the clothes for herself. For this machine is fitted with a tucker, a smocker, and an attachment for gathering and making buttonholes."

He produced from various parts of his person gadgets that looked to Captain Darling like part of a dentist's equipment.

"A child could use them," he carolled triumphantly.

"And—er—do you supply also the child?"

The young man's brightness wilted.

"And—er—the good lady?"

The young man re-collected his face and laughed hoarsely, entering into the spirit of the thing.

"Well, we haven't gone into that line as yet, but it's worth considering. But you don't mean to say you live up here, year in year out, all alone? Don't your family join you for the cold weather?"

"I haven't got a family."

"Gee!" said the young man. "I thought men with beards were always married. I'd take it off, if I was you. Then you'd have a chance. I'd go batty if I lived in a place like this, alone. All elephant——"

Captain Darling said gloomily: "There are worse things than elephants."

"You meantersay there's no society of any kind, no relaxation, no girls, women?"

"The women are not a wine for a fastidious palate. Water, in these parts, is scarce in the village. We do not waste it on washing."

"Well," said the young man. "Now you're telling me something. It never put anything like that in the books I used to read about the glamour of the wide open spaces, way back there at home."

"It never does," said Captain Darling.

"I can't fancy how a man can cut himself off like that. I couldn't do it. I like a bit of company myself. I'm getting married next month. Got a bungalow in Mandalay. Nice little place. All conveniences. I found her in a country village where I was on holiday. Nice kid, she is. Religious. I think religious women make the best wives, don't you?"

Sorrow for the girl he had never seen wrung the heart of Captain Darling. Fancy living with the horse-faced young man forever, in a bungalow in Mandalay! Sorrow for himself wrung his heart, when he saw the young man delving in a pocket book. Captain Darling was frequently forced to inspect the female relatives of strange men met in the jungle, and he never could think of anything to say.

"There you are. Taken when she was sixteen. She's twenty

now, but she's never had another. They're poor. An aunt is paying her passage out here. Thought it a good investment, no doubt. I can tell you, as far as she is concerned, I'm a bit of a catch in the matrimonial market, I am."

He laughed, recalling to Captain Darling boyish memories of cab-horses in urgent need of water.

Captain Darling took the photograph in an unwilling hand. He leaned to get it within the circle of light cast by the lamp. His eyes narrowed a little, and he looked at the young man, wondering was he bragging. The fatuous face opposite him wore an innocent look. Captain Darling regarded the girl again.

She had a dear little face, with a pointed chin, regular features, and eyes that reminded him of those little blue speedwell flowers that starred meadows near Oxford, where Captain Darling had often wandered as a youth. The eyes had a queerly gay and innocent look, as if nothing had ever hurt them very much yet. Her hair was parted and sleeked down, ending in two long plaits.

Captain Darling handed the photograph back. His first thought was, "The girl must be mad." He was about to say: "She's much too nice for you," but bit it back in time, and said, as usual, nothing.

The young man did not mind. All he wanted was a willing ear. The tropical moon rose white and wonderful over the jungle. Captain Darling, in self-defence, slept.

He dreamed a tiresome dream, distressingly life-like. He sat on his own veranda, a glass at his elbow, a good day's work behind him. The hour was sunset, and at his elbow ice tinkled invitingly in a long glass. Up the twisting pathway that led through the jungle to his bungalow, a figure toiled but, when he went to the veranda rail to meet it, it wasn't the bouncing young man at all. It was the slender girl, with sleeked fair hair and eyes like speedwell flowers. That she was in trouble was evident, for she held out her hands to him, as if imploring him to help her, and her chin quivered in a fashion he found terribly upsetting.

So upsetting, that he awoke and sat up with a start, to find only the moon and the owls, and the young man talking and talking. About women, and elephants, and free love, and free samples, commissions, gilt-edged stocks, rubber shares, brothels in Port Said, and the silk stocking business.

"You must rest," said Captain Darling firmly. He flung the young man into a bedroom. Later he noticed the whisky decanter had been emptied during his sleep, which no doubt accounted for the blithe way the young man chanted, and carolled and trilled as he fell around his bedroom over the business of undressing.

On the way to his own room, Captain Darling fell over something too. It was the self-oiling, ball-bearing, gear-changing sewing-machine (with guarantee) marooned on the floor like a small forgotten island.

Softly as an endearment Captain Darling said "damn."

For twopence, the young man would have stayed on another day. He began to complain of his feet, and he began to complain of his head. Captain Darling knew the signs. Lots of folk felt like staying where they were, when they remembered the discomfort of the river trip back to Bhamo, and contemplated the worse discomfort of the road on over the frontier.

Captain Darling was not having any. Out of the jungle a mule caravan came, jingling north. It cost little to persuade the Chinaman in charge to take the young man and his self-oiler along. Captain Darling paid. It was cheap at the price.

Now his bungalow was his own again. He returned to it in the evening, and drew a luxurious sigh of peace, as he stretched himself in his long chair, the glass at his elbow. But the young man had, after all, left something behind him, and had omitted to take away with him something that by rights was his. For in the days that followed, Captain Darling found his leisure oddly haunted by that little pointed face, those speedwell eyes that looked so gaily and innocently out of the cheap photograph. And once or twice he dreamed of her at night, which annoyed him.

The only other woman he ever dreamed of was Ma Ma Lin, half Burman, half Chinese, who drank deep and often of the juice of the toddy palm, and then tried to sacrifice her children to her ancestors, and so was a continual responsibility, and had imprinted herself deeply on a mind more sensitive than the red beard, cold grey eye, and domineering nose led people to suppose.

Clouds banked themselves behind the distant hills, making farther ranges, that linked the world of space. The monsoon was at hand, and in four days' time Captain Darling would return to Mandalay, there to temper his wit to the Burra Mem-Sahibs' conception of what was funny. He felt depressed. It was a thick, thundery morning, the whole world sweating.

With a jingling and jangling a mule caravan came downhill, bound for Bhamo in charge of one Wa Lung, silk piece and walnut merchant, and a close friend of Captain Darling, in spite of spots of trouble over opium, in the past. He stopped at the bungalow, and the mules poured all over the hillside, grazing, whilst Wa Lung delivered gifts. Strange-looking sausages, one yard; a duck, completely flattened out as if treated drastically by a steam-roller not once but several times.

He brought a letter marked "Beardie."

"From very number three not much good Master with sewing-box and eye-windows," Wa Lung explained passively. "He now sittee allee timee Teng-ue along big number one Chinese merchant. Makee marry daughter. Him wearing Chinese clothes last time see um. No good."

So that was the end of the story! The bright young man had gone native, as others before him. Convinced his own country would never miss him, Captain Darling tore open the letter so impudently addressed, and read:

"Am opening local branch here, Beardie. This is a country fit for heroes to live in, where they know a good man when they see one; but I don't relish doing that journey back this side of the tomb.

"This is just to tell you I am sending you gratis, shipped and delivered free of all charges, a sample of one of our new lines which I feel sure will interest you. I shall have no use for it personally, out here, so have instructed headquarters to let you have it. God bless you.

Yours,
Leonard Franks."

Captain Darling tore up the note, salaamed the caravan and watched it out of sight, until Wa Lung's blue trousers and vast straw hat, that served as a sunshade in summer and an umbrella in the rains, was swallowed in the lush green of the morning. The sun had no doubt melted what little intellect the young man ever had, or he would not have landed a lone bachelor with a sample sewing-machine, but Captain Darling comforted himself that he could give it, when it did arrive, to his bearer's wife, or send it along to the mission in the hills.

And he thought no more about it until the mail boat hooted at the jetty three times, which meant there was something more than usually bulky to come up.

"Run smart ship side, catching one parcel," he instructed his servant. "Better take one coolie."

And he cursed the young man, as he drew out his razor, and regretfully shaved off his beard, in preparation for the morrow's return to civilization.

Without it he was a slender, good-looking young man, tall above the average, ten years younger than when it adorned his chin. Captain Darling had no hankering after looking young, since he wanted none of those things for which youth is a bait. Also, it revealed to a harsh world how the sensitiveness of his mouth contradicted the heavy masterfulness of his nose, perhaps a secret Captain Darling preferred to keep, in a country where his humour was never understood.

When the deed was finished, and he was bathed and clad in clean white garments, his servant returned, round-eyed.

"No parcel catching, sir. Only one piecee Missie."

Captain Darling stared at him.

"She waiting." The man indicated the veranda, and withdrew.

She was standing as he had seen her in his dream, at the top of the veranda steps. She looked at him, and there was no laughter in her blue eyes. She looked tired and terrified. The coolie had dumped her box beside her, and gone away.

"Is—isn't Mr. Franks here?" she faltered.

"I'm afraid he's not."

She slumped into a chair, and began to cry. The sun popped itself behind the mountains, a golden penny going into a dark box. Captain Darling shouted "Boy—bring lamps!"

She looked so small and tired that his heart failed him. And when the lamp-light fell on her face, he saw she was without a doubt the girl of the photograph, and he had a strange feeling that all this had happened to him once before, and they were not strangers at all.

"You mustn't cry," he said gently. "I don't think you ought to cry."

"What's happened?" she said, and her chin quivered in a way that hurt him terribly. "I can't understand what has happened at all. He was to have been at the boat to meet me ten days ago. But he wasn't. All I got was a letter saying he had been kept, on business, and that I was to come here, and I'd find a man—he did not tell me his name even—he only said a man with a big, red beard—who could explain everything and tell me what I was to do. Is he here?"

In the pause that followed, the whole business dawned on Captain Darling in its blatant heartlessness. For this was what the bouncing young man had sent him, something he himself had no further use for; and of his own defalcation, the young man had told her nothing whatever, leaving to him the unpleasant business.

Pity for the girl choked him as he longed to choke the bouncing young man. He said: "I am afraid he isn't here, either, at the moment. As a matter of fact, he went away this afternoon."

"What am I to do?" she said, dazed . . . looking round the bungalow, and out into the darkening jungle. "Whatever am I to do."

And she wrung her hands with a lost and childish gesture that gave Captain Darling a queer feeling about the heart.

"But it's perfectly easy. You must just wait quietly here. There is quite a nice spare room, and you'll find we are really moderately civilized. My servant's wife used to be an amah once, looking after ladies, you know. She'll look after you. And I shall be only too delighted to have your company. It's lonesome up here, very lonesome," said Captain Darling.

She was crying quietly.

"And I'll take you round, and show you the elephants. We have a big *keddah* up here. I don't know if you're interested in elephants. And I've got a sort of court right out in the jungle, next week. You'll find it quite amusing, especially if you've never seen anything of the kind before."

"You are too kind."

"Not a bit. I'd love it. If you won't be terribly bored."

"But—I feel so dreadful, landing myself like this on a complete stranger."

"Oh, don't feel dreadful," said Captain Darling, very heartily. "I don't think you should feel dreadful."

"When do you think Mr. Franks—or the man with a beard will be back?"

Captain Darling did a little swift calculating.

"As for Mr. Franks, I can't say. But the man with the beard should be back in about a fortnight. Though quite possibly you'll be able to get in touch with him before that."

"And he'll be able to tell me what I ought to do."

"I feel sure he will."

He learned all about her over the dinner table, with its pink candle-shades, and spotless mats and silver. In that grim village where she lived with an aunt, the little salesman had seemed a glamorous figure. One almost heard that aunt, with her "Better accept him, my dear. The world is so full of girls. If you don't, you may never get another chance."

"So you fell in love with him?"

Her blue eyes met his, worried and full of doubt.

"I thought so. It seemed so lovely to come out here and see the world, and have a home. But when he never arrived at the ship—I wondered." She sat, her pointed chin cupped in her hand. "How can you ever know, in time, whether you're really in love or not?"

He fancied he could have told her, but he did not try.

"Are you a friend of Leonard's?"

That question, at least, he was able to answer with explosive sincerity. After she had gone to bed that night he wrote a despatch to headquarters, and sent it down with a runner. In it he set forth three reasons, each of them entirely convincing, why his return to headquarters was going to be delayed for a fortnight.

Not one of them was the real one.

She was an adaptable girl. After the first day, they might have been together there all their lives. She took their odd adventure quite as a matter of course, apart from worrying a little occasionally at all the trouble she was giving a stranger. And Captain Darling, for the first time in his life, got a long draught of that most satisfying wine of all, companionship. She rode with him to the elephant lines, she went with him out shooting. And he found to his delight she could cap his quotations from *Alice in Wonderland,* and was much better than he was at Lear's nonsense, and though she did not know much about the classics, when he quoted from them she never took offence and thought he was being personal.

Her mind was like a garden with which nobody had as yet taken much trouble, where all the flowers grew by chance. In the beginning she chattered a good bit about Leonard, as if he were a knight errant who would come cantering through the jungle at any moment to rescue her. But presently she talked less about him, and less, until for days on end his name was never mentioned.

Captain Darling had no definite plan of campaign. He grew his beard again perseveringly, and trusted to the inspiration of the moment. There came a morning when she eyed him quizzically.

"You look—odd."

"I am odd," said Captain Darling. "Lots of people will tell you that."

"I know what it is. You have stopped shaving!"

"I have a very tender skin. When the monsoon is hanging about, I cannot bear the touch of the razor. Do you mind?"

She did not mind. But at odd moments during the following days, he caught her looking at him, her blue eyes clouded. Once she said:

"I've been here nearly ten days, and you said I might perhaps get in touch—with that man."

"I think you will," said Captain Darling cheerfully, "at practically any moment now."

The sun burst for one moment through the gathering clouds and flooded the veranda where they sat at breakfast, rested on Captain Darling's coal-black hair, and lit in all its glory, his growing beard. She stared at him.

"Oh——" she said.

"Yes, Mary." He got up, and walked away to the edge of the veranda. "I want to prepare you for the worst, dear. The man with the beard has got home, and he will tell you anything you want him to. Also, he will tell you what he thinks you ought to do, and if you don't feel like doing it, will escort you dutifully to Rangoon and put you on the next boat home."

"Leonard——" Her hand flew to her throat. "He's dead."

"Not a bit of it," said Captain Darling heartily. "Death wouldn't bother about a little horror like him. If you really want to know, he's—rather gone to the bad. But you needn't worry about him. He's well and very comfortable."

"And—he doesn't want me——"

"If you're wise, you'll put Leonard right out of your head, once and for all."

He kept his back turned. He was so afraid her chin would quiver, and then he could not answer for what he would do.

He said presently, as casually as possible:

"Mary—do you mind very much?"

There was no answer, and in a panic he turned to find she wasn't crying. She was laughing though her eyes were wet.

"Oh, no!" she said. "No, no, no!"

Then he knew the gods were good, and had kept him in mind, when he hadn't thought for himself. He put his arms round her. Over the steaming world, the rains broke with a roar and a rattle on the wooden roof, but they never noticed.

"If you really want him to tell you what you ought to do, he can, Mary, easily. You are to stay here, and we'll get the padre over from the mission, darling. Oh, don't be silly. Of course it isn't pity. We've had such fun. I've never been so happy as these last days."

He wanted to tell her about the photograph, and his dream, and how marvellously it had all happened. All these things battled in the mind of Captain Darling, but would not clothe themselves in words. He could only hold her tight, and whisper:

"Mary! Mary!"

And later, he said:

"Just a moment, while I go and remove my beard."

THE PRISON OF SUNSET

By

SIDNEY DENHAM

The big open car rolled smoothly over the narrow but perfectly-surfaced road cut out of the mountainside. The two men in European clothes at the back, peering over the native driver's shoulder, could see the road five miles ahead where it climbed in a series of tortuous hairpin bends.

"Funny bloke this rajah must be, to build a road like this, that leads nowhere." The smaller of the two men at the back spoke without taking his eyes off the road. His companion, lanky, whose thin, long legs sprawled over the car, turned his eyes sideways. Grey hair showed under his topee. His face was that of a student, his eyes were those of a fanatic.

"He is indeed a curious man," replied the professor gravely. "To an oriental stock has been grafted the superficial culture of Eton and Cambridge, with this result. . . ." He waved his hand at the deserted road. "A twentieth-century road in a country that has been unchanged for twenty centuries. The road leads from the Rajah Sabhatur's palace to the frontier, where it ends in a track barely fit for mules. It is an astonishing revelation of the rajah's mind, Burton."

"Well, I'm hoping his education doesn't extend to the latest in safes," grinned Burton. "I haven't brought much in the way of tools with me."

"I have explained before, Burton, that the object in which we are interested is entirely unprotected." The professor spoke a little wearily, as if he was repeating a lesson to a forgetful child. "I brought you only because I needed an assistant, and in case, just in case, the rajah has recently decided upon some form of protection."

"Yes, I know. But fancy a bloke leaving a jewel like that what d'you call it?—the 'Prison of Sunset'—lying about, without so much as a safe to put it in at nights."

"I have explained to you, Burton, that the rajah relies for the safety of the 'Prison of Sunset' upon superstition. It is said that every workman who handled the jewel in its fashioning died horribly. It is said that two desperate thieves who took it were found dead, as if struck by lightning. . . ."

"Don't sound too good . . ." remarked Burton uncomfortably.

"It need not disturb us," said the professor firmly. "We, unlike the rajah's subjects, are of the twentieth century. We are not likely to kill ourselves of fright, and I have provided the fine steel gloves against the possibility of some poisoned projection in the box. On my last visit, three years ago, the rajah refused to let me handle the jewel, even refused to handle it himself."

"I don't like it," muttered Burton gloomily. "If it wasn't for the five hundred waiting for me when we get back, I'd chuck it now. All these natives looking at you cock-eyed and talking a balmy lingo . . . it gives me the creeps at nights, sometimes."

The professor laughed easily. "My dear Burton, you are getting not only five hundred pounds, but an education. I have always maintained that it is lack of education that makes most thieves the easy prey of the police . . . but in a few hours you will see the gem itself, and then you can form an opinion as to whether it is worth coming seven thousand miles to get. Your interest, of course, will be purely mercenary, in contrast to mine which is purely scientific. It is indeed fortunate that the gem, because of its unique size and quality, will be unmarketable."

Burton shook his head and for a moment took his eyes from the road, which he had been watching so intently in participation of the drive he would have to make back. "I can understand a bloke pinching an opal, or whatever it is, to fence it for a good price, or even to make into a necklace for his girl-friend," he said, "but I'm blowed if I can understand what you reckon you can do with it with those test-tubes and whatnot of yours."

A half-smile came to the professor's lips. "That is not surprising, Burton. I need not repeat my remarks about education. But this stone, which is widely known by the literal translation of its vernacular name, as the 'Prison of Sunset,' presents a scientific problem about which I have my own opinions. These opinions I wish to confirm by examination and test. The rajah refuses permission, giving as his excuse the superstitious awe with which the gem is regarded by his subjects; an excuse he does not believe himself. Therefore, knowing that all things are justified in the search for knowledge and truth, I have come to take the jewel without his permission. Perhaps it is difficult for you to understand. . . ."

Burton scratched his head. "If the stone's an opal, that's all there's to it, I should have thought; except you say it's a mighty big one. . . ."

"My dear Burton, I have spent many months investigating the history of this stone It was discovered two hundred years ago in a bed of sandy-mud of rock-salt and sandstone boulders. That means nothing to you, I suppose?" The professor barely paused for Burton's puzzled shake of the head. "But the expert 'know-alls' asserted definitely that since no precious-stone could have formed in such material, the thing must have been hurled out of space to imbed itself in that sand, perhaps thousands of years ago. . . ."

"Coo, sort of jewel from the moon, eh?" asked Burton, aroused at last.

"You put it crudely. A meteorite, they said it was; a fragment from some star or comet. And with the conceit of their kind, they left it at that. For a hundred years they quoted it in their textbooks as a wonder of the world, the only opal ever found in a meteorite. If they had stopped to think. . . ."

The professor paused, noticed that Burton had lost interest again, and then went on, talking almost to himself. "The fools! If they had stopped to think, they would realise why no gem but the diamond has ever been found in a meteorite. The opal and the emerald are soft and limey. They would never survive the journey through the earth's atmosphere, that burns up all but the hardest substance. No, that gem never reached the earth from another world. It was born in that bed of sandy-mud in some convulsion of the earth's crust, and since no opal could be so born, it must be a gem of a new genus. And there may be thousands more of them. . . ."

"Eh?" grunted Burton suddenly.

"There may be thousands more like it, lying in old sea-beds in this country, which form the land from where salt is now gathered."

Burton suddenly sat forward intently. "Look!" he exclaimed. "What's that?"

The professor followed his pointing finger, and saw a fortress with smooth walls rising sheer out of rock on the hillside in front. "The Palace," he said. "And now for the 'Prison of Sunset.'"

The Rajah Sabhatur, wearing faultless evening dress, joined the professor at dinner. Burton took his meal alone. The rajah, the professor guessed, had learned sufficient at Eton and Cambridge to distinguish between a scholar and a cockney, and so Burton had been passed off as his valet.

"And so, my dear professor," said the rajah, "you have travelled seven thousand miles and risked your life in this barbarous country, to see my bauble again!" His lips curved in a smile and it was easy to see that the smile could become cruel. "Strange that while you have what you believe to be the learning of the world, in those charming buildings of yours at Cambridge, you travel so far merely to see a bauble. . . ."

"The quest for knowledge, you know," replied the professor. "So often miscalled, the lure of the unknown. This time, I hope, you will change your mind and let me examine the gem."

The rajah shook his head. "In the west, professor, minds are changed quickly. You re-write your books as frequently as you change your clothes. But in the east, we change slowly. We do not regard knowledge as a coat to be worn sometimes, then hung in a cupboard and at last discarded for a more fashionable garment. We do not seek the explanation of all things, in terms of science. We learn that it is so, and we are content that it should be so. . . ."

"But the 'Prison of Sunset,'" interrupted the professor.

The rajah smiled again. "In the west you are always so impatient to get to what you call the point, when indeed, there is often no point at all. I was about to state that the 'Prison of Sunset' is sacred. In two hundred years no member of my family, much less a European, has touched the stone. If you ask me why . . ." he shrugged his shoulders, "I would only say that all those who have touched it have died, and my family have never shown any desire for premature death."

"But I am prepared to take the risk," said the professor earnestly. If he could persuade the rajah, it would save the risk of theft.

"My dear professor! In our country we do not allow our guests to take risks which we are not ourselves prepared to take. A foolish custom, no doubt, that has sometimes led to the host losing his life; but there it is. And as I do not wish to lose my life, I must ask you not to touch the 'Prison of Sunset.' And if that is not sufficient . . ." the rajah's voice hardened just a shade, "then I must forbid you to touch it."

"Of course, of course," replied the professor with a forced laugh. "If you say so . . . But surely you, who have travelled, do not believe this superstition. The men who have died have been uneducated men, with all the mental instability of the primitive native. . . ."

"Travel, they say, broadens the mind," the rajah smiled. "Sometimes it broadens it only in showing how little people know of one another. I could, perhaps, explain, professor, why all who have touched the 'Prison of Sunset' died within six hours. But I could not say for certain, and is it not foolish to speculate, when you know sufficient? My ancestor, to whom the stone was first brought ordered it to be polished and cut. When the workmen engaged in the task died, he did not ask questions he could not answer. He set others to take their place. They also died. They sav that altogether, one hundred men died before the stone was cut to its present shape. And then there were the thieves. I cannot say how many attempts have been made to steal it. In my time, there has been only one. My soldiers found the man, horribly scarred, some six hours later, before he had reached the frontier. . . ."

"But really, my dear rajah, this is all nonsense . . ." The professor suddenly saw the flicker of annoyance on the rajah's face and stopped short. "But perhaps you are right. I should like to be privileged to look at it again, and if I may ask a favour, I should like my man Burton to see it. He is naturally curious, although, of course, he has no knowledge of science."

"Delighted, my dear professor." The rajah ordered a servant to call Burton, then led the two Englishmen to a vast hall. In a niche of a pillar stood a heavy metal box, with an opening in the top. "There you are, my dear professor; that is what you have come seven thousand miles to see. . . ."

The professor looked in and his eyes brightened as he saw the beautiful object within. Three inches long, fully an inch thick and perhaps two inches wide, it lay on a bed of gold, the colours coming and going like liquid fire. The constant changing of hues from purple and crimson to orange and yellow, with a thousand tints between, made it seem to quiver with life.

"The 'Prison of Sunset,'" the professor breathed as he stepped back. "An opal, you think, rajah?"

The rajah shrugged his shoulders. "Chemical analysis alone would show for certain, as you know, professor. Since we cannot analyse it, does it matter what we call it?"

Burton stepped forward to look at the stone. He had been surveying the hall professionally, noting the entrance and exits. He examined the box. This was easy—just a matter of putting in your hand. He gasped as he saw the gem. What a price it would fetch! And that damned fool of a professor proposed to hide it in his laboratory. A plan he had been considering came back to Burton's mind; a plan that meant a fortune instead of five hundred pounds.

"Wonderful!" he exclaimed, as he saw the rajah's eye upon him. "But is it safe like this, without any bars or anything?"

"Very pretty," replied the rajah, "and dangerous. The professor has no doubt told you the fate of those who have taken it. . . ."

"Oh, that story!" said Burton easily, but his grin was a little sickly. He returned to the room he had been assigned, slowly, noting the way so that he could move easily in the darkness.

The theft of the gem was, as the professor had prophesied, child's play. Burton's skill was not required until they reached the

"It's gone! It's gone!" he raved, and pointed wildly over the brim of the precipice along the top of which the road ran at this point. "It's broken to pieces!"

garage below the palace, where the rajah's cars were kept, but the crude padlock gave him little trouble even in the darkness at two in the morning. The road sloped downwards for nearly a mile, and the car slid down easily so that they were out of earshot before the engine was switched on.

"And now!" whispered the professor, "for the frontier. We can make it in seven hours and there are no telegraphs. . . ."

The rajah, when a servant came running to tell him of the theft in the morning, was unperturbed. He looked at his wrist-watch sleepily, seemed to make a mental calculation.

"Six hours at, shall we say, forty miles an hour," he murmured to his secretary. "Two hundred and forty miles. You will find them between the two-hundred and the two-hundred and fifty mile-posts. You had better send a car to bring in the bodies. . . ."

"The bodies, highness?" exclaimed the secretary startled.

"Is it not known that he who touches the 'Prison of Sunset' dies?" asked the rajah, brusquely, and returned to his sleep.

The car was found by the two hundred and fiftieth milestone—Burton had driven fast. In the back seat the professor's body lay horribly burned, as if he had been struck by lightning. Of Burton or the "Prison of Sunset" there was no sign, and the search-party were about to return when they saw a shambling figure coming down the road. It was Burton, madness in his eyes and in his gestures, so that he did not seem to notice the raw burns on his hands and arms.

"It's gone! It's gone!" he raved, and pointed wildly over the brim of the precipice along the top of which the road ran at this point. "It's broken to pieces!" He shuddered as he glimpsed the corpse in the back of the car. "Gawd!" he screamed, then collapsed.

The secretary walked to the edge of the precipice and glanced down as if hoping to see the "Prison of Sunset." He saw only a wilderness of arid boulders and at the bottom a rushing torrent. The "Prison of Sunset" was probably now in a million fragments.

That might have been the end of the story, but even in a frontier state an English professor cannot die and his companion go raving mad without enquiry. A rather bored rajah, badgered by the authorities, at last condescended to offer an explanation, to a political officer.

"The thieves were struck by the curse that attends all who touched the 'Prison of Sunset'" he said.

"Yes, but if I may venture to say so, rajah, you and I don't believe that and I've got to get something better than that, for those hard-headed fellows at home . . ." The political officer wiped the sweat from his forehead and silently cursed professors whose thirst for knowledge led them to crime. "Of course, I could say it was a flash of lightning . . . but why did that fellow Burton throw the 'Prison of Sunset' over the precipice?"

"It was not lightning, my dear sir," said the rajah. "I cannot say for certain, but the smatterings of western science I gleaned at Cambridge suggest it was burns due to radium. . . ."

"Radium!"

"So I speculate. I have long thought the 'Prison of Sunset' was nothing but a bubble of unusually radio-active ore. That would explain the death of the lapidaries and the thieves. The professor evidently insisted upon carrying it—which saved his servant's life, but his death was so horrible that it turned Burton's head."

"But if it was radium, it would be of incalculable value. Cancer, you know . . ." The political officer shuffled awkwardly. "Why, there must have been more of it than in all the hospitals put together!"

"There *is,* my friend, since matter is indestructible . . . but who will collect it, in a million fragments, from the bottom of the stream? I proposed, in the near future, to present the bauble to your hospitals, since we do not know how to use it here. But your professor, who knew so much and wished to know more, has denied me the pleasure . . . and, of course, it might not have been radium. As the professor said, only chemical analysis would reveal, and since we cannot make that analysis, why should we exhaust ourselves in argument?"

The rajah stood up and barely stifled a yawn. "And now, if you will excuse me," he said, "I must go to administer justice to my poor subjects who, though they have not the learning of the professor, had the wisdom not to touch the 'Prison of Sunset'."

HUQM CHAND, AN EASTERN TRIANGLE

By

"AFGHAN"

HUQM CHAND walked from the office in thoughtful mood; for the cares of the world were his, and they pressed heavily upon him. In his household affairs was he troubled, and now in the office had further trouble been his portion. He had been promised a special increase three months back if he worked satisfactorily; but now this special increase would not be given him; he would have to wait till the end of the year. The head of his department said that Huqm Chand's work was not satisfactory; he must wait. Even at the end of the year he would not get his increase unless his work showed much improvement.

But how can a man work satisfactorily in office when his mind is troubled by household affairs? Even if one is a babu in an office one does not cease to be a man, and a man's responsibilities are many. Huqm Chand had a wife; and how can a man's mind be on his work when his wife is at home alone, with no trustworthy person in the house to watch her?

Huqm Chand was on the short side; and was slim, with drooping shoulders, a narrow chest, and an anæmic complexion of pale olive. He was what is called in India a "B.A. plucked," and was proud of the distinction, never failing to announce the fact to new acquaintances. This strange title actually means that Huqm Chand was one of those students who manage to slip through the Intermediate examination and appear for the degree of Bachelor of Arts, though they know they have not the slightest chance of passing the necessary examination. He failed, a foregone conclusion, but had now the proud distinction of being a B.A. plucked.

On the strength of his attainments, Huqm Chand secured an appointment in an office on fifty rupees per mensem, which was exactly double what he was worth. But all departments must be Indianized, and though many a young Anglo-Indian (new style) would have been glad of the appointment and would have been a cheap bargain, Huqm Chand got it.

Huqm Chand was a married man: hence his disturbed state of mind, for his wife was young and his mother was dead. Since the death of his father some years back his mother had lived with him, and he knew that when he was from home someone was there who would see that his wife behaved as a wife should; but his mother had died a month before, and when the leave he had taken to perform the funeral ceremonies expired, he had to return to duty and attend office, leaving his young wife all day alone in the house. Was she all day alone in the house? This is what troubled his soul. The boorkha is a good custom, but it may be put to a bad use; for beneath its folds a woman may go where she will, unknown of all. She may even brush shoulders with her husband in the street and he none the wiser. There was a maid in the house—he could not afford more than one maid—but of what use is a maid? She may be bought. As like as not she may have a lover of her own.

Then there was another matter for thought. Not only must he be away from home all day, he must be at home all night, and sometimes Huqm Chand wished to be away from home at night. From a youth Huqm Chand had been fond of a gay life, hence his narrow chest and pasty complexion. He liked variety; and the society of the ladies who live upstairs in a certain street is both amusing and agreeable.

During his mother's lifetime he had often been away all night, returning in the small hours of the morning; but now this must cease unless he could make sure his wife did not take advantage of his absence to have a little recreation on her own account. His friends would soon know that he had again taken to staying out all night, and many of those friends would be quite willing to take his place at home.

He must marry another wife. He could ill-afford to keep two wives; but it was the only way out of his difficulties. The two wives would watch each other, and he could go where he wished when he wished.

At first he considered this an excellent idea, but on second thought discovered several objections, the chief being that the two wives might combine forces. They would be jealous of each other; but when he started going out, they would both be jealous of the unknown third and would make friends. He sucked in his lips and shook his head. His wife was always angry when he spent the night out; the second wife would also be angry. Then they would think it a fine revenge to combine and pay him back in his own coin. Not that Huqm Chand put it exactly that way; the proverb that what was sauce for the goose was sauce for the gander did not appeal to him. Two wives would be worse than one.

But then another thought struck him. He was of the advanced

party that advocates widow re-marriage. He would not have allowed a widow of his own family to re-marry; but he was a great orator on the society platform and urged all his friends to re-marry their widowed daughters and sisters, and to marry their sons to widows so as to set a good example. As it happened, a man had heckled him at the last meeting, asking how it was that when his marriage was being arranged and a widow had been suggested, he had objected strongly. Of course Huqm Chand had objected. He wanted a brand new wife, not a second-hand one. But he did not say this on the platform; he said he had been willing to marry a widow, anxious to do so, to be an example to weaker brothers, but his father had vetoed the idea. As Huqm Chand's father was dead, nothing more could be said, and the heckler was silenced.

Now Huqm Chand could do more than silence those who talked. He would marry a widow. Not a young one, for he already had a wife to bear him children and many lady friends to amuse his leisure hours; he would marry an old widow.

It was more than a bright idea, it was an inspiration. An old woman would not expect gallantries on the part of her husband. If she did, she would be disappointed. It mattered little to her husband if she were disappointed; she could not take revenge as a young woman would by having a lover, for who would be the lover of an old woman! And yet, though the old woman might not expect much attention from her husband, she would be jealous of the young wife who did receive these attentions. Also, should the young wife complain about the all night absences of the husband, the old wife would give her no sympathy, would, in fact, be glad. She certainly would not combine with the young wife to procure a lover for the pleasure of the young wife, while she, by reason of her age, was herself debarred from such pleasures. Decidedly it was nothing less than an inspiration, and Huqm Chand decided to look up a widow next Sunday.

By the time Huqm Chand arrived at this momentous decision, he had also arrived at the door of his house. He lived in the Anarkali Bazaar, down a side street; and pushing open a wooden door, he entered a small courtyard. It was a very small courtyard, with not more than three rooms on each side, and one side belonged to Huqm Chand. Not hired, be it noted; it was his own property, left him by his father. There were three rooms in the lower storey, and in these Huqm Chand lived. One was his bedroom, one his *baithak* where he received male acquaintances, and the third was a spare room in which coal, wood, and lumber was kept. The three rooms above, reached by a small masonry staircase, were the women's apartments, and where the food was cooked.

And now to change from his office things. Huqm Chand wore a suit of English cut to go to office—was he not a B.A. plucked?—but English clothes are uncomfortable, and moreover they cost money and must not be subjected to home use, else will the knees of the trousers become baggy and the suit soon wear out. Removing his turban, Huqm Chand replaced it with a small, round cap, and divesting himself of his office clothes, donned dhoti and kurta. He was now comfortable; and seizing a charpoy that stood in the veranda, dragged it out into the courtyard where some men were already sitting, and joined in the conversation.

As it happened, the conversation turned on the subject just then uppermost in Huqm Chand's mind for they were discussing widow re-marriage.

"It is naught to me," said one, "for I am already married and do not need another wife; but were I to marry again I would not marry a widow unless——" He paused.

"Unless she were very beautiful," suggested another.

The first speaker spat. "Who wants beauty in a wife? Is it not for sale in the bazaar, and young, too? Unless she had a deal of money, I was about to say. Then indeed I might be persuaded to marry a widow."

The other man laughed. "Her relations might not be persuaded to let her marry. Nay, my friend, if thou wouldst wed a widow, thou must be prepared to take one without fortune, and that few men will do."

"That will I do," put in Huqm Chand. "I have a young wife who knows naught of housekeeping, and my mother is dead. Who will teach my wife? If I but knew of some respectable widow I would marry her so that I could have food to eat that did not half kill me. Now I eat packets of *churan* every day, and still I suffer much in my bowels from the bad food that is given me."

The other men glanced at each other, and then at Huqm Chand. They knew this was not his real reason, else he would have given another. Perhaps he had no reason, and did not intend to marry, speaking as he did merely to give himself importance in the eyes of others. If that were so, it were good to put him in his place without further delay. One of the men spoke.

"In my house there is a widow whom thou canst wed. She is not young, nor hath she wealth. Thou canst have her for thy wife."

The others grinned; but to their surprise Huqm Chand did not seem to be disturbed at being taken up so quickly.

"I will think over the matter," he replied.

Huqm Chand did not wish to be hurried. It was a serious

step. He had just thought of this way out of his difficulties, and must study it from every angle, lest his last state be worse than the first. Also this was a matter which could not be discussed in the presence of other men.

Huqm Chand thought it over. For a week he thought over this matter of marrying an old, penniless widow; for when his friend said she was not young, he knew she must be old. And indeed, had she not been old, his friend would not have allowed the marriage, for a young, widowed relation is cheaper than a servant. For a week he thought it over, and then he went to his friend's *baithak*.

He had quite made up his mind. On Saturday he came home to find the maid wearing a new chaddar. She said she had bought it. She may have; but it may have been given her—by Huqm Chand's wife, or by some gallant who wished to secure the maid's good offices. The matter could not be put off; and on Sunday he went to the house of his friend.

The affair did not take long. The woman was a widow, so a grand marriage was out of the question. The friend wanted to get rid of an encumbrance, and Huqm Chand wanted a watch-dog. In a week Huqm Chand had a second wife, and could apply himself to his work in office with a mind undisturbed by the thought of what might be happening at home in his absence.

Also, since the day the maid wore a new chaddar, Huqm Chand had remained at home every night; but now he was at liberty to resume his nocturnal adventures. He was not slow to avail himself of the opportunity.

This new wife was not a bad bargain. The maid was gone; for with the new wife in the house there was no need of a maid, and the maid's salary was saved. The new old wife could do the maid's work, and she and the old young wife could between them do the cooking and everything else that was necessary.

The new wife accepted her position meekly; but to make sure there should be no mistake in the matter, Huqm Chand bade her sleep in the room at one end, while he and the young wife slept in the room at the other end. Every night of the first week he spent with his young wife, and he knew by the look he surprised occasionally in the new wife's face that she had no love for the wife who had what she never would have, the caresses of a husband.

To make quite certain, on Saturday morning Huqm Chand rose early and went to the room where the elderly wife was making preparations for the morning meal. He looked at her in silence, and then, as she turned to pick up something from a box, he stepped up to her and swiftly passed his arm round her waist.

She stiffened visibly, and a tremor ran through her frame; but she did not turn. Huqm Chand glanced over his shoulder. It was as he had expected. The young wife, wondering what could have taken him to the other room, had followed and was now watching him with flaming eyes. Stooping forward, he whispered into the elderly wife's ear: "See that the dal is properly cooked," and stepped hastily back as if he had just discovered the presence of the young wife.

"I told her to see that the dal was properly cooked," he stammered.

Now, this had a double effect. The young wife would not believe him, and the elderly wife, thinking he made sport of her for the amusement of the young wife, would be angry. She could not vent her anger on him, so would turn it on the young wife. Here was the makings of a pretty quarrel; and Huqm Chand knew that even had they been inclined to be friends, they would hate each other now. His young wife was in safe keeping, and tonight he could go with a light heart to see one of his lady friends. Tomorrow would be Sunday, and the office would be closed, so there would be no need to rise early.

That evening Huqm Chand went out. He wore a new cap, and a silk coat over his kurta. Also his dhoti was of fine muslin, and the kurta embroidered with cunning designs. He did not go at once to the house of his lady friend, for it was yet early; for a time he roamed about the bazaar, exchanging greeting with the friends he met and trying to stare out of countenance every unveiled female he met.

Presently a boorkha passed Huqm Chand. Whether by accident or design, as she passed she bumped against him. As it happened, it was an accident, for the woman had trodden on a ball which a boy had just thrown to another in the street; but Huqm Chand did not see the ball, and was quite sure the bump was given purposely. It was enough; and when the woman went on, Huqm Chand followed.

Now, a blind woman would know if she were being followed by a man, and it was not long ere the woman knew that Huqm Chand followed her. She did not betray her knowledge, but hurried on and presently entered a house.

Huqm Chand smiled. Evidently she was new to the game. She had seen him, had been seized with an irresistible desire to touch him, to come in physical contact with him; and then, frightened at what she had done, she had fled to her home. All the better; this adventure would be exceedingly diverting, and when he was at last successful—for that he would be successful

Huqm Chand had not the slightest doubt—the pleasure would be all the greater for the knowledge that he was first in the field.

He knew exactly what she would do. When she got to her room, she would hold her heart and reproach herself for what she had done. Then she would peep from the window to see if he were still in the street. He twisted the end of his moustaches and walked up and down, humming a gay air. She must be looking at him now, and presently there would be a sign. Even if she gave no sign today, she would certainly give one soon; and he would parade this street daily till he received the sign.

Huqm Chand had a great opinion of himself. He failed to realize that his narrow chest and puny frame gave him a far from heroic appearance, else he might have hesitated; for when a woman would have a lover, she usually chooses a man with plenty of the vigorous animal about him. But Huqm Chand was hardly to blame, except for his easy credulity; for his paid lady friends, knowing his weakness, flattered his vanity so that he should be extra liberal, and he took all they said for the truth. His male friends, too, knowing it would mean a glass of sherbet, perchance sweetmeats, often told him what a devil of a fellow he was.

Huqm Chand walked up and down the street for some time; but no flower fell, no hand appeared at a window-sill, and he was about to leave when the door opened and the boorkha again came forth. He knew it by the embroidery about the edge.

Evidently he had been mistaken. She did not live there, she had merely sought refuge in the house—from him, or from herself? From herself, undoubtedly; for she had overcome her first alarm and had come forth. Now she would lead him to her house. He hurried, and soon overtook the boorkha. Suddenly the woman stopped, and threw up the front of her boorkha. Huqm Chand started back in disgust. The face was that of an old woman, a woman older even than his new wife. What a mistake!

The old woman frowned. "Thou art my son, and yet would follow me in this way! Thinkest thou I am like to one of thy women friends in the bazaar? First didst thou follow me to my house, and now dost thou follow me again!"

To Huqm Chand's alarm, she began to raise her voice. Should he flee? Nay; for then she might begin to scream and someone would seize him, and though where they stood there was no one, farther along the bazaar were many men. He must temporize; and the fact that she had stopped where none could overhear gave him courage. He raised his clasped hands to his forehead.

"Nay, mother," he said; "I followed not. I but walked idly in the streets before returning to my house."

The old woman sniffed. "Then are the men of today different from the men of my young days. Had I bumped against a young man when I was young, he had followed my boorkha to the ends of the earth."

Huqm Chand was puzzled. But at first he was greatly relieved; for the old woman was not angry, and would not create a scene. The next moment he was seized with horror, for the old woman leered at him out of the corner of her eye. She had fallen in love!

The old woman marked his confusion, and smiled maliciously. She knew what was in his mind.

"Thou art a proper man," she said, eyeing him admiringly up and down. "Thou shalt come to my home and be the friend of my son," and she leered again.

Huqm Chand drew back in terror, and looked round wildly for a means of escape. He must plunge down some alley and lose himself so that this dreadful old woman would not know where he had gone. Never again would he come near this awful street! He was just about to bolt, when the old woman smiled and leaned towards him.

"I but sported," she said. "Why didst thou follow my mistress?"

Huqm Chand breathed again. What a fright the old woman had given him! At first he was inclined to stand on his dignity, for no man likes to be made ridiculous, and the old woman had laughed at him; but on second thoughts he changed his mind. After all, he had not been mistaken; the fair one had done more than give him a sign, she had sent out her maid to him with a message, probably an assignation.

Strange to say, Huqm Chand had never before had an adventure such as this. Many of his friends had followed boorkhas, and had been admitted to the homes of these boorkhas. Many had been accosted in the streets by old women and had accompanied them; for such things will be when the husband has other loves, or is an opium-eater, or is addicted to other and worse vices. But in spite of his manly appearance, never had Huqm Chand received encouragement from a boorkha or been accosted by an old woman. This he had thought extremely strange; though had he studied himself with critical, candid eyes he perchance might not have considered it so strange, especially had he compared himself with those who were called.

But all that was now over. Here was an old woman who had been sent out to him by her mistress. He slipped a couple of rupees into the old woman's hand. A rupee would have been sufficient, but he did not know this.

The old woman smiled. This young man was new to the game; he would be rare plucking. She did not let him see the smile; instead, she turned to him a face of scorn.

"Adventures are not for those of a miserly heart," she said; "for the heart that is miserly with money is also miserly with love, taking all and giving naught in return. Take back thy money."

"Nay," and Huqm Chand hastily took out another three rupees, the last of the money he had upon him, "I am no miser," and he pressed the money into her hand. "I am liberal with my money as with my love."

The old woman was mollified; and drawing Huqm Chand aside, told him why her mistress had sent her forth.

He must not linger in the street, for her mistress's husband was a man consumed with jealousy. Presently she would show him a *galli* (alley) behind the house. This *galli* was dark, with no lamp, and it approached even to the door of a small courtyard at the back of the house. There must he come the following night, and she would open the door of the courtyard for him. But, and she smiled knowingly, she opened to a liberal heart only; and though five rupees might open the lips, it would not open a door, the door of Paradise. Let him be outside the courtyard door at ten o'clock.

Dropping her boorkha, she hurried away, and Huqm Chand followed. Presently the woman stopped at the mouth of a *galli* and pointed down it. Huqm Chand nodded, and the old woman disappeared down the *galli*.

Huqm Chand walked home on air. At last adventure was his, adventure such as he read of in the Urdu novels he bought in the bazaar. True, it was like to be an expensive adventure, for the old woman's hint meant in plain words that he must take more than five rupees if he would pass through the door of that courtyard. But what mattered? He had drawn his pay a few days before, and he had money in the Post Office Savings Bank. This was real adventure, and he was not going to begrudge a few rupees.

Such was Huqm Chand's impatience that he was in the street even before it was dark. But he was wise enough to keep away from the end of the *galli*, though he could not refrain from passing in front of the house once or twice to let the fair one see that he was there. For a while he sat before the shop of a sherbet seller and sipped sherbet. Then he went opposite and had a cup of tea; but when he had finished the tea, a glance at his cheap wrist-watch told him that it was yet only eight o'clock.

Another two hours! He walked down other streets. He sipped more sherbet. He drank more tea. He slipped for a while into an inner room where cards were being played and where dice rattled.

But he did not join in these diversions, for he might lose his money; and that would never do. In that case the adventure would be over before it began, for unless he had money the old woman would refuse to admit him, would tell her mistress he had not come. At last his wrist-watch told him that it was a quarter to ten, and filled with blissful anticipations he went to the *galli*.

It was a dark *galli* and narrow, with a vile drain on either hand, open sewers, in fact, and Huqm Chand held his nose. He did not mind strong smells, he was inured to them, but this was more than even he could stand. Holding his nose, he approached the door and waited.

He had not long to wait. Softly the door opened and the old woman stepped forth, her finger on her lips.

"So," she whispered, "the ardent lover waiteth impatiently to be admitted to the chamber of his beloved," and she held forth a crooked hand.

Huqm Chand slipped ten rupees into it, and the woman's hand disappeared into the folds of her boorkha. He would now have entered the courtyard, but the old woman pulled him back.

"Not yet," she whispered. "A woman friend is with my mistress. She will leave in a moment, for even as I left the room she donned her boorkha. When she is gone, then will the gates of Paradise open to thee."

Suddenly she started; for from the little courtyard without which they stood came the unmistakable sound of a man's voice. The old woman seized Huqm Chand and dragged him frantically from the door.

"My master!" she gasped. "He hath returned! Flee, lest he open the door and find thee here!"

Huqm Chand fled. He did not waste a precious moment in hesitation. A jealous husband was not to his liking at all, and God knows what the size of this husband was. Huqm Chand abominated violence; and picking up the skirt of his dhoti, he fled with all speed down the *galli*. He did not hold his nose this time, he had other things than smells to think about. He stopped running when he reached the street, for he did not wish to attract attention; but he nevertheless walked as fast as he could put foot to the ground, and it was not till he reached home that he breathed freely.

This sort of adventure was not to Huqm Chand's liking at all. There was too much danger in it. Suppose the husband had not spoken in the courtyard. Suppose he had opened the door without warning and discovered Huqm Chand without! Huqm Chand turned cold and shuddered in his soul at the dreadful thought. Decidedly, this adventure was far too dangerous; he would go no more to that house.

But he had spent fifteen good rupees, and the more he thought over his lost money the more unwilling he was that it should indeed be wasted. The husband had returned unexpectedly that night, but he would not return unexpectedly every night. At last one afternoon Huqm Chand walked up and down the street in which stood the house of his beloved. He had never seen her; but she was his beloved and he was madly in love with her, for this is the custom of the east, to love the unknown.

Six times he passed before the house, and he was almost in despair. But he passed the seventh time, and the old woman came forth. He followed her, and when they were some distance from the house she stopped. This time she did not throw up her boorkha in front.

"A hot lover!" she said scornfully. "He hears the husband's voice, and flees, his ardour cooled in an instant!"

Now, this talk of fleeing annoyed Huqm Chand excessively. He was ready to acknowledge that he had walked hurriedly away; but that was merely because there was no use in staying, and because he did not wish to be mixed up in a vulgar street brawl. As for fleeing, or fearing the husband, by this time Huqm Chand had quite convinced himself that had the husband come forth unexpectedly, he, Huqm Chand, would have trampled on that husband, and would have walked into the house over his prostrate body. That was how the heroes in the romances he read behaved, and he would have done the same. He was greatly annoyed with the woman, and turned haughtily away.

But she plucked him by the sleeve. "O hasty one," she said soothingly, "may not an old woman have her jest! Business detained thee, is it not so? And therefore thou couldst not come before. Now that the business is finished, thou art here. But the days have been long to my mistress, and ever she sits mourning thy absence, weeping for the sight of thy beloved face. Surely thou hadst time to walk in the bazaar that she might see thee from the window!"

Huqm Chand settled his cap at a rakish angle and twisted his moustache. His vanity was immensely flattered, and he showed it.

"I am a man of business," he said importantly, "and I have much to occupy my time. Even love must give way to business sometimes. But now I am at leisure, and therefore have I come."

Another meeting at the door of the courtyard at the back was arranged for that night at ten o'clock, and at nine o'clock Huqm Chand was again in the bazaar. He came later this time, for the former occasion had been a lesson, and so he had not so long to wait. Nevertheless the hour dragged, as such hours will, but at length it was a quarter to ten. He passed down the dark *galli*.

Again were his nostrils assailed by the vile stench from the drains; and this time it was worse than before, for there had been no rain for many days, and the drains had been unwashed. Holding his nose, he walked delicately down the centre of the lane and reached the door.

This time he had to wait nearly half an hour ere the woman came; but at last the door opened, and the woman came forth.

" My mistress hath friends," she whispered. " When they leave I will tell thee."

Huqm Chand cursed these infernal friends in his heart, and pretended not to see the outstretched hand. The old woman sniffed.

" It were idle to wait here," she said, " for the friends may stay late. Come another day."

Huqm Chand had brought ten rupees, and he slipped five of these into the old woman's hand. The woman's fingers closed over the money, but still her hand remained without the boorkha.

" My master is a man to be dreaded," she said. " If he should hear of this, he would turn me out to starve. And starve I would, for I have no money of my own. Perhaps it would be well for me if I had no more to do with this matter."

With a sigh Huqm Chand slipped the other five rupees into her hand, and this time the hand disappeared beneath the boorkha.

" I will now go within," she said, " and as soon as these women——"

She stopped suddenly, for at that moment the door of the courtyard was opened and a couple of veiled forms emerged. Huqm Chand and the old woman stood in the shadow and she seized him by the neck.

" Down till they have passed!" she hissed, " else will they see thee and spread the news abroad that a man waited without our back courtyard! Down!"

Huqm Chand crouched instinctively. But crouching did not satisfy the old woman, and she pressed him lower. Huqm Chand tried to save himself; but this infernal old *churail* had the strength of two men and forced him down relentlessly, till his foot slipped and he fell prone in the gutter. The next moment the women passed, and the old woman went with them, talking as if she had come without the courtyard merely to show them the way through the *galli*.

It was no use waiting there. Even if the door of the courtyard were now opened Huqm Chand could not go within. He rose from the gutter and went home, holding his clothes away from him with one hand, and holding his nose with the other. That vile gutter! It was not till he had bathed three times, and rubbed himself with scented oil that he could get rid of the stink. Even then the memory of that vile effluvia lingered and he shuddered every few minutes.

This adventure did not work out on the same lines as the adventures he had read of in the books, and he decided to have nothing further to do with this particular fair one. His experiences had been intensely disagreeable, and might prove dangerous. Last time the husband had nearly caught him, and this time he had nearly been seen by the two women who came out of the courtyard. Had they seen him? He thought not, he hoped not; but he seemed to hear a giggle as they passed. Had they seen him in the drain? If they had, by this time the news that a man had been outside the door of his back courtyard may have reached the husband's ears. Huqm Chand shivered at the thought. Decidedly, he must give up this adventure.

But what about the twenty-five rupees? The more Huqm Chand thought of the wasted twenty-five rupees, the more sad he became. What pleasure he could have had with those twenty-five rupees had he taken them to his lady friends in a certain bazaar! Now they were gone. Wasted.

But the days passed, and gradually Huqm Chand's courage returned. This husband, after all he was only a man; and no hero of romance ever feared a husband. Let this husband come forth; he would find Huqm Chand a difficult proposition. Five and twenty rupees had he spent, and he would have a return. The more he thought over the twenty-five rupees, the braver he grew. That afternoon Huqm Chand went to the street of adventure.

He had not long to wait this time. In a few minutes the old woman came out, and Huqm Chand followed her. Again did she chide him for a cold lover, and again did he plead business. She told him to be at the back door at ten o'clock, and at a quarter to ten Huqm Chand was there.

Again the five rupees were given, and again after a moment's hesitation the other five. Huqm Chand hoped that the rest of the previous programme would not be adhered to. He looked at the gutter and shuddered. The old woman leant towards him and whispered in his ear.

"This is thy lucky day," she said, "and shortly shalt thou be in Paradise. My mistress is alone in the house, and she will herself admit thee. I go to tell her thou art come." Slipping through the door, she closed it after her.

At last! Huqm Chand twisted his moustache and settled his cap. He heard a shuffling within the courtyard, and placed his ear to the door. She came. The door opened softly, and Huqm Chand sprang forward.

Alas! It was not she! A great, burly brute of a man stepped forth, and seized Huqm Chand by the throat.

"Ha! So thou wouldst dishonour my house?"

Huqm Chand recognized the voice he had heard in the courtyard the first night; it was the husband! He tried to wriggle loose; but this brute had the strength of a giant. Lifting a stick he carried, he rained blows on Huqm Chand; and though Huqm Chand raised his clasped hands in piteous appeal, even fell on his knees to beg the other to desist, the villain did not leave off, and the merciless rain of blows descended till Huqm Chand was sore from head to foot. Then the monster threw Huqm Chand into the gutter and returned within the courtyard.

Huqm Chand crept sadly home. What a terrible fate had been his! He had been beaten, he had been again cast into that vile gutter—and he had wasted thirty-five rupees!

It was a very chastened Huqm Chand who sat in the courtyard of his house the next few afternoons. What a dreadful ending to his first real romance! Never had he read a tale that ended that way. In the novels the lover was always successful, and the fool of a husband duped. If there were any rolling in stinking gutters, it was the husband who did the rolling while the lover looked on and laughed. Huqm Chand decided in future to content himself with imagining himself the hero of one of his favourite romances, and to leave romance at first hand severely alone.

But time heals all wounds; and at last Huqm Chand began to go out again. But not to see his lady friends; thirty-five rupees were gone, and he must be careful with his money for some time.

Nor did he go near the street of adventure. That devil of a woman would tempt him again, and he had borne enough. Not even for the sake of a peri would he again undergo what he had suffered that night. He kept to the other bazaars, and stared at the unveiled women he met. One afternoon, about ten days after his terrible experience, he entered the shop of a sherbet seller, one of the better class with a room, and called for a drink.

There was a partition in the shop, and Huqm Chand sat without the partition sipping his sherbet. Presently he heard the voice of someone on the other side of the partition. The voice was unknown to him, and he listened idly. But not for long. Soon he was listening with bulging eyes to the words of the one behind the screen. Huqm Chand could not see the men who sat there, nor could they see him.

"This Huqm Chand thinks himself clever," the man was saying, "but he is a fool!" and the man laughed. "When his mother died it was well, and there was no need for assignations in strange houses; for the maid was greedy of gifts, and many a pleasant day did I pass in his house while he was away at office—nights too!"

Huqm Chand's hands clenched convulsively; but it might be that the man spoke of another Huqm Chand, and he waited. The next words convinced him that he was indeed the Huqm Chand of whom this vile wretch spoke.

"But the fool grew uneasy," continued the man, "and married another wife to keep watch on the first one. He chose an old woman, a widow, so that they should not join forces and deceive him," again the man laughed loudly. "The fool! Is ever a woman too old for a lover! I have money. I hired a friend; and while my friend made love to the old wife, I made love to the young one."

Huqm Chand's jaw dropped and he gazed stupidly before him. But the man was again speaking.

"I know not if he afterwards guessed, and would have repaid me in my own coin," said the man reflectively, "but he came to my house, trying to play the gallant. My wife told me about it, and in truth it is a diverting tale. He followed her one day in the bazaar; so, after she entered the house, she sent out her maid, an old woman, to him. Five and thirty rupees have they wrung from the fool, and great sport have they had," and he chuckled.

Huqm Chand's jaws closed with a click, and he sat up in his chair. Did his ears deceive him? If this was true, then indeed was the villainous old woman a *churail,* a *bhootni,* a—but his feelings overpowered him.

"What was this sport?"

It was another man who spoke, and Huqm Chand started as if he had received an electric shock. Too well he knew that voice! It was the voice of the husband by whom he had been beaten! Huqm Chand half rose from his chair to flee; but the voice continued and he sank back, a puzzled frown creasing his forehead. This was the man who had beaten him, the man whose voice he had heard in the courtyard the first night; yet it was the other man who told the tale, as a tale, moreover, of his own house. Here was matter for wonder; and he listened eagerly for what would follow.

"What was this sport? Thou callest it a diverting tale. I have seen this Huqm Chand, he is a small man with a narrow chest."

"The first night," said the first speaker with a laugh, "my wife spoke with a gruff voice from the courtyard; and thinking it was me, the fool fled. The maid says his thin legs twinkled down the *galli* like the spokes in the wheel of a bicycle. The second time my wife and her sister went forth, and the maid forced this Huqm Chand down till he lay in the foul drain that runs beside the wall of the courtyard. La! How did he remove the stench from his body? The third time the three, my wife, her sister and the maid, set upon him with sticks. They beat him well, threw him in the gutter, and there left him!" and the man laughed loudly. "Of a truth; never more will this Huqm Chand seek adventure in the houses of other men!"

Huqm Chand passed his hand across his forehead in bewilderment. He gritted his teeth when the man spoke of the vile drain in which he had been twice rolled; but he was greatly puzzled by what he heard.

He was positive it was a man's voice he had heard in the courtyard the first night, the voice of the man who had afterwards beaten him and thrown him in the gutter. Why did not the husband say it was he who had meted out this punishment to his wife's would-be lover? Why relate it as a tale told him by his wife? But hark! The other spoke.

"It is indeed a diverting tale," said the other man, "and thou art a lucky man. A faithful wife is above riches."

There was a laugh in his voice. The husband thought his friend laughed at the tale; but Huqm Chand knew otherwise. That voice! He would know it among a thousand! Never would he forget it!

At last Huqm Chand saw light. Rising softly, he went without the shop and waited a short distance down the street. One of these men had dishonoured him in his house, the other had beaten and rolled him in a filthy drain; he would have revenge!

Presently the men emerged from the shop, and Huqm Chand strolled towards them. They met, and with a well acted start, Huqm Chand stepped back a pace and stared at one of the two men. The next moment Huqm Chand had him by the clothes.

"Thou art the man!" he cried excitedly. "The *galli* was dark, but I know thy figure!"

The man wrenched his cloth from Huqm Chand's grasp. "What *galli?*" he asked roughly. "Let me pass."

But Huqm Chand was not to be denied. By this time a small crowd had collected, and Huqm Chand turned to them appealingly.

"This man beat me," he said, "and for no fault. But a few nights since, returning home from a friend's, I met an old woman.

She took money and led me to the door of a courtyard. But within the courtyard we heard a man's voice, this man's, and I left. Another night I met the old woman. Again she took money from me, and again she led me to the door of the courtyard. Then this man came out, beat me, and threw me in the gutter. It was not my fault, the old woman took money from me and led me to the door. This man was waiting for me, so he must have sent the old woman forth. And yet he beat me! Then was I unprepared and he beat me; but now I am ready, and I will break his face!" And knowing the crowd would not allow them to fight, Huqm Chand struggled to get at the man.

"Fool!" and the man scowled angrily, "I live not in the Sadu *Galli.*"

"How knowest thou the name of the *galli?*" cried Huqm Chand triumphantly. "I mentioned not the name; I call on thy friend as my witness."

"Thou didst mention the name!" said the man desperately, for his friend looked at him strangely

"I did not," insisted Huqm Chand. "I call on all present to witness. Thou art the man who was within that courtyard, and thou art the man who came out of that courtyard! If that be not thy house, thou art the lover of its mistress, for thou wert two nights in that house!"

It was enough; the man's face convicted him. Huqm Chand went home to interview his two wives, while the crowd tried to remove the hands of one man from the throat of the other.

PAIN BESTOWING CONSEQUENCES

By

COUTTS BRISBANE

HIS belt heavy with the well-filled purse, token of the gratitude of his patient, Hang Loo, a dealer in comestibles whom he had relieved of a tumour, Dr. Hi Ho, the beneficent and well-esteemed physician of Sen Yang, climbed the mounting-block in the courtyard of the little country house and glanced apprehensively at the lowering heavens. Soon the invisible sun would set.

"Let your honourable feet be moved to celerity," he growled. "This person desires to reach the city before darkness falls."

"I hasten, honourable uncle!" grunted the servant, leading out the doctor's plump and lethargic steed. "It is well to hurry, the more so that a brigand, one who has but recently come hither to plague us, is said by travellers who paid tribute to his valour with all their possessions, to lie close to the southern gate. Moreover, he questioned them severely concerning the dwelling-place of the honoured Dr. Hi Ho, using words of no respect concerning him."

"Eh? And what is the dishonoured name of this infamous person?" asked Dr. Hi Ho with well assumed indifference, yet allowing his moonlike countenance to assume the aspect of cold mutton fat.

"The name, honourable uncle, is Ting Wei. It is said that he is the son of that Ting Lung who for long provided stimulation for all travellers on this road, but perished mysteriously with all his band, leaving only his son to carry on his calling."

With carelessness that bespoke absence of mind, Dr. Hi bestowed a handful of small silver taken from his purse and not from the pocket, where lay the pieces of light weight and doubtful quality usually reserved for such donations.

"My son, if any make question concerning my abode, let word be given that I have departed for Hang'tse," he said. "May your shadow continue to cover an extensive and ever-increasing area!"

And loosening in its sheath the broad-bladed sword that hung by his saddle, Dr. Hi Ho rode forth to the road which resembled a watercourse in every respect save that it lacked water. Then he urged his horse to its best efforts.

"Without doubt, this must be the ill-conditioned offspring of that well-deserving accumulator of substance to which, by the inscrutable decrees of the high ones, I became heir," he reflected. "Without doubt, by some trick of despiteful demons, this fellow Ting Wei has heard a rumour that I attended the passing of his sire to the Upper Beyond. It would be well to offer a reward for his atrocious and evil-designing head, and meantime be wary lest it appear, still attached to his body, accompanied by weapons."

So thinking, Dr. Hi Ho rode with care, giving to the dreary landscape all the attention that he would have bestowed upon the tongue and pulse of a wealthy and benevolent patient. Thus it was that presently he observed that a flock of sparrows about to alight upon some bushes by the wayside before him suddenly circled about and fled hastily, instead of alighting.

"A bush may conceal a tiger or a hare!" muttered Hi, and incontinently turned his horse off the road.

But a few moments later his wisdom was made manifest, for a puff of smoke jetted from the brushwood and a bullet whistled so close to his body that it seemed certain he would have fallen had he but continued on his way.

"For this time my feet have escaped the stirrups of the heaven aspiring steed!" quoth Hi, and urged his earthly mount over the rough ground at a pace that forbade any further manifestation of no good will.

Even as darkness descended he clattered up the Street of the Evening Star, and, alighting in the courtyard of the House of the Fortunate Frog, slammed the gate and shot the bolts with a sigh of thankfulness.

As he alighted, Sung, once his barrow man, now his faithful and well-deserving assistant in the art of healing, for it was he who held reluctant patients or administered anæsthetic taps on the skull, glided from the house.

"One waits," he murmured. "He is but an ill-looking fellow, and his face is as a countenance bruised by the heels of a horse."

"Bid him begone into the illimitable, and hasten his going with a sharp spear if need be!" growled Hi. The little incident of the road had upset his usually placid temper.

"Let the reins of discretion bridle your tongue," whispered Sung. "This one who waits announces the name of Yip Hi, adding, moreover, that he is a long lost but well beloved cousin of the honoured Dr. Hi Ho. Wherefore, since he might perchance be speaking truth, I did not cast him forth, but allowed him to repose in the outer chamber, providing fitting refreshment."

Dr. Hi Ho allowed himself the solace of a groan.

"Well is it said that he upon whom fortune bestows a smile should prepare his back for rods. Know, oh Sung, that an evil designing brigand, one Ting Wei, son of that Ting Lung now passed into the Beyond, desires my life, shooting at me as I neared the gate. Now, that the measure may be filled to overflowing, comes this ill-omened Yip Hi. Truly the back of probity shall be scarified!"

"A flea may instruct a many-examination-passing scholar in the art of leaping," murmured Sung sympathetically. "It may be that this humble and stony-headed person may instruct the learned one in the art of butting down the barriers to repose of spirit, even as the war elephant butts down the gate of a city. Ting Wei lies outside the city, but Yip Hi lies in your house. Therefore let us consider him first. Is he truly your cousin?"

"He is but the son of an uncle five times removed. Yet he was the friend of my youth. Has he made mention thereof?"

"Much, and in a loud voice. It was, therefore, that I gave him to drink of wine wherein was mingled a sleep-bestowing potion," replied Sung. "Is it true, beloved master, that you and he together, in the guise of beggars, robbed a temple of the offerings, beating the priest with clubs from behind so that his senses forsook him? Also that for a while you were the leader of a band of blind beggars, till on a day you led them to a broken bridge above a flooded river and there forsook them, carrying with you the week's takings?"

A noise as of a female dog lamenting for her young ones escaped from the constricted throat of Dr. Hi Ho, while his cheeks became suffused with tints like to the glowing of a stormy sunset. Sung held the lantern he carried higher and continued:

"Also that for the space of five years and four moons you, oh honoured master, were in the service of a learned doctor, mixing the potions and holding the hands of patients, even as I. Also that, the time being fulfilled, you did mingle a substance of no nutriment with his rice so that he died, and departed, taking his drugs and all that was his."

"Lies, lies, lies!" moaned Dr. Hi. "Yet in them all there is a grain of truth mingled, even as salt is mixed with pottage to give it savour. Thus it is true that being hungry, we partook of rice offered in a temple, yet the priest freely forgave us after he had broken a stout rod over our backs. As for the blind beggars, half of them could see. While the honourable Yat Foo, he from whom I learned the beginnings of my art, died full of years and duck stewed in wine, bequeathing to me his stock of drugs and instruments and his blessing, after I had served him faithfully for five years and seven moons. Yet of what avail is truth against calumny? A stoppage of the mouth of this execrable Yip Hi is indicated lest he open it wide in the market place. Behold, the night is dark, he sleeps heavily. Let us bear him through the hole in the wall at the bottom of the spacious if ill-tended garden and lay him amidst the tombs outside the city. It may be that an evil demon will assail him and bear him away, or deprive him of breath."

Sung shook his head, assuming the aspect of an heir who, having paid an avaricious undertaker for the obsequies of a wealthy relative, finds him revive ere the ceremony is begun.

"Honoured master, Yip Hi made announcement of his destination in a loud voice to certain of the watch, bestowing upon them the last of his money ere he entered and bidding them visit him tomorrow to drink with him. If therefore a demon should have conveyed him hence the matter would be known. It might even be that the voice of calumny would be uplifted against the honoured name of Hi Ho, to the pleasure and profit of those dogs, Dr. See Hop and Dr. Lu, whose takings have been greatly diminished by your unsurpassed skill. What says the proverb? 'He who crosses a melon field should not stoop to tie his shoe strings.' We must avoid the appearance of evil."

"Truly. Yet if this accursed dog remains under my roof he will assuredly devour much substance. If he is driven forth he will blacken the name of Hi with his base inventions. Therefore apply the hammer of necessity to the stone of your skull that sparks of wisdom may fly forth for my enlightenment."

"This person is of the unalterable opinion that the thrice welcome Yip Hi should be promoted to the position of a desirable though misguided younger brother. Clothing of quality equal to that of the revered Hi Ho should be placed upon his excellent body while nourishment fitted to one who has by habit subsisted chiefly upon liquid should be bestowed within. Thus tranquillity being restored, the tongue that reviled shall be turned to the uttering of words in praise of the munificence of a beloved elder brother."

"And for how long shall the elder brother endure the presence of this reptile, more poisonous than the teeth of serpents?" demanded Hi Ho, acidly.

"For as long as shall suffice to increase the rotundity of the thrice welcome and ensure the placidity of his tongue."

"And when these ends are accomplished, what then?"

"Then, it may be, he will take a journey. Who knows whether he will return? Yet if he does not none will make question of the matter, seeing that he will have spoken much of the loving kindness of his elder brother."

Dr. Hi Ho pondered for a while, then nodded assent.

"It is well. And if the desirable younger brother but absorbs nourishment as in the days of his youth, rotundity will be achieved in no great time. To you, O monument of wisdom, is allotted the task of keeping his bowl full even to overflowing."

"On a fortunate day, at a fortunate hour, came I to the House of the Fortunate Frog!" murmured Yip Hi. "Of surpassing excellence is the nourishment bestowed, only exceeded by the excellence of the wine. All the days of my life will I extol the estimable Dr. Hi Ho. You tell me, purveyor of delectable things, why it should be that the elder brother is thus filled with milk of benevolence? Otherwise was it in the days of our youth."

"There speaks the voice of no wisdom," replied Sung, refilling the chop bowl with spiced apricots stewed in honey and garnished with ginger. "Is it not written: 'The prosperity of a house is written on the bodies of the dwellers therein.' And again: 'The skill of the physician is written on the countenance of the patient.' Many beheld you at your first coming, lean as a mountain fox, clothed in garments of no seemliness. Now, though but few days have passed, you present a comely circumference fitting well with the garments of the revered Hi Ho which you wear, so that all who behold you reposing in the outer chamber marvel at the change and give praise to his skill and benevolence, so that he acquires therefrom much merit. Many of meagre habit are encouraged thereby to come to him. His coffers grow heavy."

"And is no other service than this demanded?" asked Yip. "Would it not be well that I should go about the city, spreading the fame of his skill and benevolence?"

"That assuredly. Also, since many need him, little time remains to him for visiting those who live beyond the city walls. Therefore it would be fitting that you, who now greatly resemble him in body and somewhat in countenance, should ride forth to the house of one Hang Loo, bearing medicines and the assurance of well being, saying also that the honourable Hi Ho will attend him tomorrow. A good horse is provided. I myself will attend you."

"I go. It is but little in return for loving kindness so freely bestowed," murmured Yip Hi and would have risen, but that Sung shook his head.

"Not yet, well esteemed, but later, when the sun declines. It would not be well that you should lose any of your substance by sweating in the heat of the day. Compose yourself for refreshing slumber," said Sung, and hastened away.

Presently, when the tide of patients had abated, he betook himself to the southern gate of the city and hurried forth. No travellers were upon the road. Indeed there had been but few of late, for the fame of the brigand Ting Wei was spread abroad and none travelled alone but only in companies too strong to attack.

"Small pickings have been the lot of Ting Wei," meditated Sung. "Therefore, it may be that he is alert. Yonder bushes offer concealment—and though no wind blows their upper branches quiver. Being now beyond sight from the gate it may be——"

Almost immediately it was. Ting Wei, a person of villainous aspect, but armed with many weapons, all in excellent, life-depriving condition, appeared, smiling as might a dragon who perceives before him a young and plump maiden suited for nutriment.

"Honoured uncle, bestow upon me the supreme delight of relieving you of garments too heavy for the season," he observed politely. "One of your magnitude will walk more easily in the garb of a newly-born infant."

"Will the honourable and perspicacious Ting Wei sacrifice great gain and the gratification of avenging the sending hence of a revered male parent for the sake of a few garments not in their first freshness?" returned Sung. "Know, valiant reaper of unsown harvests, that this inconsiderable person is servant to the ill-bespoken Dr. Hi Ho. Aggrieved by the acerbity of an ungoverned tongue, he seeks means to convert the doctor into an ancestor if it may be accomplished without danger to himself."

At once the countenance of Ting Wei assumed a horrible aspect of mingled rage and delight.

"Of what will the gain consist?" he demanded. "What is in your mind, oh aggrieved one?"

"Today, an hour before dark, the well-esteemed doctor rides to the house of Hang Loo, bearing a bag of two thousand taels in payment for land purchased. This person will accompany him, riding before him to give him warning of any danger by the way. For the small consideration of a hundred taels, this person will fail to note any such warnings as waving boughs, trodden grass, or the gratifying odour of recently cooked food," replied Sung. "Afterwards, it may be, this person will join with Ting Wei bearing arms and such money as he may find in the coffers of the deceased."

"The hundred taels shall be yours!" cried Ting Wei. "Also you shall be as the beloved offspring of the same father. At an hour before dark shall the estimable Hi Ho be prevailed upon to mount the skyward ascending steed. Go!"

And, greatly elated, Ting Wei vanished into the covert, leaving Sung to return to the city, bearing a bunch of herbs which he gathered by the wayside.

Bestriding Dr. Hi Ho's easy pacing steed, clad in Dr. Hi Ho's garments, bearing a packet of health-bestowing drugs, Yip Hi rode out of the southern gate, preceded by Sung. Great thoughts filled the mind of Yip Hi, fruit of long meditation after soul-satisfying meals.

"Behold, it comes to this person's mind that, though clad in well-filled garments of superior silk, no money is in his purse," he remarked. "Will it not be well that the lack should be supplied, and freely?"

"And if in his wisdom the honourable Hi Ho should see fit to refuse the desire thus delicately indicated?" queried Sung, one eye on the brushwood ahead.

Yip Hi allowed yellow teeth like fangs of a dog to show between opened lips.

"At his first coming, this humble one, weakened by privations, allowed the tongue of indiscretion to wag loosely concerning certain doings of the elder brother. It may be that deprivation of money may ere long lead to a similar loosening."

"Would not gratitude for rotundity bestowed suffice for a bridle?"

"Nay, this person thinks the bridle should be golden," returned Yip in a voice like the sound of a blunt saw cutting hard wood. "This person knows well wherefore benevolence has been lavished. Let it be extended and silence is upon him. Let an unwise parsimony deny and consequences of a pain-bestowing nature may follow."

At these words, Sung, perceiving their fitness, loosed the laugh of derision.

"Truth is sometimes spoken unawares, oh estimable Yip!" he cried mockingly, and at the bushes urged his horse forward.

A few moments later a gush of smoke and a thundering report announced the bestowal of the consequences, followed by Ting Wei, who, bending over the passed on as he fell from the saddle, omitted to note the proximity of Sung till a short blunderbuss was pressed against his ribs.

"Four thousand taels is the reward for the taking of the greatly desired Ting Wei alive, but two thousand only for him dead. Yet prudence impels this person to accept the latter," observed Sung, and pulled the trigger.

Then, with satisfaction of a mathematician who has solved a difficult problem, he loaded the horses with the deceased and turned back towards the city, there to claim the reward of meritorious elimination and consult with his master about the fitting obsequies due to a highly esteemed if misguided younger brother.

THE HUT IN THE PADDY FIELDS

By

REGINALD CAMPBELL

"REVERTING to our conversation before dinner," said Jennings leisurely, as he helped himself to one of my cigars, "do you mean to tell me, Anderson, that you *believe* in this extraordinary tale?"

"Of course he doesn't," grinned Barnes. "He's merely pulling our legs."

I flushed. "The fact remains," I said at length, "that no native will go near the place after dark."

"How far is the hut from here?" asked Jennings.

"About half a mile from the bungalow," I replied. "An eight minutes' walk through the jungle brings one to the edge of the paddy fields, which are circular in shape and about a hundred yards in diameter, and the hut is slap in the middle of them."

"Let's have the yarn again, and in slow time," suggested Barnes.

"The story, according to the villagers, is this," I said slowly. "A few years ago a man was stabbed at the edge of the scrub surrounding the fields in question. He apparently crawled, with the knife still sticking in his back, across the fields to the hut where he lived, in which he stayed, according to tradition, about one hour. He then crawled out again and over the fields till he disappeared into the jungle at the side opposite to where he had received his fatal injury."

"But why," queried Jennings, "did he leave the hut again if he was dying?"

"It is presumed he was in search of water," I answered. "There was a small pool near where the body was discovered."

"And the ghost, apparition or what not?" asked Barnes.

"On one night of every month, at full moon, the man's ghost is said to repeat the performance in every detail," I told him

"Let's get this right," said Jennings. "The fields are circular in shape, you say, with the jungle all around them. The ghost appears from where, the western side of the fields?"

I nodded.

"Then," he resumed, "it crawls to the hut, which is in the

centre of the open space, and stays in there an hour. Then it comes out again, and continuing its previous course, disappears into the jungle at the eastern edge of the fields."

"Right first time," I laughed.

"And to-night the moon is full," said Jennings significantly.

There was a pause; then Barnes spoke. "Do you think there's any foundation for the story, Anderson?" he asked me.

I helped myself to a whisky and soda before replying: "If I do not actually believe it, I do not disbelieve it," I answered at length. "Why should I? Although ninety-nine ghost stories out of a hundred are utter nonsense, you two must admit that there *have* been authentic cases of apparition or whatever you like to call them having been seen from time to time in England. And if there are such things at home, why not also in Northern Siam?"

"Have you ever tried to see the spook yourself?" asked Jennings.

"No, never," I replied.

"Yet here you live in your bungalow not half a mile from the place."

"Granted," I replied. "But two of my coolies went out one night a few months ago to test the truth of the tale."

"And what did they see?"

"I don't know."

"*Don't know?* Why not?"

"Because," I said nonchalantly, "they are dead."

"Good God! What happened?"

"It appears they had been drinking in the village grog-shop, where they boasted they would spend a night in the hut. They went, and the moon was full. Next morning their bodies were found there. From the look on their faces they had died of sheer fright."

"Pah," sneered Barnes. "The rustle of a cobra, a barking deer coming out from the jungle, the hoot of an owl, devils. Then heart failure. You know these natives." He spread eloquent hands.

"Nevertheless," said Jennings slowly, "this intrigues me."

"It doesn't me," said Barnes. "I've a long journey before me if I'm to reach my forest tomorrow, so I guess I'll turn in shortly."

"You don't often go to bed so early, Barnes," I broke in.

He rose, yawned, and stretched his arms. "Dunno why, but I feel devilish tired tonight. Heat perhaps. Let me see, my room's the end one on the left, isn't it, Anderson?"

"Yes," I began, "you'll find——" but Jennings interrupted me.

"Look here, you fellows," he said excitedly, "what about us three spending the night in the hut? It's the chance of a lifetime."

"Not for me," laughed Barnes. "Sheer waste of time."

"Nor me," I agreed.

"Come on, Anderson," urged the first speaker. "Be a sport. You're host after all, and it's up to you to provide any excitement there is going round here. Lord knows, we don't get much to relieve the monotony of living in a teak forest in Northern Siam."

I remained silent.

"Of course if you're afraid."

"I'm not afraid," I said somewhat stiffly.

"Then why not come?"

I frowned, for another aspect of the affair had suddenly struck me. Both my guests, whom I was putting up for the night in my bungalow, were confirmed practical jokers, that well I knew. I had told them something of the story before dinner, and Heaven knows what they might have planned together in the interval that had since elapsed. I think I can say that I am no coward, but practical joking is not in my line, and never has been. Moreover, when it is coupled with ghosts, it is a dangerous game and liable to lead to tragedy at times. Which is very bad medicine indeed.

"Poor old stick-in-the-mud," Jennings' voice broke in on my thoughts.

"Don't tease him," smiled Barnes. "Personally I don't blame him. I expect he wants his sleep as much as I do."

I rose to my feet and faced Jennings. "All right, I'll come, damn you," I cried. "But look here, no fooling. No monkey tricks from either you or Barnes, you understand?"

"Of course not," replied Jennings.

"Poor devils," said Barnes pityingly. "A night out for you two: a good sleep for me. So long, see you both in the morning, I suppose." He crossed over the veranda in the direction of his bedroom, and Jennings and I were left alone.

An hour later Jennings and myself, laden with a bottle of whisky, a flask of water, and some cigarettes and sandwiches, strode through the bungalow compound that I had had cleared from the heart of the forest, and, swinging through the little gate of the fence that ringed the garden, we struck down the narrow path that ribboned in and out between the towering trees that mantle the rolling forest hills of Upper Siam.

The heat was simply stifling, for the month was March, when the hot weather is at its worst, and the pitiless sun has scorched and baked the jungle till it is a mere collection of charred, dried-up bamboo clumps, interspersed with the blanched, naked trunks of thousands of giant trees from which the leaves have long since fallen. The stillness as we walked along was absolute, and I remember that, although we did not hasten unduly, the perspiration fairly streamed from us out of every pore, soaking the loose cotton garments which we were wearing till we were literally wet to the skin.

After some eight minutes' progress we had reached the fringe of the paddy fields and, halting, we gazed over the moonlit space before us. The rice had been harvested many weeks before, and a yellow stubble was all that covered the flat, hard-baked earth that now met our eyes. In the centre of the field, which was about two hundred yards across, was the deserted attap-roofed hut. Raised, as it was, some six feet above the ground on four poles, it looked gaunt, dreary, ghostly in the pure, pale light of the moon.

"There it is," I whispered to my companion, pointing to the structure.

He clutched my arm with a strength that made me wince. "*What's that?*" he cried hoarsely.

"Where?" I shied like a startled horse.

"Nowhere," he laughed. "Your nerves are not as good as they might be. Too many cigarettes, old boy."

"Quit your nonsense," I said roughly. "And let's get on with the job."

A minute later we had reached the foot of the hut, and, having climbed up the rickety ladder that connected it to the ground, we squatted down on the hard, bamboo flooring and looked around us.

The sides of the hut were, like the roof, composed of attap, or dried grass, which, in the passage of time, had withered and dropped in places, leaving large holes through which we could get a clear view of the dry, moon-gleaming space of stubble that surrounded us, beyond which was the unbroken wall of jungle, showing us against the horizon, grim and austere, in the glittering darkness.

Having settled ourselves down as comfortably as we could under the circumstances, we lit our cigarettes and gazed in silence through one of the larger apertures in the attaps towards the western edge of the scrub.

After some thirty minutes had passed, my companion nudged me: "What . . . what time is it supposed to come?" he breathed, and I could see by the whiteness of his face gleaming in the rays of the moon filtering through the rushes that his heart was tense.

"I don't know exactly," I whispered. "Somewhere about midnight, I believe." And then it was I that gripped his arm:

"*Look.*"

"Where?"

My hand shook as I pointed to the forest.

"*There,*" I quavered.

"My God," he choked. "It's something black coming out from the jungle, *and it's crawling.*"

To my dying day I shall never forget that moment. Numbed, dazed, with prickling skin and thrilling spine, I watched the thing crawling, painfully and slow, over the glittering waste towards the hut in which we were crouching. Although, as I have said before, the night was stifling, yet the sweat that rose to the pores of my skin literally froze as with terrorstruck, fascinated eyes, I watched the horror. By the time it had approached to within some forty yards of where we were, I could see the form almost as plainly as if it had been daylight. The thing was clothed only in a loin cloth, the whites of its eyes gleamed horribly against the background of its dusky skin, while in between the shoulder blades was the haft of a knife, round which was a crimson stain.

An overwhelming desire to run assailed me, to flee anyhow and anywhere from the ghastly monstrosity, but I felt like one in a nightmare whom invisible arms hold back. I could not move, I could not even raise a hand; I was tied, earth-bound, and in the agony of that moment I very nearly knew death. Then a sound came from my companion, and the spell was broken:

"I shall go mad in a second," he gasped, and I can hear yet the dry catch in his throat as his heart sobbed: "Out of it, man, out of it."

And then we fairly flew. How we got down the ladder to the ground I haven't the faintest notion, all I remember is the desperate pound, pound, pad, pad, pad of our feet on the dry earth as we tore madly back to the bungalow and safety.

Once again in the living room, with shaking hands I lit a lamp, for the whole place was in darkness, and, white to the lips, we stared at one another across the table on which I had placed the lamp.

"Are you satisfied now?" I asked at length, and my teeth were chattering in my head as I said the words.

Jennings sank down on to a rattan chair and buried his face in his hands: "My God," he whispered, "my God." This was his only answer.

I hastened over to a cupboard that stood at one end of the room, seized a tumbler and a bottle of brandy, poured out a stiff tot into the glass, and gulped down the contents. Then I refilled the tumbler with another generous measure of the spirit, and returning, handed it to my companion. A splash of colour returned to his pallid cheeks after he had drained the glass to the dregs, and he rose to his feet.

"I'm going to tell Barnes of this," he said unsteadily. "Most extraordinary thing I've ever heard of. His room's at the end of the veranda, isn't it?"

"Yes," I replied, "but why disturb him now? Tomorrow will do." I, too, was in a fever to break the news to the man now sleeping, but I knew he had a long day's journey before him in the morning, so with an effort I restrained myself.

"I'll never sleep till I get this off my chest," muttered Jennings, thus echoing my own unspoken thoughts. "Come on."

Snatching up an electric torch from the table, I followed him across the veranda into Barnes's room, where I flashed on the light. Then we both started in surprise. The bed, though slept in, was empty. I circled the arc of light round the hot atmosphere. There were his day clothes, suspended over a chair. I switched the torch on to the floor, and noted that a pair of sandals that he had been wearing that evening were apparently missing.

Jennings drew in a deep breath, then turned to me. "Fooled, by God," he exclaimed. "The pair of us."

"Well, I'm damned," was all I could say at first.

"We'll get even with him, though, by Jove we will," muttered Jennings at last. "Now quick, get a haft of a knife, a long piece of black tape, some burnt cork, and some red ink or paint. Then come into my bedroom."

"What's the idea?" I ventured.

"Why, play his own game on him, of course."

"Don't be an ass, man, I don't like it."

"But he deserves it, doesn't he?"

"I suppose he does," I admitted.

"Well then, come on and help me."

"But how do you know he'll still be in the hut when we get back there?" I objected.

"We can't be sure, of course, but the chances are ten to one that he will. Think of it, Anderson, he'll be able to come back in the morning, laugh at us, and say he's stayed there all night on his own. I know Barnes, it's just the sort of thing he would do for bravado. Remember, it's the hot weather, so there are no mosquitoes to worry him in his rig-out, and he's got our whisky and sandwiches with which to regale himself."

"I don't like it one little bit," I repeated. "He might, for instance, have his revolver with him."

Jennings took the electric torch from my hand and flashed it on to the dressing-table. Then he swung round towards me: "You can see for yourself it's here. I tell you, there's no danger at all, man. By the way," he added hurriedly, "what's the time?"

"Twenty-three minutes past twelve," I replied, glancing at my watch.

"And what time do you reckon it was when we legged it from that hut?" he queried.

"It must have been just about midnight," I answered. "Though naturally I wasn't concerned with the hour when we ran for it. Why do you ask?"

It may have been my imagination, but I thought I saw a smile flit, for the fraction of a second, over my companion's features as I put the question.

"Nothing," he said briefly. "Now stop talking and come and help me make up. And for the Lord's sake get a move on."

"I hate this tomfoolery," I grumbled, "but why the hurry?"

He made no reply, but hastened towards his bedroom. For a second the moonlight shone on his profile as he passed a window, and this time I could have sworn the grin was real.

Some twenty-five minutes later, for the hands of my watch pointed to five minutes to one, I was standing just within the western edge of the scrub, watching Jennings crawling slowly over the field in the direction of the hut.

The moon was now sinking, but its light still shone strongly and I shivered, for Jennings certainly looked and played the part of the spectre to a T. The fellow's appearance was simply ghastly as he crept, simian-like, over the ground, and, what with the burnt cork on his skin, the haft of the knife tied with black tape round back and belly, and the red paint between his shoulder blades, he would have made a serpent shiver.

Personally, I didn't know whether to laugh or to cry over the business as I crouched there, motionless, at the edge of the jungle. It was an asinine affair, to say the least of it, but when three men who live at the back of beyond or a bit further foregather, they are apt to do the maddest tricks to relieve the drab monotony of existence that is, contrary to general belief, the lot of those who lead lonely lives in the wild places of the earth. Barnes, I knew thankfully, had strong nerves, or I would never have countenanced the trick, and I wondered whether I should shortly see him burst from the hut and leg it in wild panic for the bungalow as we two had done not so long ago, or whether presently would come the sound of laughter from the structure as he saw the joke.

Jennings was half-way across the space that intervened between the jungle and the hut when he halted in his crawl and made a slight, very slight, movement with his right hand. The light was tricky, of course, but my eyesight is exceptional, and I blinked in astonishment, for the motion was as if he had been signalling to the occupant of the hut. It looked almost as if he wished to ***warn*** the man inside.

Then on he went again, nearer and nearer to his goal, and still no signs of Barnes taking fright. At last he scaled up the bamboo ladder of the structure and disappeared from view.

Curious, I awaited developments. They did not take long to come, for scarcely a minute later a form, whether it was that of Barnes or Jennings I could not tell, crept down the ladder again and commenced crawling away over the field towards the *eastern* edge of the scrub.

For a second my brain stood still at this unexpected denouement, and then, like a blinding flash of light, I saw the who scheme as clearly as if I had been Jennings himself. The two of them were going to fool *me* now. Whether or no the whole thing had been planned from the very start, I was doubtful, for I could have sworn that Jennings' fear when the horrible apparition came creeping towards us was genuine. But now, now matters had assumed a very different complexion.

I stood for a while doing a rapid bit of mental calculation, when I came to the following conclusion. Jennings had had the brain-wave to turn the tables on me when we had got back to the bungalow and discovered Barnes's absence. He had calculated that, if we could get back to the field within the hour, he could play a very pretty little game on me. Provided he could warn Barnes somehow that he was not the real ghost, and get to the hut without the man taking fright, then he could persuade Barnes to crawl off to the other side of the field just as the real ghost was supposed to do, for the time would be just right. Then he, Jennings, would remain in the hut and when I, anxious, appeared on the scene, he would pretend to be dead of fright, and give me the shock of my life.

" My God," I muttered to myself as I strode out boldly across the field, " I'll have the laugh on the pair of you yet."

I had not made more than a few yards' progress when I became aware of two things: one, that the black form that I had seen crawling over the field to the edge of the jungle opposite had by now disappeared between the trees; the other, that a heavy thunder-cloud was gradually enveloping the sky and was threatening at any minute to obscure the moon. And as I saw that cloud I grinned.

Having reached the bottom of the ladder I paused with one foot on the lowest rung. " Barnes, Jennings," a terrible cry burst from my lips. " Speak, for God's sake."

No answer.

And then I climbed up into the hut, where I saw exactly what I had foreshadowed. Jennings was lying, grotesque and sprawling, on the bamboo boards, and his eyes were starting, horrible, as one whose soul has fled from a nightmare monstrosity.

And then did I feign madness. I was down that ladder in the fraction of a second and, screaming to the full extent of my lungs, I raced as hard as I could for the surrounding jungle, but *not* in the direction of the path that led to the bungalow. Even as I ran the moon clicked off with startling suddenness and I was left in a blackness that was absolute, but I heeded not, for I knew the locality like the back of my hand.

Once back in the jungle again, I proceeded more circumspectly, till an opportune flash of lightning showed me what I was looking for. This was a second path that, unknown to the others, also led back to the bungalow, but by a slightly longer route. As I hastened along this I grinned, for I pictured Barnes bursting out from his hiding-place amongst the trees, Jennings leaping out from the hut, and the two of them, guided by my screams, fairly legging it after me in the pitch darkness of the night.

A quarter of an hour later I was home, when I sat down at my writing desk. Taking two pieces of paper from the drawer, I inserted a carbon between them, and wrote as follows:

"Dear Barnes and Jennings,

"Please don't wake me when you return. It is late enough already and I want my beauty sleep. I congratulate you; it was a very pretty little scheme. I think you will agree, however, that I have had the last laugh, especially in view of the thunderstorm that I think is now approaching. No, I didn't go mad with fright and bolt off anywhere into the jungle. I was quite sane at the time and knew exactly what I was doing. I hope you have had an enjoyable time looking for me, though I fear it will turn out rather wet from the look of things.

"Bye-bye. See you at breakfast if you have returned by then.

"Yours sincerely

"A. H. Anderson."

I had hardly completed my signature when, with a roaring and a thrumming on the shingled roof of the bungalow, down came the tropical rain, and I smiled grimly as I heard the sound. Then I slipped the carbon from between the two sheets of paper and, taking a couple of pins in my hand, entered first Jennings's room, then Barnes's. Having pinned a copy of the letter on each of their deserted pillows, I yawned and went into my own room.

I was in the act of slipping off my shirt when a sound on the veranda outside attracted my attention, and, opening my door, I gazed out.

"Hello," said Barnes. "Back again?" Dropping the rattan chair he was holding on to the floor, he gazed into the pattering gloom outside. "Lucky you didn't get caught in that," he muttered. "*I've* just been. Damned nuisance, this rain. After you two fellers had gone to the paddy fields I tried to get to sleep, but in spite of being tired out I couldn't sleep a wink. The bungalow, my dear chap, was like an oven. Then I had a brain-wave. Slipped on my sandals and took this chair out to the lower end of the garden. Beautifully cool out there: slept like a log until this infernal rain . . . but, good Lord, man, what am I talking about? Tell me, did you see——" the words suddenly died in his throat as his eyes caught the expression on my face.

With a supreme effort I pulled myself together. "You . . . you give me your word of honour," I cried hoarsely, "that you have never left the compound tonight?"

"On my word of honour I never did," he said quietly, for he saw the terrible look in my eyes.

I laughed wildly. "Then it was the *real* ghost after all," I shrieked, "and Jennings is *really* dead."

And he was when we found him.